"You have so much to give,"

she said. "It's time you gave it to someone who could give it back to you."

"Do you have someone in mind?" Joshua reached across the table and took her hands, wiping them clean with a slow, sensuous motion.

Maggie watched in fascination as the napkin moved over the palms of her hands and between her fingers. She couldn't tear her eyes from what he was doing. "Why didn't we meet under different circumstances?" she asked softly.

"Do you want me to say something comforting and theological? Or probing and psychological?"

She shook her head.

"Then truthfully I don't know. Maybe we both needed a lesson on looking beneath the surface."

Dropping the napkin, he laced his fingers through hers and lifted them to his mouth. Maggie shut her eyes as he kissed each one. Even after he released her hands, she sat with her eyes closed, savoring the feeling of Joshua's lips on her fingertips. When she finally opened her eyes it was to the warmth of Joshua's.

Dear Reader,

When two people fall in love, the world is suddenly new and exciting, and it's that same excitement we bring to you in Silhouette Intimate Moments. These are stories with scope, with grandeur. These characters lead the lives we all dream of, and everything they do reflects the wonder of being in love.

Longer and more sensuous than most romances, Silhouette Intimate Moments novels take you away from everyday life and let you share the magic of love. Adventure, glamour, drama, even suspense— these are the passwords that let you into a world where love has a power beyond the ordinary, where the best authors in the field today create stories of love and commitment that will stay with you always.

In coming months look for novels by your favorite authors: Maura Seger, Parris Afton Bonds, Elizabeth Lowell and Erin St. Claire, to name just a few. And whenever you buy books, look for all the Silhouette Intimate Moments, love stories *for* today's women *by* today's women.

Leslie J. Wainger
Senior Editor
Silhouette Books

Emilie Richards

Lady of the Night

Silhouette Intimate Moments

Published by Silhouette Books New York

America's Publisher of Contemporary Romance

SILHOUETTE BOOKS
300 East 42nd St., New York, N.Y. 10017

Copyright © 1986 by Emilie McGee

ISBN: 0-373-07152-3

First Silhouette Books printing July 1986

America's Publisher of Contemporary Romance

Printed in the U.S.A.

EMILIE RICHARDS

grew up in St. Petersburg and attended college in northern Florida. She also fell in love there, and married her husband, Michael, who is her opposite in every way. "The only thing that we agreed on was that we were very much in love. We haven't changed our minds about that in the sixteen years we've been together." They now live in New Orleans with four children, who span the years from toddler to teenager.

Chapter 1

In the beginning there was nothing. An absence of form and sound. An absence of pain and fear. She created the void, and the void was good.

Then there was the voice.

The voice was life. It was life calling back life. And the voice would not be silenced.

The voice moved through the shattered wreckage that had once been a soul, slowly weaving it back together. I will not be denied, it insisted. Once again, you will exist.

Then, as always, the voice was extinguished.

The young woman opened her eyes and there was light. It beat against her eyeballs with an intensity that sent shivers of pain dancing through her body. Pain. Pain was familiar and to be avoided.

Protecting herself instinctively, she sought the darkness. But this time there was no escape.

When she reopened her eyes, they were wide in helpless terror. Words formed to summon back the void, but words spun it farther away. *Please. Please. Not again.* Each word brought her closer to reality. Each word burned away another layer of the mist that cloaked her vision.

Finally, there was sight. On a stark white backdrop lay a hand. The fingers were long and graceful, with nails cut to the quick. As she watched, the hand moved convulsively, forming a fist, then relaxed. Over and over it practiced until, as if now ready for the long journey, it moved toward her hair.

Suspended in midair the searching fingers stilled. It's not too late, the woman called into the darkness. But the blessed darkness was gone. She was irrevocably alive.

Her hand found her head. Trembling fingers fluttered through the impossibly short strands that layered it. Slowly, inch by inch, she covered her scalp, coming to rest on a thin scar that zigzagged from her forehead to the middle of her skull. Her body twitching in terror, she dropped her hand and focused her eyes on her lap.

The training of a lifetime stilled her quaking limbs. She had gained a tenuous control when at last her eyelids fluttered up once more. Careful not to touch herself again, the young woman began a slow examination of her surroundings.

The white backdrop was a sheet; the firm support behind her, a bed. The light was from a small window to the side. It was covered with heavy mesh, more than a screen, less than bars. There would be no escape through it.

Her visual range disclosed white walls, a steel door with a small window covered with the same mesh. There was nothing else to distract her. The images were pieces of a puzzle, an old-fashioned cardboard jigsaw with no picture on the box to use as a model.

Then, finally, there was sound. A low keening came from the side of the room the woman had not yet examined. As she turned her head by terrified inches, the source of the noise was revealed.

An old woman sat on a bed like her own, rocking back and forth, her eyes blank, her body rigid. The old woman's arms tensed as they spasmodically gripped her body in a fierce, unloving hug. Back and forth she rocked, her rhythm as certain as anything in the universe.

The young woman snapped her head to the front and squeezed her eyes shut as the familiar terror overwhelmed her. But there was no longer a void to which she could retreat. The sound of her own screams destroyed the darkness forever.

Joshua Martane quietly closed the door to room 815 behind him as he stepped out into the dimly lit corridor. Closing the door quietly was one of those habitual responses that made no sense upon examination. The two women on the other side of the door would not have cared if he had slammed it loudly enough to be heard in the emergency room on the ground floor. Both of them were so out of touch with reality that the sound would have been completely ignored, if indeed it even registered.

Old Mrs. Tryon would not have stopped rocking. Years of therapy, medication and finally electric shock treatments had failed to make her take notice of the world surrounding her. A loving but resigned daughter had recently admitted Mrs. Tryon to this the psychiatric ward of New Orleans City Hospital as the first step toward permanent hospitalization in the state institution in Mandeville. There she would probably rock away her days, locked forever from the world that she hadn't acknowledged in almost a decade.

And then there was the patient in the other bed. Joshua leaned against the wall beside the door and thought about the young woman lying inert in the room behind him. Jane Doe. The "Doe" part fit. She was delicately boned and sleek. Her hair, cropped brutally short, was the soft, misty brown of a yearling. If she moved, he knew it would be as gracefully as a deer running through the woods. But she didn't move. She lay quietly in her bed, sometimes opening huge blue eyes to stare straight ahead. The eyes were like a doe's, too. A doe who has not survived her encounter with the hunter.

Jane Doe affected Joshua in a way that no other patient ever had. In all the years of his training, in his experience with hundreds of patients, no one had touched him like the young woman lying in room 815. It wasn't the huge eyes or the almost transparent skin stretched tightly over a delicate bone structure that was much too prominent. It was who she was and who she wasn't. It was the mystery that surrounded her, the secrets that would never be unlocked. It was the waste of potential.

Perhaps if she were to awaken from her long slumber, she would sit up in the bed and destroy his fantasies forever. Certainly if she was what the police insisted she was, the aristocratic features were inappropriate. If she was truly what everyone assumed, then she was a woman who had already given up on herself long before she was found bleeding and abandoned in a vacant lot.

"What planet are you on?"

Joshua lifted his eyes to those of the big black woman standing in front of him, hands on her hips and a smile twisting her full, painted lips. "Betty, I didn't hear you coming," he said, pulling himself back to the present.

"You looked a million miles away."

"It's been a very long day."

"Come get some coffee."

Obediently—because everyone obeyed Betty—Joshua followed the waddling woman down the hall. Betty St. Clair ran the eighth floor of N.O.C.H. with an iron hand she didn't bother to encase in a velvet glove. She knew everything, everyone and every nook and cranny of the extensive ward. Nothing escaped her notice, including one Joshua Martane and his interest in the young woman in room 815.

"When are you going to start dressin' like a psychologist's supposed to?"

"When I start acting like a psychologist's supposed to." He watched her face light up in a huge grin that revealed sparkling uneven teeth.

It was a familiar exchange. Joshua was a tall, broad-shouldered man who wore his faded blue jeans, long-sleeved white shirt and carelessly knotted tie with the flair of a gentleman dressed in formal attire. Betty was one of the few women who encountered him who was not impressed. Her methods of trying to get him to adhere to her standards were always well meant and completely lacking in subtlety.

"Just once I'd like to see you in a dark suit and a tie that matched what you were wearin'," she drawled. "Then we could tell at a glance that you were on the staff."

"You'll just have to tell by the good work I do."

"Been doin' any good work in room 815 today?"

Joshua lifted one shoulder in half a shrug. The pervasive disappointment he felt at not seeing any changes in Jane Doe settled back over him.

Betty nodded in sympathy then turned, squeezing past the nurse's desk to the medicine room where a pot of hot coffee was always in residence. Joshua followed her, nodding to the two psychiatric aides and another R.N. who were leaning against the long counters, sipping cups of the dark, rich New Orleans brew.

"A party and I wasn't invited?" Betty asked with a toss of her black curls.

"Trish and Malcolm are out on the floor," the blond nurse explained in a voice that conveyed her boredom. "Most of the patients are in occupational therapy."

"Thank you, Sarah. I know where the patients are," Betty said.

It was a familiar battle, and Joshua leaned back to watch. Sarah, aloof and elegant, disliked her job and disliked Betty's authority even more. Betty wouldn't give an inch. To Joshua they were symbolic of the two kinds of people who worked on the unit. Betty was strong but compassionate. Sarah was strong willed and judgmental. Luckily the staff had more Bettys than Sarahs.

Before the discussion could intensify one of the aides turned to Joshua.

"How was your girlfriend?"

All eyes focused on Joshua, and and he attempted a smile. "Quiet."

"He likes 'em quiet," Betty confided to everyone. "He likes to do the talkin' himself."

"I get my chance in room 815," Joshua agreed, purposely keeping the lingering sadness from his voice. The hospital staff, trained to pick up on every nuance of a conversation, did not need any more fuel for their teasing. His special interest in the young woman in room 815 was already a favorite topic of gossip.

"I was working the emergency room when that girl was brought in," Sarah said. Sarah rarely teased. Early in her assignment to the eighth floor, she had realized that Joshua would not support her rebellion against Betty. Sarah had worked hard since that day to pay him back. "You were filling in for the chaplain that night, weren't you, Joshua?"

He nodded, unsmiling now.

Joshua was an ordained minister who had found that his call to serve God and man had led him out of the path of the parish ministry and into psychology. Now he only reluctantly donned his clerical collar if he was needed to fill in during a crisis. Working with patients, helping them to make strides toward health, was his greatest skill. It was the long-term interactions, the giving of himself over and over again that made his job worthwhile. The night the young woman had been brought to the hospital in a police ambulance, bleeding and unconscious, had been the beginning of just that kind of involvement.

"You should have seen our Joshua that night," Sarah recalled smugly. "He was a young lion. He was everywhere, in everybody's way, trying to make sure that girl got only the best of care." She paused, minutely adjusting the belt on her crisp white pant suit. "I had to shave the girl's head. You'd have thought Joshua was going to cry."

Joshua's eyes didn't flicker, nor did his expression change. His rugged features remained under strict control. It was a skill he had developed to perfection in his youth.

The others took up the discussion turning it away from Sarah's venom back to good-natured teasing. Joshua sipped his coffee and remembered.

Jane Doe had been brought in five months before. It had been late at night. Joshua had survived that particular evening on black coffee and the knowledge that he probably would never be asked to substitute for the hospital chaplain again. The hospital had finally agreed to hire another minister to assist the beleaguered young man who now held the job.

There had been two dead-on-arrivals already that night. One had been a fatal stabbing in a barroom brawl, another a car accident. He had comforted relatives, repeated prayers, held hands. He had jounced a colicky baby on his knee and wiped away a little girl's tears as she was prepared to go to radiology for a broken arm.

When the police ambulance came to a halt at the emergency room door once again, its siren still screaming, he had steeled himself for another crisis and waited quietly by the door as the well-trained emergency team did their job. The young woman who had been carried past him on a stretcher was too pale and still to be alive, but the team had refused to give up on her.

It was in the young woman's favor that she had been brought to this particular hospital. Used to just such emergencies, the staff was prepared. The faint flicker of life had been nurtured. Joshua had watched as a cheap, flashy red negligee was pulled from her body and life-saving machinery was attached instead. Her waist-length hair, matted with mud and blood, had been cut, and her head shaved to prepare her for the surgery that had to be performed to close a gaping head wound. Her face had been scrubbed of its gaudy makeup. The impersonal touch of the nurses had angered him, and he had protested. They had laughed and continued to treat their patient with rough precision. And they had saved her life.

Later he had retreated to the coffee shop with the police sergeant who had followed the ambulance. The man was a lifelong friend. Joshua Martane and Sam Long had grown up on the same block in the Irish Channel section of New Orleans. Together they had fought their way from poverty and petty juvenile crime to a different life. Native sons, both were determined, in different ways, to improve the city that was their home.

"What do you know about the girl?" Joshua had asked Sam.

Golden-haired Sam, with male model looks and a deadly aim that had found a target more than once, shook his head, signaling the sleepy coffee shop waitress for a refill. "Another prostitute murder. Only this time he didn't quite finish the job. If the girl survives, we may be able to nail the bastard."

"Tell me what you know."

"Why?" Sam was curious. Although he and Joshua stayed in touch, it was rare for his friend to ask him about a case.

"I may have to deal with her. I'd like to know what to expect."

"Your kind doesn't 'deal' with her kind," Sam said bluntly. "She's a lost cause."

"Tell me."

"We found her facedown in the mud in the vacant lot behind Hootie Barn's Tavern off Basin Street. One of his 'patrons' tipped us off."

"How long had she been there?"

"Not too long, or she'd be dead. Have you been outside lately?"

Joshua shook his head.

"It's cold out there, and she wasn't wearing much. Between the blood loss and the exposure I'll be surprised if she makes it."

"What makes you think she's a prostitute?"

Sam laughed, his perfectly formed lip curling back to reveal strong white teeth. "Hootie Barn's neighborhood isn't for ladies. I don't think the girl was doing social work. You saw how she was dressed, how she was made up. All the details fit with the rest of the prostitute murders we've seen. Only this time the man got careless."

"Go on."

"Well, usually, he beats them good. And then he strangles them with a scarf he leaves around their necks as his personal calling card. He did everything exactly the same this time, but he forgot to make sure she wasn't breathing when he was done."

"Don't you think that was a pretty big error?"

"I'm sure he'll think so when he reads the story in tomorrow's paper. Of course, she may be dead by then."

"No."

"You know something I don't?"

"She's going to make it."

Sam had searched his friend's face. As always he wondered how someone who looked so much like a fallen angel could ever have chosen a more unlikely profession. Joshua was obviously tired, his wavy hair in disarray around his haggard features. Only his slate-gray eyes were still snapping with life. Sam revealed his cynicism. "You got a direct pipeline to the Almighty, Josh? Did they give you one when you graduated from your fancy seminary?"

"She's going to live."

"After what she's been through, that may not be a blessing."

She had lived. Although sometimes Joshua wondered if Sam had been right. What sort of celestial joke was it that the beautiful young woman had hovered near death for three months, finally to come out of her coma unable to respond to the world around her?

At first the doctors thought that she had suffered serious brain damage from the head wound she'd sustained. Now the opinion was that the shock of her near encounter with death and the traumatic circumstances leading up to it had thrown her mind into a place it would never find its way back from. Five months from the day of the tragedy, she was catatonic. Alive and completely unaware, she was one of the living dead.

"Martane here just won't give up, will you?" Betty was addressing her question to Joshua, giving him an elbow in the ribs. "If sheer willpower could cure anyone, he'd have that girl walkin' and talkin' in no time."

"I thought I saw a flicker of response today," Joshua said, finishing the last of his coffee. "When I was talking to her, her head turned slightly as if to follow the sound, and her eyes seemed less dull."

"And old Mrs. Tryon walked on water," Sarah scoffed. "We have a miracle worker among us."

Joshua allowed his eyes to drift to the coolly elegant Sarah. She stood defiantly, but her arms were clasped across her breasts in an instinctive effort to protect herself. Joshua's scathing tongue was a well-documented fact. It was just one more way that he had never fitted the stereotype of the kind, forbearing pastor. This time, however, he let Sarah's sarcasm pass.

"Did you know," Betty asked seriously, "that Dr. Bashir has started the procedure to send Jane Doe to Mandeville along with Mrs. Tryon?"

Joshua hadn't known, but it came as no surprise. The young woman had shown no real signs of progress. Medically she had improved enough not to need any special attention. She could not be allowed to continue to take up a bed needed for other patients. At Mandeville she would receive custodial care. She would be kept alive.

"It's been coming," he said, running his long fingers through his springy dark hair. "I'm surprised Bashir hasn't done it before—"

A piercing scream interrupted the rest of his sentence. It was followed by another and then another. Joshua slammed his coffee cup on the counter, turning to run out of the room, around the desk and down the hall in the direction of the screams. Patients were gathering in the corridor, some talking excitedly, some crying like lost children. A small group trailed out of the door of the cafeteria where voluntary occupational therapy was held. One old man clutched a green-and-red pot holder with the reverence of a child snuggling a favorite blanket.

Trailing behind Joshua, the rest of the staff stopped to organize the milling patients, leaving Joshua and Sarah to confront the source of the screams. Six paces ahead of the blond nurse, Joshua stopped at the door of room 815. The terrified sounds were coming from behind it.

"Let me handle this," Joshua told Sarah quickly. "If we both go in, it will scare her even more." He pushed the door open and strode to the screaming young woman's bedside.

The change in Jane Doe was so vast that for a moment Joshua could only stare. She was sitting up, although when he had left her she had been supine. Her hands were covering her face. As he watched, her screams quieted to whimpered pleas of "No, no," that seemed to be wrenched from the deepest part of her being.

"Procedure for dealing with a patient coming out of a catatonic state." Joshua searched his memory for just such a topic in the hundreds of journals and textbooks that he had studied. Nothing he could remember began to address the present situation. Throwing the part of him that was a careful, objective psychologist out the window, he assumed the role of comforter.

"You're all right," he said quietly. "You're in a safe place. You're all right." Since Jane Doe never had any visitors, there was no chair by her bedside. Joshua pulled one from the side of Mrs. Tryon's bed and sat on its edge. "You're all right," he reassured the young woman.

Flinging her hands from her face, the young woman turned her head and stared as if she recognized him. Joshua was flooded with feeling. He couldn't begin to count the hours that he had sat by her bed, talking to her, asking her to begin the return to life. Now she had. Successes were few. He had not expected one from his work with Jane Doe.

Her hand lay stiffly on the bed, and Joshua reached for it. Immediately he knew he was making a mistake. He could frighten her back into herself by moving too fast. Her return must be gradual and nonthreatening. But the young woman did not pull away. Her hand felt fragile and surprisingly cool. He clasped it firmly but without force, letting her know that she could pull away at any time.

"You're going to be all right," he repeated. "You're safe here. Nothing is going to hurt you."

She was trembling. The delicately boned hand was alive in his. Her whole body was reacting to the ordeal. But she seemed to be trying to relax, to gain control. The whimpering was less frequent, interspersed with short periods of silence. As he soothed her, Joshua studied the terrified blue eyes. No longer blank, they were sparkling with tears that caught in the heavy fringe of charcoal lashes surrounding them.

"You're going to be all right," he said again as he smiled at her.

The door opened with a bang, and Sarah stalked into the room. "This'll calm her down," she stated. "Fifty milligrams of Thorazine. It should put her out for a while."

"Get out," Joshua said calmly, not taking his eyes off Jane Doe.

"It's a standing order Dr. Bashir left on her chart. Move out of the way."

"Sarah, get out of this room right now." Joshua's voice rang with calm authority, but the tension between the psychologist and the nurse was affecting the young woman in the bed between them. She began to whimper again. Snatching her hand from Joshua's, she thrashed helplessly in her bed.

With a sigh, Joshua stood and strode to the side of the irate nurse. "If you don't get out of here right now," he said with perfect control, "I'll toss you out on your aristocratic little behind. Savvy?"

Joshua was a six-foot-three tower of authority. Sarah turned and stomped out, muttering threats and slamming the door behind her. Joshua ran his fingers through his hair before he moved once again to the bedside chair.

"They're trying to help," he said to reassure the thrashing young woman. "But I think you need something else, don't you? I know you're frightened, but you can get through this without a shot. I know you can."

She stopped her restless movements, calming at the sound of Joshua's voice. He saw her take a deep breath and let it out slowly. With fascination he watched her do it again. It was a healthy response to fear, a search for control that was encouraging. She whimpered twice, taking deep breaths in between until finally, she was silent. Her eyes were focused on her hands, but slowly, inch by inch, she raised them to his.

Joshua fought down the urge to reach for her hand again. Instead he put all the comfort he wanted to give her in his eyes and in his voice. "Are you feeling better now?"

She nodded. Joshua drew in a harsh breath. He had not expected an answer. "You look as though you are," he said carefully.

"Where am I?"

Her voice was sweet, filled with long-suppressed music. Joshua wanted to dance or sing to its notes.

He tried not to show his excitement. "You're in the New Orleans City Hospital."

"New Orleans?" She lowered her eyes to her hands again, twisting her fingers relentlessly in her lap as she tried to absorb his meaning. Joshua watched as a single tear trailed a path to her chin to fall unnoticed on the sheet below. "I don't understand."

"I'm sure you must feel very confused."

"Who am I?" She lifted her eyes to his as though she might find the answer to her most crucial question in them. "Who am I?" she repeated. "Please tell me."

He had not considered the possibility that she would remember nothing. Joshua would have given the young woman anything he could, but her identity was something he could not help her with. She was Jane Doe, brutalized prostitute. Beyond that, no one knew anything.

The police had made a detailed investigation into the facts surrounding the attempted murder. They had circulated pictures, talked to everyone who might know, searched for information among their informants. When the trail had ended with no clues, they had stopped trying. Had she been something other than what they knew her to be, they might have continued trying to learn her identity. But in the scheme of things, what was the identity of one comatose hooker worth?

"Can you remember anything at all?" Joshua asked.

Her eyes were the deep velvety blue of a forest wild flower. They were also clouded with fear, and she shook her head. "Who am I?" she repeated with a trace of desperation.

"I'm sorry. I don't know."

She drew in her breath in a low wail, tears rushing down her cheeks to fall on the sheet tucked over her breasts. "Oh, my God," she moaned.

Joshua sat on the bed. Instinctively he reached for her and pillowed her head against his shoulder. Across the room, Mrs. Tryon was rocking back and forth, unaware of the drama unfolding beside her. Joshua took up the old woman's motion, soothing the shattered patient crying helplessly against his shoulder.

The door opened suddenly, and a short, olive-skinned man marched in. "What's going on in here?" he demanded, his voice a heavily accented intrusion in the quiet room.

The young woman stiffened, throwing her hands to her face as Joshua rose to stand beside her. Dr. Bashir moved to the bedside, grabbing her chin with a fat, soft hand. "So there's been a change." He jerked her head up, pushing her hands away in irritation. "Do you know where you are?"

Wide-eyed, she tried to shake her head.

"Still can't talk," the psychiatrist noted.

"She can talk," Joshua said between clenched teeth. "Give her a chance."

"Do you know where you are?" the psychiatrist repeated.

The young woman began to shake her head, which was now free from Dr. Bashir's grasp. She stopped and then nodded slowly. "Yes, I'm in the New Orleans City Hospital."

"Good." He lifted her wrist as if to feel her pulse. "Tell me your name."

"I . . . I don't know." She began to cry again.

"She's disoriented," Dr. Bashir pronounced. "Confused, probably hallucinating. I've ordered Thorazine for her. Don't interfere again, Martane, or I'll have you thrown off this ward forever."

"If you load her full of tranquilizers she'll never remember anything."

"Are you questioning my authority?" The two men moved to stand beside the door.

"Yes."

"How dare you!"

"If you don't rescind that order, I'll take you to the hospital ethics committee, Bashir."

"And what will they say about your involvement with one of the patients? You were sitting on her bed, hugging her."

"I was comforting her. Touch is an important part of healing. I'm sure you learned that in medical school, Bashir."

"Don't interfere where you know nothing, Martane," the psychiatrist said with disdain. "On paper you may be a member of the therapy team, but in my book you're an untalented do . . ." His English slang failed him.

"Do-gooder?"

"Yes."

"Bashir, I'm warning you. If you do anything to this patient that sets her back, I won't close my eyes. I won't be satisfied until I have you before the committee."

Both knew it was an empty threat. Psychiatrists willing to work in hospitals like N.O.C.H. were few and far between. Unless he murdered a patient, Dr. Bashir was assured of a job until he retired. But even though the psychiatrist would not be fired, Joshua could make his job more difficult for him. And there was nothing that Dr. Bashir liked less than having his life made difficult.

"I'm warning you," the psychiatrist said, opening the door to storm out into the hallway, "either you stop interfering with my patients or I'll have you working on the housekeeping staff."

Joshua stood quietly by the door, waiting for Sarah to reenter with her medication and her orders. No one came. Satisfied that the psychiatrist had backed down, at least temporarily, Joshua returned to the young woman's bedside.

If possible, she was whiter than before, her dark lashes the only relief against the paleness of her skin. As if she sensed his return, she opened her eyes and tried to smile. "Thank you," she whispered.

Joshua was sorry that she had been subjected to his exchange with her psychiatrist. It couldn't possibly have increased her feeling of security. "Dr. Bashir is a good doctor," he said carefully. "He's just a bit overzealous. We keep each other in line." Joshua sensed that she knew he was lying, and he tried to smile reassuringly.

"You were trying to help me. I appreciate it."

The words and the careful, cultured speech were at odds with what he knew about her. Joshua studied the sculpted, feminine lines of her face. The young woman's speech fitted them exactly. She sounded like a finishing school graduate, not a prostitute. There was a graceful tinge of the South in her words, but they lacked the abrasive twang of New Orleans. The mystery was compounded.

"You're here to be helped. I'm doing my job."

"Tell me how I came to be . . . here." She gestured to the four walls. Joshua watched her glance fall on Mrs. Tryon and move quickly away.

"The police found you." Joshua turned the chair, straddling it. "You were badly injured and they brought you here to recover."

"Injured?" She raised her hand to her hair, touching the long thin scar. "My head?"

"You sustained a serious blow to the head. You were very ill from it."

"My hair is so short."

He smiled at the completely feminine response. "Not as short as the new styles dictate." She frowned and he smiled again. "I'd say it was about two or three inches all over. It's beginning to curl."

"It feels ugly."

"It suits you." Standing he walked to the door. "I'll be right back."

In the hallway he waved down Betty who had just helped a patient back to his room. "Do you have a mirror?" he called to her. In a minute he was holding a plastic compact.

"Bashir is out for your blood," Betty said casually as she watched him open the door. "You've done it this time."

Joshua shrugged, taking the compact as he strolled back into room 815. "Here, see for yourself," he told the young woman.

She stared for a long time, her fingers combing through her hair once as if to test its reality. "That's not me," she said finally, her voice choked with tears.

Joshua cursed his intuition. He had thought that the sight of her face in the mirror would help jog her memory. He had not meant to cause her pain.

"What's different?" he prodded.

"I don't know. But that's not me."

"Your hair was very long," he explained. "Down to here." He gestured to her waist. "They had to shave your head when they brought you in."

A sob echoed in her throat.

"Your nose was broken," he explained, wishing that he didn't have to. "It's possible that it looks a little different now that it's healed."

"It's crooked," she wailed.

"No, it's not. Well, maybe a tiny bit. It adds character to your face."

Her huge blue eyes went dark with disapproval. "You're just trying to make me feel better."

He almost laughed at her righteous anger. "Exactly," he agreed.

Surprisingly, she giggled, then followed it with a hiccup and a small sob.

"You are really very lovely," he said gently. "And that's the truth. But you've lost a lot of weight since you were admitted. With everything combined, it's no wonder you don't recognize yourself."

"It's too much for me to understand," she said plaintively. "I don't understand any of it."

The strain showed in her face. Carefully Joshua covered her hands with one of his own. "You've had a number of shocks in the past half hour. Don't try to figure it all out. Just rest." Even as he said the words, her eyelids drifted shut. It was all too much for her to cope with. Joshua watched the tiny lines of tension dissolve as she began to slip into the blessed oblivion of normal sleep. Her voice, when it came, was very far away.

"Will you be here when I wake up?"

He was entranced with the obvious trust in her voice. His feelings were irrational, but he had to admit he wanted to be there for her. He wanted to watch her awaken, to help cushion her shock at the unfamiliar hospital surroundings. He wanted to hear her musical voice with its hint of gracious living and sultry summer nights. He wanted to hold her hand and anchor her firmly in the world she had chosen to be part of once again.

But he could not stay. She should not become dependent on him. There were others who could play a part in her recovery. "I'll be here tomorrow morning. If you wake up before then, I'll have one of my favorite nurses take care of you."

"Will she hurt me?" Her head inclined toward Mrs. Tryon's bed.

"She may get noisy occasionally, but she's absolutely incapable of hurting anyone or anything."

"Good." With a small sigh the young woman drifted off to sleep.

Joshua sat beside the bed, watching her even breathing. When it deepened and slowed, he got up quietly and went out into the hallway.

The change from day to evening staff was taking place. Joshua saw Sarah and two of the aides waiting to be let through the locked door by the nurses' station, one of the two exits from the ward. Betty was still at the desk, sharing information with the woman who would take her place on the next shift. When she looked up and saw Joshua coming toward her, she frowned and shook her head slightly, as if in warning.

The sight of the tall man coming out of the medicine room was all the explanation Joshua needed. He had hoped that Dr. Nelson, the chief of psychiatry, would wait until the next day to confront him. Obviously, that was not going to be the case.

"Martane? I want to see you in the staff lounge. Immediately."

With a nod, Joshua followed Dr. Nelson down the hall. As usual, there was no one in the tiny lounge when they entered. Since the room was at the end of the hall, it was seldom used. The nursing staff preferred to have their coffee in the medicine room, where they could escape for brief minutes to gossip.

Joshua seated himself in a chair next to the chief psychiatrist's and waited.

"I suppose you've figured that Dr. Bashir has spoken to me about your interference." Dr. Nelson was a distinguished-looking man whose voice was always calm and well modulated. He managed to convey all the emotion he needed with the lifting of an eyebrow, the tightening of a muscle in his jaw, the flash of a brown eye. Joshua clearly understood the anger that was present behind the carefully chosen words.

"I expected him to speak to you. I was hoping it would be tomorrow."

"Why?"

"Because—" Joshua looked at his watch "—as of this minute, I've been here for twelve hours straight."

"Then we'll make this short and to the point. You have no right to try and countermand any doctor's order."

"I know that." Joshua could barely keep his irritation from echoing in his voice.

"And do you also know that I could have you barred from this floor?"

"Yes."

"Then why did you tangle with Bashir?"

"Because his order was harmful to the health of the patient. I've worked extensively with her. To Bashir she's a name on a chart—no, not even that. She's a pseudonym on a chart, a body in a bed that he sees probably twice a week for a minute at a time."

"You know what his caseload's like."

"Yes. And I know what he's like, too."

"Meaning?"

"Meaning that his answer to everything is a shot of Thorazine. The patient made incredible progress today." Joshua's voice softened and pride shone through. "She's made no response in five months, Jim. Today she talked to me; she asked questions. For someone who has been totally unaware of her surroundings, she behaved completely appropriately. Bashir didn't even look at that."

Dr. Nelson was quiet, assessing Joshua's words. Both of them knew what was at stake. Joshua understood that Jim Nelson had to protect the doctors on his staff, but he also knew that the chief psychiatrist was a fair man. He had not hired Dr. Bashir; he probably didn't approve of many of his decisions. An excellent psychiatrist himself, Jim was caught exactly in the middle. It was not a good place to be.

"You're very involved with this patient, aren't you?"

Joshua nodded. "I'll admit I am. But I'm not too involved to know what's good for her."

"Tell me what you've been doing for her."

"Talking."

"Elaborate, please."

"I've been sitting and talking to her. When she was still downstairs in a coma, I'd sit by her bedside every chance I got and talk about anything that I could think of. If she was listening, she knows everything there is to know about me."

"And when she was transferred up here?"

"More of the same, but I've been spending longer hours with her."

"Do you understand why?"

"That's a psychiatrist's question if ever I heard one," Joshua answered with a frown. "I did it because I care what happens to her."

Jim Nelson was only twenty years older than Joshua's thirty-three, but for a moment he seemed much older. "I guess," he admitted, "that it's been a long time since I let myself care that much about what happens to one of my patients."

Joshua sympathized. "I can understand that."

"That's a psychologist's answer," Jim said, a tiny smile touching his lips.

"Look, Jim, you and I both know that I'm not up here just to perform tests and write up reports. I'm here as a therapist. I'm trained for it, I'm good at it, and as such, I will not sit by and watch Bashir destroy a patient."

"How did you make it through school, Martane?" The psychiatrist leaned back in his chair, forcing it onto its hind legs. "With that chip on your shoulder, how did you convince any examining board you could humble yourself enough to do anybody any good?"

"I managed it with great difficulty."

"And when you were in the ministry?"

"That was even more difficult."

"It's going to be difficult here, too, if you don't temper your opinions a little."

"My judgment in this case is completely sound." Joshua leaned forward slightly. "And we both know it."

There was a long silence. Joshua knew that the chief of psychiatry was carefully weighing all the factors. Calmly he waited.

Jim Nelson was nothing if not fair. "I'll tell Bashir that he is not to prescribe anything more than mild sedatives for the girl," he said. "Her treatment plan will have to be cleared with me."

Joshua let out a slow breath. "I owe you one."

"Several." Jim Nelson examined the younger man. "I like you. But your disrespect for authority worries me. The first time I think you're letting it control you and interfere with your judgment, I'll have you off this floor."

Joshua nodded.

Dr. Nelson stood and extended his hand. "Go home and get some sleep."

They parted company at the nurses' desk. Joshua explained to the new staff about the changes in the patient in room 815. Taking aside a dark-haired young nurse, he asked her to keep a close eye on Jane Doe.

He added some notes to several charts, made a phone call to a patient's anxious wife and prepared to leave. But there was one thing he felt compelled to do before he asked to have the front exit door unlocked.

The young woman in 815 was still sleeping soundly when he checked on her one last time. Her hands were tucked under her head and she lay loosely curled on her side like a child who has never experienced anything except love and acceptance. There were no hints of a darker past, nothing to indicate the life she had led except the intriguing lines of her slender body under the thin white sheet.

"I don't know who you are, and I don't know why it matters so much to me," Joshua said softly. "But whatever your secrets are, I'm going to make sure that you have help unlocking them."

In her sleep, Jane Doe smiled slightly.

Chapter 2

There were so many things the young woman didn't understand. The window was just one small piece of the puzzle, but it confused her as much as anything else she was trying to grapple with. The window was designed to keep patients from trying to jump out of it. What kind of hospital worried about such things? And then there was the woman in the next bed. She didn't seem old enough to be senile, and yet she lived in a different world, a world of her own imagination.

Curled up in a near-fetal position, the young woman in room 815 watched the early-morning sunlight fight its way through the closely knit mesh of the escape-proof window. She tried to quell the panic that threatened to overwhelm her thoughts. The night had been endless. Nurses had come in several times, waking her from her restless slumber. They hadn't expected a response from her, and she hadn't bothered to let them know she was awake. Instead she had watched them busy themselves with small tasks around the room.

They hadn't taken her pulse or her temperature. That had surprised her because, without knowing how she knew, she was sure that nurses in hospitals were supposed to check such things. Why was this place so different? •

Why was she here? She tried to fight back the most frightening question of all, but it had hovered at the edge of her consciousness all night long. Who was she? What series of circumstances had brought her to this place and wiped away all traces of her past life?

Panic churned through her body, sending pulsating messages to every cell. She knew that if she gave in to it, it would make it impossible to find any answers at all. But the panic seemed to be larger than she was. Encompassing, annihilating.

In desperation she turned to the wall and pictured the face of the dark-haired man who had come to her rescue the night before. It was a strong face. Not good-looking in a classical sense, but wonderfully male. His eyes dominated sharp, almost harsh features, giving his face warmth that it would have lacked otherwise. She couldn't remember the color of his eyes; it was the life that was reflected in them that had impressed her. He had been completely comforting, sensing and understanding her distress. But there had been another facet of his personality that had shone through his steady gaze. He wasn't a man who liked to be crossed. He would fight for whatever he believed in.

Vaguely she remembered words of anger that had left quiet echoes in the room after he had gone. There had been another man with a strange accent that the first man had argued with. Involuntarily she shivered. She felt sorry for anyone whom the dark-haired man disliked. At the same time, she wasn't afraid that he would be angry with her. He had been gentle in all their interactions. He had held her with the tenderness of a lover. She held on to that memory as the room steadily brightened with day's arrival.

A rustle at the doorway pulled her out of her reverie. Instantly she tensed, waiting for pain to be inflicted. Tears sprang to her eyes, and she moaned involuntarily. Desperately she tried to retreat inside herself but that escape was gone. The dark-haired man had taken it from her, and he had told her she was safe.

She knew he was wrong. She could feel her persecutor approach, could feel the terror well in her throat, feel the unseen menace threaten her very existence. With the small store of courage left inside her she turned in the bed to try one more time to fight for her life. But there was no persecutor standing beside her. There was only a nurse with a tray.

The wave of terror subsided slowly, leaving nothing in its wake except a tormenting absence of memory and a body that was trembling with relief. For the moment she was safe. She was alive.

The nurse was watching with careful detachment. "I've brought you breakfast. I'm going to set it here and feed Mrs. Tryon first. I'll be back to feed you when I'm finished." The words were said in the same tone of voice a mother uses while talking to a child not old enough to answer. They sparked a small flame of rebellion in the young woman lying in the bed, and they burned away the last of her lingering terror. The night before she had allowed the nurses to feed her dinner, too exhausted and confused to respond any other way. This morning would be different.

"Thank you," she said with effort. "But I'll feed myself. Can you help me find the bathroom first?"

The nurse gasped, the tray in her hands rattling with her surprise. To her professional credit, she didn't drop it. Instead she set it carefully on the window ledge and walked to the young woman's bedside. "With the greatest of pleasure," she said with a big smile.

The young woman tried to smile in return. She understood very little of what was happening around her. She understood nothing about her fears. But one thing was perfectly clear. She had to regain her strength. She had to regain her memory. Because only with the return of both could she face her persecutor and defeat him. With a deep breath she sat up and swung her legs over the side of the bed.

Joshua slept the sleep of the dead. It had been well past midnight before he unlocked the door of his Esplanade Avenue apartment and found his way to bed. After leaving the hospital he had not wanted to face the solitude of his home, a solitude he usually appreciated. He had wanted a woman's company.

Antoinette Deveraux, a psychologist friend from his graduate school days, had not seen his last-minute invitation as an insult. They had dined at a Korean restaurant near her home in the Mid-City section of New Orleans, and they had talked until neither of them could keep their eyes open. Rather he had talked, and Antoinette had listened.

Antoinette, a declared feminist, could still play the gracious Creole belle when she felt it was called for. Completely sure of her own power and independence, she did not mind exercising the nurturing part of her personality to help a friend. She had sometimes asked the same of Joshua when she'd needed support.

He had not consciously called her to talk about Jane Doe. He thought he had just wanted someone whole, someone who could laugh and flirt and demonstrate the zest for life that was always conspicuously absent on the eighth floor of City Hospital. He had wanted the smell and sight and sounds of a beautiful woman. A woman who would make no demands on him.

Antoinette understood his needs. She had admitted to Joshua once that she was half in love with him; she also had no expectations that their relationship would ever be more than a close friendship. They had met at the wrong time in their lives. The first tentative steps into intimacy had shown what was really important to each of them: their careers, their independence, their need to guard some part of themselves that lovers cannot guard. Now she was available for long talks, for quiet support, and for an occasional, warm, what-might-have-been embrace.

"You've never talked this way about any of your other patients," Antoinette had observed after Joshua told her about the young woman in 815. She sat back in her chair for an afterdinner cigarette and waited for him to explain himself.

Joshua had watched the way the overhead light picked up the blue gleam in Antoinette's long black hair. She smoked as she did everything, with quiet, natural grace. Her hands, long fingered and slender, wove tapestries of smoke and smoldering flame. It was not the only time he had regretted that she was only a friend.

He brought his thoughts back to Jane Doe. "She's captured my imagination, I guess. She's so incredibly vulnerable. It's a miracle that she's alive and aware at all."

"But all your patients are vulnerable, Joshua. That's why they're in the hospital. Why is she so different?"

He hadn't been able to answer. Jane Doe was different. She inspired feelings in him that no one else ever had. He had shrugged.

"Joshua, you need a woman in your life."

He had shrugged again, wondering if Antoinette was seeing something that he could not see himself. "I thought we agreed that I don't want to invest as much of myself as a relationship takes."

"That was months ago. Now it seems you're ready to try."

"I'm not so ready that I'd consider getting involved with one of my patients."

"Then perhaps you should take yourself off that case. I think you're already involved."

Joshua had gone to bed with Antoinette's words still tugging at his consciousness. It was past ten when he awoke. It was his day off, but there was no time to lie quietly in bed and contemplate plans for the day. He had promised Jane Doe that he would be at the hospital to see her that morning. He had no intention of breaking that promise. It was possible that Antoinette was correct. He might be too intrigued with the soulful-eyed prostitute to be as objective and insightful as a therapist had to be, but one thing was certain. Abandoning her now would be cruel. It might hinder her recovery.

At eleven o'clock, freshly showered and shaved, he rang the buzzer that would assure his admittance to the eighth floor. Betty was waiting for him. "It's the miracle man," she said in greeting. "I thought you had a day off."

"I do. But I wanted to see a patient."

"Let me guess," she said smugly.

"How's she doing?"

"Go see for yourself. Just don't go gettin' her too excited. She's still got a long ways to go."

He nodded. "I'd like to take her to the sunroof."

Betty frowned. "She's real weak in the knees. You'll have to take a wheelchair."

"Fine."

"Then I don't see why not."

It was symbolic of the changes in room 815 that Joshua felt compelled to knock in warning before he entered. Mrs. Tryon was rocking monotonously on one bed, but the other bed was empty. Standing at the window was the painfully thin figure of Jane Doe.

"Hello." Joshua announced his presence as casually as he could.

She turned, surprised by his voice. A pink blush tinted her skin and her fingers grasped self-consciously at the back closing of her hospital nightgown. She was obviously embarrassed by her skimpy attire.

Although she had lost too much weight as a result of the trauma her body had undergone, she was still gracefully shaped and her delicate bone structure was clearly emphasized. She held her head proudly, its lovely contours starkly visible beneath the short curling hair that covered it to fall softly against the back of her neck. The muted brown wisps had been fluffed around her face and parted to cover the scar that would fade into oblivion with time and a longer hairstyle.

"I'm not dressed," she said softly.

He could tell her that he had seen all there was to see of her the night they had stripped the skimpy nylon negligee from her bruised body, but instead he smiled slightly and averted his eyes. "I'll get the nurse to bring you another gown. You can put it on over that one with the closing in the front like a robe."

Out in the hall he flagged down Betty to make his request.

"I'm surprised she's worried about her modesty," Betty said with a shrug. "Considerin' what she used to do for a livin.'"

But she had been worried, and Joshua found it endearing. He waited a few minutes after one of the aides arrived with the second gown before he reentered the room. She was sitting on the side of the bed, a sheet drawn over her lap. "I'm glad you came back," she said, as if in apology.

Joshua turned the chair and straddled it, examining her face. She was trying to smile, although the haunted expression in her eyes was making the effort almost useless. "How do you feel this morning?" he asked.

"Confused."

"That's understandable." He waited.

"Weak."

"Also understandable."

"No one will tell me anything."

Joshua frowned. He knew that the nurses were afraid they might throw her back into her state of oblivion. But the apprehension she must be feeling because no one would give her any information might set her back even more quickly. "I'll answer your questions as best I can."

She seemed to relax visibly. He watched her long lashes flutter down as she looked at her hands in her lap. "Tell me about this place."

"Better yet, I'll show it to you." Joshua went out into the hall and discovered that the wheelchair was waiting. Pushing the door open with his back, he brought the chair beside her bed. "We'll go for a ride."

She hesitated, her hand unconsciously smoothing the sheet over her legs. He could almost see the struggle she was undergoing. Her bed was a safe place, the wheelchair an unknown. "Are you going to stay with me?"

He nodded.

With a small sigh, she stood, transferring her body to the chair. Joshua pulled a blanket off the bed and tucked it around her. She was so slight that there was substantial space between her thin frame and the sides of the chair. "We're going to have to fatten you up," he said, sensing that she was uncomfortable with his casual touch.

"Food tastes funny."

"Then you're obviously getting well. Hospital food is supposed to taste funny."

There were patients milling around in the hallway, and Joshua stopped and spoke to them as he pushed the chair toward the exit. Once there he waited for Betty to unlock the door.

"Do you have Dr. Bashir's permission to take this patient off the ward?" Sarah came to stand beside the wheelchair, her gaze lingering distastefully on the young woman sitting in it.

"I have Betty's permission, which is all I need."

"I'm going to make a note of this in her chart."

"Thank you. It will save me the trouble."

Sarah's cheeks were stained with red as she turned to march back to the desk. In a minute Betty was at the door with the key, and they were through the door and standing beside the elevator.

Joshua observed how the young woman's hands gripped the arms of the wheelchair. Her knuckles were white with the effort. Casually he squatted beside her so that they were on the same level. "If this is too frightening right now, I can take you back to your room."

For one moment she considered his offer. She was torn between her desire to begin the return to life and her terror that by doing so she would be forced to face the unknown menace lurking behind the locked door of her conscious mind. "Everything is too frightening," she said softly. "But I don't think I've ever been a coward." She sat a little straighter. "I want to see where I am."

"I'm just going to show you part of the hospital. I'll tell you about the rest of it."

In the elevator, he pushed the button to take them up one floor to the sunroof. "New Orleans City Hospital is a five-hundred-bed general hospital. It's well known for its fine emergency room, its ongoing work in public health, its cardiac and intensive care unit and its psychiatric ward," he recited.

She stiffened at his last words.

On the ninth floor, Joshua turned the chair toward the sunroof, nodding in greeting to other members of the hospital staff. It was a warm day. April in New Orleans was flexible, sometimes hot, sometimes cool. Today the sun shone down with spirit. Joshua pushed open the glass doors leading to the flagstone terrace and pulled the wheelchair through. Choosing a spot where the shadow of the building would provide his patient with shade, he steered the wheelchair to a halt.

Her eyes were tightly shut as if the introduction to the outdoors was too much stimulation to handle, but with satisfaction, Joshua watched her make the supreme effort to open them. She took a deep breath to chase away the stale air of the hospital room, and for long minutes, both of them were quiet.

Finally he left her side to pull a chair into the shade next to her. By the time he rejoined her, her cheeks were streaked with tears. "Do you know why you're crying?" he asked gently.

"It's the sunshine."

He waited.

"I'd almost forgotten."

He understood. She was reacquainting herself with the simple things. They would be groundwork for the more difficult things that must follow.

"I'll try to bring you up here someday when it's raining. The drops of water scamper across the flagstone and pool in the cracks. The whole terrace sparkles."

She ignored his attempt to make small talk. "Why were the exit doors locked?"

"To keep patients from wandering out of them."

"Why aren't patients allowed to wander?"

"Because they could hurt themselves."

Joshua knew what her questions were leading up to. He wanted her understanding to expand in small stages. The truth would be less traumatic that way.

"Why don't the nurses take temperatures? Why does the old lady rock all day? Why am I in a psychiatric ward?" By the third question her voice was an unsteady plea.

Joshua reached into his pocket for the clean handkerchief he always carried. "Because you've been out of touch with reality."

Her head was in her hands, and he saw the sobs shaking her thin shoulders. There was such defeat written in the posture of her slumping body. He wanted to take her pain and share it, but he knew that no one could. After he placed the handkerchief in her lap, his hand reached to stroke the short strands of hair. His fingers were surprised by their silky feel.

"How long?" she asked finally, her voice still choked with tears.

"You were admitted in November. It's April now." She lifted her head, and he could almost see the mental arithmetic.

"Five whole months!"

"You were in a coma until after Mardi Gras. Then gradually you improved."

"I don't remember!"

"No. I know you don't."

"It's all black. And the time before that. All the time. Everything is black."

He didn't want her to dwell on the horror of a lifetime that had suddenly ceased to exist. "You're beginning to establish memories now. Tell me what you remember about yesterday."

She was trying hard not to give in to her fear, and she grabbed on to the excuse for conversation. "I remember opening my eyes. The light hurt them, and I was afraid. Everything was strange. I wanted to go back to sleep, but I couldn't. The harder I tried the more awake I became."

"That's very good," Joshua reassured her, reluctantly removing his hand from her hair. "Go on."

"Then I recognized my hands. I lifted them and found the scar on my head and I was terrified." She took a deep breath. "I think it was much later that I began to notice other things in the room. Finally I saw the old woman. And I began to scream."

"You must have been very frightened."

She gave a ladylike snort at the understatement. "You were there for the rest of it."

"I came charging into the room to see what was happening."

"And you were familiar. I felt safe when I recognized you."

He was taken aback by her words. "Recognized me?"

"Your voice." She was quiet so long that Joshua was beginning to think that she was drifting back into eternal silence. Finally she turned her head to look at him. Her eyes were luminous with the aftermath of tears. "Your voice was familiar. In the darkness I would hear it calling me. I hated it at first."

Joshua fought for his objectivity, but he could feel it slipping away. He no longer felt like a therapist asking the correct questions. He felt like a man struggling with something much more elemental. "And later?"

"Later, I didn't hate it."

Joshua knew that patients in comas or in catatonic states were thought to hear and understand voices around them. Having it confirmed so matter-of-factly by the young woman he had spent countless hours monologuing to was humbling. "Do you remember what you felt?"

"Safe."

"I'm glad." He watched the huge blue eyes search his face.

"Were you in my room earlier yesterday? Before I screamed?"

He nodded.

Her face was grave as she tried to find the right words to express her feelings. "I remember feeling as though I had been deserted. That's when I opened my eyes and the light hurt them."

They had come full circle. It was inconceivable that they could be sitting on the sunroof talking rationally about her recovery from a mental paralysis that had seemed incurable the day before. But Joshua knew that psychiatry, like every phase of medicine, had its miracles.

"Your mind had to take that time to heal itself," Joshua explained carefully. "And it's going to take longer for you to begin to put everything that's happened in its proper place. With more time, you'll begin to remember the past."

She shuddered involuntarily. "I'm not sure I want to remember." Her fingers sought the scar on her head.

"When you're stronger you'll want to remember."

"Will you tell me everything that you know?"

Joshua tried to quell the rush of sympathy he felt. He wanted to answer her questions, but he knew that all the facts were too brutal to confront her with so soon. "I told you yesterday what we know about you."

"You said that the police found me."

"That's right."

"Where?"

He tried to soften the truth. "In a lot behind a restaurant." Hootie Barn's Tavern was hardly a restaurant, but the small exaggeration seemed appropriate.

"I didn't have any identification?"

"No." Nothing but a scarf left by a madman.

"Do you know what I was wearing?"

"A nightgown."

"Only a nightgown?"

Joshua wasn't sure, but her primary reaction to that piece of information seemed to be embarrassment. What a contradiction she was. "Your X rays indicate that you're about twenty-five. Before the trauma to your head you were in good health, although there were some signs of previous bruises and dehydration."

The young woman shook her head as if to rid herself of the picture he was painting. "There must have been something else."

"I wish I could be more help," he said. It wasn't a lie. He truly wished he could. He wanted to pull her into his arms and comfort her. The silky feel of her hair still lingered on his fingertips, and he wanted to touch her again. But the strength of his own response was a warning.

Jane Doe was not the first patient he had let himself care about. But she was the first who had captured this much of his heart. His own strong physical reaction to her was like a red flag. Antoinette was right. Therapists should not get involved with their patients. But repeating that intelligent piece of advice didn't seem to help. Beyond his role as her therapist was a personal reaction that had started the night she had been brought into the hospital.

From the beginning he had been fascinated by her, emotionally moved by her life and death struggle. He was a former minister, but his interest had nothing to do with wanting to set her on the right path. And it was more than the completely normal reaction of a man to a woman who has made her living pleasing others. The closest he could come to putting a name to his feelings was to say that he felt a bonding with the young woman whose name he didn't even know. Sitting beside her bed when she was comatose he had felt a commitment to her that was as strong as any feeling he had ever had. And in spite of it, or because of it, he should begin to back away. Soon he would be no good to her at all.

One major complication was on the horizon, however. The young woman trusted him. He had called her back from the darkness, and with him she felt safe. It would take time for her to develop that feeling for someone else. And she didn't have time. She was scheduled to go to the state hospital in a matter of days. Joshua was effectively blocked from doing what he knew he must. He could not take himself off this case, no matter what it cost either of them.

"Did the police try to find out who I was?" There was a slight frown crinkling her forehead. "Didn't anyone report me as missing?"

Joshua forced himself to sound as reassuring as possible. "The police tried, but no leads turned up. So far, no one who knows you has come forward. Of course that doesn't mean that they won't." He didn't add that some of New Orleans's most notorious pimps had been called in to try to identify her. More than one had volunteered to take her off the hospital's hands when she recovered.

She folded her hands in her lap and stared at them, rearranging her fingers until she felt calmer. "Why don't you tell me about yourself? Are you a psychiatrist?"

He smiled at the prejudice apparent in her pronunciation of the last word. "No. I'm a psychologist, a therapist."

"I don't know your name."

"Joshua. Joshua Martane."

"Dr. Martane?"

"Joshua."

She managed a small smile. "Now I'm supposed to tell you who I am. Only I can't."

"You were admitted as Jane Doe."

She wrinkled her nose in distaste.

"There's nothing sacred about it. Why don't you think of something you like better?"

She ignored his suggestion. "Do you see many cases like mine?"

"No."

"That's going to make it difficult to help me, isn't it?" Years of not knowing her identity stretched in front of her.

"There are some problems that we see every day and we still haven't found a way to cure them. Familiarity is not a guarantee of success. Personally I think your prognosis is good."

She raised her eyes slowly to his. "Because you want it to be?"

He was surprised at her skill in asking questions. Her thought processes were completely rational, her expression, or "affect" as psychiatrists referred to it, was completely appropriate at all times. The human mind was a mystery. Researchers probed, developed hypotheses, formulated theories, and still the mysteries could outwit the sharpest intellect.

"Why are you looking at me like that?" she asked.

"You astound me," Joshua said truthfully. "You're recovering right before my eyes."

"And for a long time you hadn't expected me to recover at all."

Now she was even interpreting facial expressions. Correctly. He smiled. "I never gave up hope."

"Thank you for that."

Their roles were disintegrating. She was no longer patient; he was no longer therapist. They were two people who believed in each other. They were two people who had shared in a miracle. Once again Joshua realized how perilous was the line he walked.

"I'm going to take you back now." He stood and moved behind the wheelchair.

"Joshua?"

He wondered how his name could sound so sweet. "Yes?"

"I'll never forget what you've done for me."

"You've done it yourself."

"Not by myself."

He watched as she wearily leaned her head against the back of the wheelchair. By the time they were at the elevator, she was fast asleep.

"She was still sleeping when I moved her back to her bed." Joshua was telling Betty about his conversation with Jane Doe. For a moment he let himself remember the fragile, feminine feel of her body as he had lifted her in his arms to tuck her back between the sheets. She had slept right through it, too exhausted to do more than sigh in gratitude.

"I've only seen this kind of recovery one other time," Betty mused. Betty, who never attempted to impress anyone, was probably the most astute and well-educated psychiatric nurse whom Joshua had ever run across. When she made an observation, everyone listened. "It was a child, a little boy abused by his parents. The courts finally had him put in the hospital 'cause his teacher at school began to complain about his bizarre behavior."

"What happened?" Joshua leaned back against the nurses' desk, mentally filing away the case history that was unfolding.

"Well, he was talkin' to doorknobs, hoppin' on one foot twice, then the other once. Just like a Bourbon Street tap dancer, only nobody was throwin' coins at him." Betty fluffed her hair. "His folks got scared 'cause the social worker started to uncover some of the stuff that was goin' on at home."

"What stuff?"

"Bad stuff. Beatin's, lockin' him in closets. Finally, his folks left town." Betty smiled, remembering. "I had to be the one to tell him that they'd gone. He just looked at me. It was the first time he'd ever looked me in the eye. Then he said, just as clear as anythin', 'Are you sure?'"

Joshua shook his head, bemoaning lost innocence.

"I told him yeah, I was sure. Then he smiled and asked me what we were havin' for lunch. He never talked to another doorknob or danced again. Last time I heard, he had finished high school and was sellin' cars on the West Bank, makin' a fortune."

"And, of course, everyone said they had known all along that he was really going to be fine," Joshua concluded.

"Goes without sayin'. But I don't think this girl's too different. She's been waitin' until she felt it was safe to get well. Takes a strong person to have that much control."

"I'm not sure she thinks that it's safe, even now."

"She might be right." Betty laughed softly at Joshua's raised eyebrow. "We get so used to discountin' what the patients up here say. After all, they're crazy folks. But this girl just might have a point. Someone tried to kill her once."

"He won't try again. As long as she's not out walking the streets, she's safe from that maniac."

Betty shrugged. "I don't know about that. But I do know that it pays to listen carefully. Even when the words aren't bein' said out loud."

Jane Doe smiled wanly at the middle-aged woman who was introduced as the daughter of Mrs. Tryon. There was no way that the surprised woman could hide her amazement that her mother's roommate had made such a startling recovery. As she fussed around, preparing her mother to get in a wheelchair for a ride around the ward, she continuously sneaked glances at the opposite bed.

"Could my mother get better like that—" The daughter's words were directed at a nurse who was helping her maneuver Mrs. Tryon's wheelchair through the doorway, and as it closed, shutting off the rest of the question, tears gathered in Jane Doe's eyes. It was inconceivable to her that only the day before she had resembled Mrs. Tryon. "Perhaps it would have been better if I'd never improved," she whispered to herself. "The miracle happened to the wrong patient. The one who didn't deserve it."

She had been sitting up most of the day except for the nap she had taken before lunch. Tired, and completely discouraged, she lay back on the bed and shut her eyes. She wanted to shut off the voices in her head, too, but they faithfully replayed the conversation she had engaged in with her psychiatrist several hours before. It was too bad that her memory of the rest of her life wasn't as crystal clear.

There were no tears to cry. She lay perfectly still, willing her mind to retreat from the truth Dr. Bashir had bestowed on her like a gag gift at a birthday party. Only the truth wasn't funny at all. It was sordid and frightening.

The door opened and closed softly, and as always, she tensed, afraid to open her eyes. Her persecutor might be waiting for her. She had no other name for the mist-enshrouded man who tormented her, instilling fear in every cell of her body. Helplessly she waited for pain to be inflicted, and when it wasn't, she forced her eyes open to search for it. Joshua was standing beside the bed, and relief flooded through her body, washing away the fleeting memory.

"I thought you were asleep."

Dr. Bashir's words returned to haunt her. They were almost as horrible as her vision of the persecutor. Tears welled in her eyes again, and she closed them tightly. "Go away."

She heard the sound of the chair being pulled beside her bed, and she turned in the opposite direction, willing Joshua to leave her alone. "Go away," she repeated.

"Not until you tell me what's wrong."

"Don't waste your time."

There was no answering scrape of the chair. Self-consciously, she threaded her fingers together, hoping that she could outwait him.

"I have all night," he said finally. "I'm here to visit—I'm not on duty."

"You're wasting your time."

"I don't think so."

His perseverance angered her. She pulled herself up to a sitting position and slowly rotated to face him. "Trying to save a soul, Reverend Martane?"

Joshua heard the anger in her voice. "Are you upset because someone told you I used to be a minister?"

She ignored the soft-spoken question. "Are you here to hear my confession? Sorry, I can't remember any of the glorious details."

Joshua searched her face, trying to figure out what was causing the suffering he saw. "What's upset you?"

"The truth!"

Joshua waited.

"The truth you didn't bother to tell me."

"And what truth is that?"

She couldn't make herself say the words. They stuck in her throat, burning away her speech. Lowering her head, she gazed through misty eyes at her fingers.

"You've been talking to someone."

She didn't move; only the tears slipping down her cheeks signaled that she had heard him.

"A nurse?"

She shook her head slightly.

"A doctor?"

She didn't move, but the deep breath she took told Joshua he was on the right track. "So Dr. Bashir has been here to see you."

"Why didn't you tell me I was a...prostitute?" Her voice cracked with the effort it had taken to say the last word. "Why didn't you tell me that someone tried to murder me? God, I wish he'd succeeded!"

For a moment, Joshua wanted to shake her. His anger at Bashir for telling her the truth when she was not yet ready to hear it knew no bounds. But he was angry at her, too. She was giving up. "Your life is precious," he said finally.

"At least I understand your interest in me now." Self-dillusionment and bitterness dripped from every word. "If anyone on the ward needed your Christian attention, it was me, wasn't it?"

"I'm here because you need help, and for no other reason."

"And of course, if you just happen to make a good woman out of me in the meantime, you won't be disappointed, will you?"

That she could be this angry and challenge him so openly was a good sign. But the human part of Joshua Martane, the part that was emotionally invested in this young woman, was hurt by her words. Still, when he answered, it was as a therapist. "What you do with your life is up to you. I'm here to help you put the pieces back together, but how you put them together is your decision."

She had been sure that her words would drive him away. She obviously did not deserve to have Joshua Martane in her life. His forbearance completely dissolved her weak defenses. "I'm sorry," she said with a sob. "I'm so sorry." She hid her head in her hands, wiping her tears on the sheet.

Joshua itched to comfort her. Instead he forced himself to watch as she sobbed out her pain. "You have nothing to apologize for."

"Evidently I do," she said, struggling to stifle her misery. "Evidently I have a lot to be sorry about."

It was apparent to Joshua that Dr. Bashir's talk with her had not unlocked any new mysteries. She was still wandering in the dark, trying to fit the pieces of information they gave her into one intelligent whole. She had no memory of her past life. It was as if she had been born again, but she felt no forgiveness for her past mistakes. Indeed, they were mistakes she didn't even remember.

Finally she was calmer. "I don't want to talk about this anymore."

"Fine. We don't have to." He cast around for a safer subject. "I'm having trouble with something, and I need your help."

She lifted wet eyes to his. "What?" she asked suspiciously.

"I don't want to call you the patient in room 815 anymore. And you've already let me know that Jane Doe has no appeal for you. I want you to come up with a new name for yourself." He didn't add that beginning to establish a new identity could be helpful if her memory didn't return before she had to leave the hospital.

"I don't care. Call me what you want."

Joshua continued to prod. "Is there a story that you remember, a character you'd like to name yourself after?"

"How about Mary Magdalene?" All the bitterness she felt about the revelation of her background resounded through the suggestion. "It's such a good analogy. The prostitute saved by the man of God."

"You're no longer a prostitute, and I'm no longer a man of God. I'm just Joshua and you're a woman who needs a name." Joshua tilted his head, placing his fingers beneath her chin to lift her gaze to his. "But I like the name. Mary Magdalene led a useful, important life. I'm going to call you Maggie."

She refused to look at him, closing her eyes against the warmth and compassion in his. But his words rang in her head. Maggie...Maggie. She felt herself moving into darkness, anchored only by Joshua's touch.

Maggie, darling. Don't run down those stairs. There was a man's voice calling to her through the black fog. Unlike the persecutor, he was not mist enshrouded, only very far away. *Maggie, darling...* He was gone.

She had no idea how long she had been silent. When she opened her eyes, Joshua was still watching her, his fingers resting beneath her chin. Her eyes locked with his. Behind the compassion was a subtle flicker of something more primal. Joshua was not oblivious to her. She understood instinctively that she was not a patient like every other patient to him. That thought and the tiny sliver of memory lifted her feeling of anonymity. She was, after everything, still a person worthy of his concern.

"Maggie will be fine," she whispered. "Just fine."

Joshua noticed the change, the slight lifting of the cloud of depression enclosing her. He dropped his hand. "Maggie what?"

She shrugged.

"Maggie sounds Irish. How about Kelly?"

She shrugged again. "With a name like that, I'll have to dance jigs and eat corned beef and cabbage."

"If you can dance a real jig, we might be on the trail of something."

"Sure. If I'm Irish American, I might be one of millions instead of billions."

She was trying to joke, and Joshua smiled his encouragement. "We'll find out who you are, Maggie. In the meantime you're to work on getting well, not on regretting a past you don't even remember.''

"With that attitude, I can understand why you left the church.''

Her perception was amazing. Maggie was a woman with keen intelligence and sensitivity. More than ever Joshua found himself drawn to her. "Now my job is simply to help you get well. While I'm doing it, let's both throw away our stereotypes, shall we?''

She lowered her eyes and drew a deep breath. "Thank you, Joshua. I've been feeling so . . . soiled.''

He wanted nothing more than to gather her in his arms and give her the physical reassurance she needed. But he knew that touching her that intimately was no longer safe. Instead he stood, squeezing her shoulder for a moment, before he turned to leave. "Sleep well tonight.''

"Thank you.'' She watched him disappear through the door, and she struggled to convince herself that her courage and strength were not disappearing with him.

Chapter 3

Maggie was sitting on her bed reading a February issue of *Newsweek*. It didn't matter to her that the magazine was completely out of date. She hadn't been aware of the world situation in February. She hadn't been aware of anything.

It was one of the tricks of the amnesia that gripped her that she could remember general facts like the name of the president and the capitals of forty-three of the fifty states. Arguments about the economy and the environment seemed familiar. Titles of television shows came easily, and sometimes she found that she could sing along with songs on the tinny radio that played incessantly in the patients' cafeteria. Unless the songs were new, that is. Then they were totally foreign to her.

She had just washed her hair, and the soft wisps were curling around her face. She had changed into a clean hospital gown, using another one as a robe. The rough cotton chafed her thighs, and she wished for a real nightgown or casual street clothes like those the other patients had. But there was nobody to bring her anything from home. It was possible that there wasn't even a home. Trying to shake off that melancholy thought, she forced herself to concentrate on the article about nuclear disarmament.

"Maggie?"

The familiar voice sent a warm rush of sensation through her nervous system. "Joshua. Come in."

He came to her bedside, noticing with satisfaction that they were alone. It was always easier to talk without Mrs. Tryon rocking in the next bed. He pulled the straight-backed chair beside Maggie's bed. "You look cheerful."

"I'm working on it." She smiled and her face glowed with the first steps toward health. Joshua examined her closely. In the week since she had begun to make her recovery, Maggie had gained some weight, beginning to fill out the sharp contours of her body. Color was returning to her face, tinting the white of her skin with a pale rose. Her hair seemed to grow almost daily, and she had learned to cleverly conceal her scar. Looking at her this evening, it was more and more difficult to discern signs of the trauma she had undergone.

"Where's your roommate?"

"Her daughter has her out on the floor in a wheelchair. I've never seen such devotion in my life." Maggie stopped when she realized what she'd just said. Her lips turned up in a small smile. "I wonder if that's true? How do I know what I've seen? Sometimes I forget for a moment that I've lost my memory."

"Somewhere inside you it's all still there. You haven't lost your memory, just your memories. They'll come back."

"Joshua, why do you suppose I don't remember?" She began to twist the sheet. "You say it'll all come back to me, but suppose it's something physical that isn't going to change?"

Joshua leaned forward and covered her hands with his. "Suppose you tell me why you don't remember."

"What do you mean?" Maggie liked the feel of his hand on hers, and for a moment she allowed herself to imagine that it was something other than a comforting gesture.

"What happens when you remember anything at all?"

"I haven't remembered anything. Nothing except a man's voice calling 'Maggie, darling.' But I told you about that already." She searched Joshua's face for a clue to his meaning.

"You have another memory that keeps trying to make itself known."

Maggie shook her head. "No, nothing..." She stopped and Joshua could feel her hands become fists.

"Maggie," he prompted.

"My nightmare." She watched Joshua nod solemnly. "But that's not a memory, it's just a terrible dream."

"Your nightmare is one way that your memories are trying to get in touch with you. When you can begin to face it, you may begin to remember pieces of your past." Joshua squeezed her hands and then withdrew his. "I want you to tell me about it."

"No!"

The seconds ticked by as Joshua waited. "Tell me," he said finally. "Are you afraid you'll remember the night you were brought here, or are you afraid of the life you led before that night?"

The challenge in his tone coaxed Maggie's response as silence never would have done. She lifted her head and stared straight into Joshua's eyes. "It's easy to sit beside my bed and be judgmental, isn't it?"

"I'm not judging you."

"Aren't you? You're assuming that my guilt about being a prostitute is what's keeping me from remembering my past."

"What do you think about that theory?"

"When I try to look into the past, I feel terrified, not guilty." She lifted her chin another notch. She wanted to hurt him. "Maybe I liked what I did."

He tried not to smile at her display of pique. "Tell me about the nightmares."

Maggie saw the softening of his features. She sighed. It was difficult to stay angry with Joshua, even when he pushed her further than she wanted to go.

She tried to put the dream into words. "It's always the same one, over and over again. I'm lying in bed in a small dark room. A man comes toward me. I can't see his face because there's always mist surrounding him. But I'm terrified that he's going to hurt me. I try to get away, but I can't. He bends over and whispers to me."

"What does he say?"

Maggie ignored Joshua's question. "Then just as he reaches for me, I wake up."

"What does he say?"

She tried to control the humiliation in her voice. If she refused to tell him, then Joshua would know how much it hurt her. "He calls me what you and everyone else assume I am."

Joshua could almost see Maggie withdrawing from him. "I'm sorry, I don't like to see you in pain," he said honestly. "I know you didn't want to tell me that."

Maggie tried to shrug it off. "It's just one more piece of evidence, isn't it? Even the man in my nightmare thinks I'm a whore."

"It's what *you* think that's important."

"What I think is that nothing makes sense. I go over and over it in my mind, but it doesn't help."

"It will come. In the meantime, you're getting stronger."

"And the nightmares are coming less often."

Joshua put his hand on her shoulder, his fingers brushing the soft skin of her neck. "I'm glad for that." For a moment their eyes locked, and both felt the communication that neither would dare put into words.

A noise at the door signaled the return of Mrs. Tryon and her daughter. Joshua stood. "I'll see you tomorrow, Maggie. I hope you sleep well tonight."

As always, Maggie felt a wrench as Joshua disappeared through the doorway. As he'd said, she was getting stronger. She no longer needed his support to make her feel like a whole person. That part of their relationship had ended. Instead, in its place had appeared a whole new set of yearnings that were impossible, and painful, and very, very real.

And there wasn't a hope in the world that her feelings would ever be reciprocated.

The new hospital orderly wasn't orderly at all. In fact he was the most disorderly staff person that Ida Collins, the head nurse on the sixth floor, had ever seen. And he was lazy. And insolent. She shook her head and bit back the curse that had almost escaped. She had been complaining for a week that the sixth floor was shorthanded on the night shift. A near epidemic of spring fever had cut her staff by a third. Personnel had finally heard her pleas and sent her a new man to train. If she fired him, personnel would never take her seriously again.

"After you've washed your hands," she said, addressing the man with distaste, "you can begin giving the patients fresh ice water." She almost hated to send him to any of the patients' rooms, clean hands or not. There was something disagreeable about the man that soap and water could never wash away. She hoped it wasn't catching.

"They're not going to be drinking ice water at 2:00 A.M. I've got a break coming." Under the man's heavy growth of reddish whiskers, his mouth curled up in a snarl.

"Fine. You can take care of the water when you come back. But don't forget your break's only fifteen minutes."

Fifteen minutes would just about do it. Wiping his hands on his white uniform, the man sauntered down the hall to the stairway. Inside the stairwell, he listened for footsteps. There were none. As quietly as he could, he began to climb. One flight, two...

This was where his plan had broken down the night before. He had reached the eighth floor, taken the stolen key out of his pocket and begun to insert it when the door on the floor above had slammed. He had realized that he wouldn't be alone long enough to unlock the door and disappear through it before he was discovered.

He had pocketed the key and begun the climb to the top floor as if he were going there for his break. Then he had heard the voices. He passed a couple on the next landing.

Listening as he climbed, he knew that the two young interns were having a private assignation on the stairs. He had cursed his bad luck and given up for the night.

Tonight would be different. It was later. He was calmer. Tonight he would succeed. He had already done the hard part. Stealing the key had taken real brains. In contrast, killing the girl would be easy.

He took the hard-won key from his pocket, slipped it into the lock and turned it slowly. He had already peeked through the wire-woven glass window to determine that the hallway was empty. The patients were all sleeping soundly, doped up and unaware. The staff? Well, they were probably snoozing at the nurses' station. Everybody knew that the staff on the psychiatric floor took their rest whenever they could get it.

If anyone saw and questioned him, he could tell them that he had gotten confused, that the stairwell door had been ajar and he had thought he was on his own floor. After all, the locks were to keep patients in, not to keep staff members out.

His white, rubber-soled shoes creaked softly as he crept down the hallway. Finding out the girl's room number had been surprisingly difficult. He'd had no idea what name they'd brought her in under. But he had managed to figure it out. Just as he was going to manage to sneak in her room and hold a pillow over her face.

For a moment he stopped as he imagined her slender body twisting with the effort to dislodge him. The thought excited him. He only wished he hadn't waited so long to do it. He should have killed her when he'd had the chance to take care of it at his leisure. But he'd had dreams then, dreams he'd thought she'd make come true for him.

The man stopped in front of room 815. There was still no one in the hallway. He opened the door and slipped inside. His dreams were gone. Soon the girl would be, too.

Maggie lay awake listening to the small sounds around her. She could hear Mrs. Tryon's harsh breathing and the gentle swish of the cars on the steets below. In the hallway she could hear the soft squish of hospital rubber-soled shoes. One of the nurses must be making rounds.

It was a comforting thought. She was used to the hospital routine, and Joshua had convinced her that there was nothing here to fear. There was always someone nearby. Now if she was awakened by her nightmare, it took her less time to adjust to her surroundings and less time to get back to sleep. Tonight would be such a night, especially after finally describing the dream to Joshua. The images had come again, their impact no less frightening, but already she was calmer. She knew where she was. The dream had only been a dream. No one could harm her here.

Maggie heard the footsteps stop at her door. She fought back the lingering effects of the nightmare. This was not the faceless persecutor. This was only a nurse checking on her patients. Still, it was only when the door opened and closed softly that Maggie forced her eyes open. She resisted the urge to call out in order to hear the reassuring answer of a female voice. She had to learn to grapple with her fears by herself and defeat them.

The room was dark, and Maggie's eyes adjusted slowly. She could make out a white blur beside the door as if the nurse couldn't see well, either, and was waiting for her eyes to adjust to the darkness. Slowly the nurse began to move toward her bed. Maggie could feel her pupils widen, feel the beginnings of real panic. The white blur was too tall, too angular to be a woman. It was a man, faceless in the dark of the room. Suddenly she was immersed in her own nightmare. She wasn't awake. She couldn't be. She tried to fight her way to consciousness, but there was nowhere to go. The white blur was by her side, tugging on her pillow. Maggie opened her mouth to scream and a hand was clapped over it.

"Well, you're awake. Didn't they give you a sleeping pill?" The man's voice grated with a hoarse, familiar sound. Maggie struggled, using her small reserves of strength, but she was no match for the man from her nightmare. "Go ahead, keep trying to get away. I like to feel you moving against me."

Maggie could feel her terror overwhelming her. Bile rose in her throat and she could feel herself choking. "I hate to make this so quick," he said in false apology, "but I can't stay too long."

She had no fingernails to scratch with; she could only hit him as he covered her face and his own hand with the pillow. She could feel the weight of his body on top of it as he pulled his hand off her mouth. There was no more sound. She bucked and kicked and tried desperately to push the pillow off her face. Her despair was total. She was going to die. Just as the blackness began to envelop her, she thought of Joshua.

"Why in the hell didn't somebody call me?"

"Nobody called you because you're not related to the girl. You're not even her psychiatrist." Betty watched Joshua pace the floor of the staff lounge. Each time he smashed his fist into his hand, she winced in sympathy.

"I'm the only person in the world she trusts, dammit. I could have calmed her down. She doesn't belong in that cell."

"From what I hear it was a madhouse up here last night." Betty lifted her shoulders as Joshua stopped to glare at her. "Sorry about that. Anyhow, they were so busy trying to stop all that screamin' that I'm sure it never occurred to anyone to get in touch with you. They finally put Maggie in 809 so she wouldn't hurt herself."

"And Mrs. Tryon?"

"She's her old self this mornin'. Which isn't necessarily good."

Joshua ran his fingers through his hair. "What could have brought it on?"

"Maggie won't say anything now. Near as anyone can figure out, she had another bad dream or hallucination and started to scream. Mrs. Tryon woke up and started screamin', too. Or Mrs. Tryon screamed first. We just don't know.''

"Something must have triggered it."

"It's just possible that Maggie's a lot sicker than any of us thought." Betty put her hand on Joshua's shoulder. "Are you gonna try to talk to her?"

"Of course I am."

"Then there's somethin' else you should know."

Joshua understood that he hadn't heard all the bad news. "What else is there?"

"Dr. Bashir is going to go through with his plan to send Maggie to the state hospital in Mandeville. He's arranged a commitment hearing for day after tomorrow."

"On what grounds?"

"That she's a danger to herself. She has no memory of her previous life, and she's incapable of caring for herself until her memory returns. After last night, he shouldn't have too much trouble convincing a judge." Betty's face radiated her concern. She understood just how much of himself Joshua had invested in this patient.

"Jim Nelson won't go along with this."

"Dr. Nelson's out of town for the next week. Dr. Timmes is takin' his place. He won't go against Dr. Bashir."

"Who's Maggie's lawyer?"

"Crofton from the public defender's office."

Joshua knew that having a lawyer speak on Maggie's behalf was proper legal procedure. He also knew, in this case, with no family or friends protecting her rights and a public defender who was probably only nominally acquainted with the details of her case history, Maggie's chances of escaping commitment were not the best.

"She's going to feel like we're coming at her from all sides. All the breakthroughs she's made aren't going to be worth a thing," he said, slamming his fist in his hand again.

"If you give up, too, then there won't be anybody fightin' for that girl."

Joshua nodded, but his expression was becoming one of resignation. "I'll need you to unlock the door to 809."

Betty was sympathetic. "If she stays calm for twenty-four hours, Bashir will probably have her moved back into 815."

"Just in time for her commitment hearing."

Maggie counted the dots in the acoustical tile on the ceiling. She wondered why the ceiling wasn't padded, too. Everything else certainly was—the floors, the walls. This is where crazy people ended up. But then, she was probably lucky. At least they hadn't put her in a straitjacket. She suspected that was next on their agenda if she got upset again. The next time someone tried to murder her, she'd have to remember to be calmer about it.

Everyone had given up on her. Even Joshua hadn't come to see her. Maybe they thought that if she huddled there on the padded floor by herself, she'd see the error of her ways. Maybe they'd learned their techniques from some Far Eastern prisoner of war camp. It was brainwashing in reverse. They weren't trying to make her talk; they wanted her to shut up. Well, it had worked.

She was still counting dots when she heard a key turn in the lock and the door swing open. Her persecutor only came in the dark. She wasn't afraid.

"Maggie?"

She started at the sound of Joshua's voice. She had a sense of sudden shame. He shouldn't be seeing her this way. She was dehumanized, an empty shell. There was nothing left inside her.

She pulled together whatever shreds of pride were left. "I'd offer you a chair if there was a chair to offer." The tranquilizers they'd pumped into her the night before were wearing off. Her voice was distinct. She was glad for that one piece of herself that still seemed to be intact.

"Maggie, I didn't know about last night. I came as soon as I heard."

She had screamed his name over and over and over again. How could he not have known? "It's all right, Joshua. You have other obligations."

She felt rather than saw him kneel beside her. Her eyes were still turned to the ceiling. "Maggie, what happened?"

"I'm sure it's in my chart."

"I want to hear it from you."

"Do you know that there are over 368 dots in each tile in this ceiling?" She looked at him for the first time. The sympathy in his eyes was almost her undoing. She steeled herself to ignore it and turned away. "Every time I count that high, I lose track of where I am. If they really wanted patients to get well in here, they'd put in tile with symmetrically arranged dots. These wavy patterns would push anybody over the edge."

"Are we going to play games?" Joshua sat back and crossed his legs, campfire-style.

"Why not? It might while away the time until somebody tries to murder me again."

Joshua felt cold chills run through his body. He didn't know whether to hug her or slap her for her flippancy. He could do neither. "Tell me what happened," he said evenly.

"You'd find it a fascinating study in true insanity. You'd probably even want to take notes." Maggie carefully avoided his eyes.

"You're very angry."

"That's insightful."

"I can't help if I don't know what happened."

She gave a bitter laugh. "Do you want the unexpurgated version? The one nobody will believe? Last night I was sure someone was trying to kill me. It was the man out of my nightmare. He came into my room wearing a white uniform and tried to smother me with a pillow. Just as I was passing out, Mrs. Tryon began to yell. I guess it scared him away. When I could breathe again, I began to scream, too. Then they shot me full of something and when I came to, I was in my own, wonderfully plush private room."

Joshua was shaken to the core. Patients often thought that someone was trying to kill them. But Maggie had never shown any signs of paranoia before. She had always been

able to distinguish her nightmares from reality. "You said
that last night you were sure. What about right now?"

Maggie could feel her self-control crumpling. She knew
what Joshua must think of her story. After all, he was
trained to probe beneath the surface. He would never believe that she was telling the truth.

"What's the right answer, Joshua?" she asked in a voice
devoid of emotion. "The wrong answer got me thrown in
here last night. Just tell me what I'm supposed to say? That
I know it was only a nightmare and I'm sorry? That I was
just trying to get attention? That I was confused but I've
been straightened out since then?" She lowered her head to
her hands. "I've got to get out of this place. Just tell me the
right thing to say to make it happen."

Joshua ached to comfort her, to pull her into his lap and
hold her until some of his strength was infused into her
body. But her misery was inside him, too. He could do
nothing but continue to question her. "The right thing to tell
me is the truth."

She shook her head. "The truth won't set me free."

"You believe what you described really happened?"

Maggie refused to answer.

"Do you have any idea why someone would try to murder you again, Maggie?"

She sat a little straighter and lifted her head from her
hands. "The man who left me for dead in a vacant lot may
not be thrilled to know I'm alive. Is it too crazy to think that
he may have come back to finish the job?"

"I've thought of that."

Maggie felt a jolt of hope. Joshua wasn't trying to talk her
out of her story.

He went on. "But the doors on and off the ward are always kept locked. All the permanent staff on this floor have
keys to the stairs in case of fire, but it would be very difficult for someone else to get hold of one. And I gather that
nobody saw a stranger around during the commotion last
night."

"Nobody looked." Maggie lifted her chin. "After all, it was only me trying to tell them what had happened. No one was listening."

"I'm listening."

"Are you? Or are your ears tuned to psychologist frequency?" Her hopes had died with the doubt in his voice.

"My ears are tuned to Maggie frequency, only Maggie is so busy putting up defenses that she's not communicating as well as usual."

"What do you expect?" Maggie hit the padded floor with the palm of her hand, and she knew her voice was too loud. "Everyone here thinks I'm crazy! No one has taken a thing I've said seriously. It's much easier to assume I was hallucinating than to ponder the possibility that I just might be telling the truth." With great effort she lowered her voice. Joshua's expression was intense; she couldn't tell if he understood her distress. "Look," she began again, "all I care about now is getting out of here."

"If you stay calm, you should be back in your old room by nightfall." Joshua watched Maggie turn paler at his words.

"I don't want to go back to my old room. He'll know where to find me again. I'd rather stay here. At least it takes two keys to get to me when I'm in this room."

Joshua ached with sympathy, but he kept his voice level. "You just said that all you cared about was getting out of here."

"Out of the hospital. Out of this town. I want to sign myself out, Joshua. Can you arrange it?" She turned and faced him. The palms of her hands were held out as if in a plea. "It's all I'll ever ask of you." Her voice broke and tears turned her eyes a misty gray. "Please help me."

Joshua had been able to remain in strict control under the force of her anger, but her tears were his undoing. He reached for her in a moment of weakness and brought her to rest against him. She felt impossibly fragile as she trembled in his arms. He stroked her hair and cursed whatever had brought her to such a state. He cursed the total lack of his own objectivity and the not-so-subtle response of his body to the feel of hers against him. Her soft breasts grazed the back of his arm, and he couldn't seem to ignore it. He could smell the sweet, clean fragrance of her skin. No, he had never felt this way about a patient before.

He tried to keep his feelings out of his voice. "Maggie, I want to help you. But it's not as easy as you think it is." She was silent, and he tightened his arm around her. "When you were very ill, the hospital placed you in the intensive care unit. You stayed there for a long, long time. Later, when you were finally out of danger, they moved you up here."

"Why are you telling me what I already know?" Maggie tried to pull away, but Joshua wouldn't allow it.

"In order to bring you here, your doctor had to sign what they call a Physician's Emergency Certificate. Since you weren't able to agree on your own, that's how it had to be done from a legal standpoint."

"And?"

"Because of the nature of your case, you've been on this floor much longer than the usual stay. But when it became apparent that this hospital wouldn't be able to do anything else for you, procedures to transfer you to another hospital in Mandeville, Louisiana, began."

"I'm not going to another hospital. I just want to sign myself out!"

"I'm afraid you can't. Legally, you're under the control of the state. The wheels were set in motion before you began to improve. Now a hearing's been set up to determine whether you should go to the other hospital or not. It's scheduled for day after tomorrow." Joshua could feel the rigidity of her body as she absorbed his words.

"If it's a hearing, then that means they'll want to hear my side of it. Won't they?"

"Yes."

Maggie's mind was whirling with this new piece of information. "If I go to another hospital, will I have to stay more than a week?" Joshua's silence was answer enough. "A month? Two?"

"The commitment will probably be for a year with reviews of your case every three months."

"No!" Maggie's voice was a wail. "That's a prison sentence."

"Maggie, you're going to have to stay calm. When they ask you questions at the hearing, you have to answer as completely as you can."

She wrenched herself out of his arms and turned to face him. "I have no answers. I remember nothing about my past. I can't even tell them my name. And what if they ask about last night? God, what if they ask about last night?"

"That's the first thing they're going to ask you about."

"I don't have a chance."

"Maggie, it's going to be all right."

She heard the doubt in his voice again, and she trembled harder. "Don't try to lie. You don't do it very well."

He lifted her chin in the palm of his hand to force her gaze level with his. "Whatever happens you're going to get through this. Even if you go to the state hospital, you'll be out in three months."

"What's the hospital like?"

He tried not to remember. No matter how well run such an institution was, it was not the right place for Maggie. He could think of no hopeful way to answer her question. His silence was all the response she needed. Joshua watched her begin to retreat. He could almost see her draw into herself. "It's not the best place in the world," he said, grasping for anything to stop her reversal, "but you'll be taken care of. There'll be people there who will help you."

"And somewhere nearby there's a man who will track me there and kill me." She shook her head, moving back against the wall. "Please, leave me alone," she said quietly. His presence had become too painful to bear. She couldn't adjust to the new bleakness of her future with Joshua sitting companionably at her side. She couldn't risk letting him touch her again. He had entered her life only to disappear without warning. She must face her punishment alone.

"It's not a foregone conclusion that you'll be sent to Mandeville. I'm sure the judge will be impressed with how remarkable your recovery has been."

Twisting her head slowly from side to side, she stared in front of her. Joshua could see her will her eyes to become vacant, her expression to become rigid. She was fighting the truth by trying to block her feelings. And he couldn't blame her. Under the circumstances, it was an understandable response. She was no different from anyone, anywhere, who has just been found guilty of a crime they didn't commit.

"You can't give up," he said, his hands coming to rest on her shoulders. "You have to try."

"I'll try," she said, her voice a monotone. "I'll go in there and I'll tell them I don't know who I am, where I'm from or what my life has been. I'll tell them I've been told that I used to be a prostitute, and that someone tried to murder me because of it, but I don't remember.

"I'll tell them if they just let me go, I'll go back out on the streets and try to get an honest job. Of course, I don't know if I have any skills, any skills besides prostitution, that is, but that doesn't matter. I'll give my word of honor that I'll start a brand-new life, free from any illegal activities."

She paused, finally raising her eyes to Joshua's. "I'm sure they'll believe me. Especially after my exemplary behavior last night. Aren't you?"

As usual, she had seen the truth much too clearly. Joshua willed himself to try to infuse her with hope. "You have a chance."

"Please go away. I appreciate your trying to help, but I need to be alone."

He wanted to stay, to take her in his arms again and let his hands and presence comfort her. Instead he rose from the floor. "I'll be back this evening."

Maggie's eyes were shut and her nod was barely perceptible. When the door closed behind him she didn't even flinch.

There was only one person who could halt the process that was destined to end in Maggie's move to the state hospital. Joshua knew that he should be the last person to confront Dr. Bashir and request that Maggie's case be withdrawn from the hearing. He also knew that there was no one else to make the request. Wearing stern self-control like a bulletproof vest, he found the physician in the staff cafeteria on the fourth floor.

Ignoring the food line, Joshua strode right to the two-person booth in the corner. "Dr. Bashir? May I join you?"

Dislike flickered across the psychiatrist's features, but he closed the newspaper he was reading to make room for Joshua.

"I want to talk to you about the commitment hearing."

Dr. Bashir chewed with calm precision. "Then talk."

"I want you to withdraw Maggie's case from consideration. Surely it's just an error that she's still being considered for placement in the state hospital."

"It's no error. That's where she belongs, and I intend to see that the transfer is made."

"Why do you want her transferred when she's made such remarkable progress here?"

"Do you call last night progress?"

Joshua ignored him. "I know her term of involuntary commitment is ending, but I'm sure she'd volunteer to stay until we can make suitable arrangements in the community."

Dr. Bashir stopped chewing, washed his last bite down with a swallow of iced tea and turned slightly to examine Joshua. "It is very apparent, Martane, that you are too involved with Jane Doe to see anything clearly. You've questioned my authority repeatedly, and you've blocked my attempts to use drugs to help her regain her memory. It is clear to me that in this atmosphere, the girl will not improve. She will become more and more dependent on you and less capable of accepting the reality of her position. I want her out of your sphere of influence. Especially after last night."

Joshua's eyes glittered with barely controlled anger, but his voice was calm. "So you admit you're sending a patient to the state hospital because you dislike me."

"I dislike you, yes. You are lacking in objectivity. You are too emotional to be of any use to anyone on the eighth floor. But since my opinion is not shared by my superiors, I can do nothing about my convictions. Nothing except get one patient off your caseload. And that I will do."

"Using a patient to carry out a personal vendetta is unprofessional, Bashir. Who's being emotional here?"

Dr. Bashir shrugged. "Your words, not mine. My concern is for the patient alone. It is the patient I am trying to protect."

"You do know that when Dr. Nelson comes back from his conference, I'll discuss this with him."

"I am sure you will. In the meantime, the patient in question will already have been transferred." The little man stood, leaving his tray for some hapless cafeteria employee to dispose of. "Since the hearing is open to staff, I'm sure I'll see you there. Until then, Martane."

Joshua watched the psychiatrist strut out of the cafeteria. He had not expected help from Bashir, but neither had he expected the overt hostility that he had encountered. The psychiatrist was in deadly earnest about Maggie's commitment. He would view it as a personal triumph; he was willing to go to almost any lengths to be sure that it was carried out.

Joshua's alternatives were few. Although he planned to talk to Dr. Timmes, the acting chief psychiatrist, he suspected that the conversation would only be a formality. The man had neither the authority nor the knowledge of the case to put himself on the line. He would sympathize; then he would tell Joshua to back off.

And backing off was one of his alternatives. Joshua could admit defeat. There were times when submitting gracefully to the inevitable was the better part of valor. He could humble himself, admit that he was not going to be able to change the future and help Maggie prepare for her transfer.

He wasn't infallible; he could not predict what effects the state hospital would have on her.

Joshua shut his eyes and leaned his head against the back of the plastic booth. He was lying to himself. He could predict what would happen just as surely as he could predict that the sun was going to rise the next morning. Maggie would be terrorized in the new environment. She would retreat; they would medicate her; she would retreat even further. His Maggie, alone and afraid, crying out for help that might never come.

And what if her story about the man from her nightmare was true? It was farfetched, Joshua could barely admit the possibility, but there was still a slim chance that someone had gotten a key and attempted to murder her again.

Desperately he searched for an answer. He could go to the hearing and make a case against commitment. If he was calm and completely rational, the judge would listen carefully, but Joshua knew that his word weighed against that of a psychiatrist would not have much importance. If he was passionate in his insistence that Maggie be allowed to stay at N.O.C.H., he would surely lose Maggie and possibly his own job.

The only other alternative was to get her out of the hospital before the hearing took place.

He wasn't sure where that idea had come from. It was so ridiculous, so impossible that he discarded it immediately. And immediately it came back, begging to be reexamined. If he could remove Maggie from the hospital, the hearing would have to be postponed. Joshua knew that if Dr. Nelson was in town, the hearing would never have been scheduled. If he could spirit her away until the chief psychiatrist came back, Joshua knew that Dr. Nelson would agree to release her, especially if Joshua had arranged suitable accommodations and out-patient follow-up.

He also knew that he would surely lose his job. No matter what the provocation, no matter what the motivation behind his act, removing a patient from the hospital would be immediate grounds for dismissal.

He opened his eyes, smiling automatically at one of the pretty young nurses who was always trying to catch his attention. Through his concern and caring for one patient, he was being forced to face the issue that had haunted him throughout his adult life. He could be objective and predictable, working to change the world by careful inches, or he could be the rebellious reformer, the man who goes where he isn't wanted, demanding changes where changes aren't desired.

He was neither. He was simply Joshua Martane, ordained minister and psychologist, a man who didn't want to see one woman's life destroyed. What power was forcing him to make a choice between his own needs and the needs of one fragile female patient who had begun to mean too much to him?

He could no longer deny the feelings he was developing for her. Joshua Martane was completely entranced with the amnesiac prostitute with the huge blue eyes and the soul that cried out to his own.

Was he entranced enough to sacrifice his job for her? He made a difference in the lives of the patients he worked with. Cut off from this opportunity, what would he be worth to anyone?

There were no easy answers. He only knew that the time was limited to wrestle with the questions and to listen to the still, small voice inside him that would give the only answer he could live with. He stood to find his way to the exit.

By nightfall Maggie was back in room 815, but there was no hope of sleep. She tried to comfort herself with the prediction that the man from her nightmare would not be stupid enough to try to kill her two nights in a row.

It was little comfort.

The man from her nightmare had shown a desperate recklessness by coming on the eighth floor and trying to murder her with dozens of people nearby. That same desperate recklessness might push him to try again. Tonight.

Maggie knew that she was not going to be able to hold out indefinitely against her exhaustion, but she was determined to try until the early-morning hours when the activity level on the ward would begin to pick up and nurses in the hallway would make it more difficult for a stranger to hide.

Awake and alert she was able to suppress the panic she had experienced the night before. This time, if the man came into her room, she would find a way to keep him in there until her screams could bring a staff member to investigate. If she could do that and survive the encounter, her sanity would be vindicated. Perhaps she would even be released from the hospital.

That hope wasn't bright enough to illuminate a shoebox, but she held on to it as the night wore on and the noises in the hallway diminished. She felt more and more vulnerable as the ward settled in for the night. Mrs. Tryon, who had probably saved her life the night before, was sleeping restlessly, but her presence gave Maggie little sense of comfort. The old woman often moaned or screeched in her sleep. There would be little possibility that her timing would ever be so perfect again as to scare away an attacker. No, Maggie was completely alone. Even Joshua hadn't believed her story.

Joshua. She was only a patient to him, a patient who believed that a sinister nightmare was reality. She was just another one of the many people on the ward who couldn't tell fact from fiction. His doubt had even caused Maggie to question her own recollections of the night before. There had been moments during the day when she had asked herself if perhaps everyone else was right.

But finally, irrevocably, she had put her doubts behind her. She was still physically weakened from her long illness, she was emotionally vulnerable and confused about her past, but she knew that she was able to distinguish the real and the imaginary. The man from her nightmare had been real.

Reality. She gave a short, humorless laugh that sounded strangely loud in the quiet room. She was going to have to face the reality of her feelings for Joshua Martane. He had abandoned her, shown her clearly what a distance there was between them. She had become too dependent on his approval and on his warmth. Foolishly she had let herself believe that she was important to him as a person, not only as a patient. Now she could see clearly the fallacy of that belief.

There had been too much time to think and to daydream during the past week. She had made too much of Joshua's comforting embraces, his concern for her well-being, the intensity of his gaze.

A noise in the hallway brought her sharply back to her present situation. Someone was coming down the hall. Maggie could hear the footsteps slow outside her room. With her eyes wide open and perfectly adjusted to the darkness she lay quietly in bed and waited.

The door swung open with its characteristic squeak. For a moment, a man's figure was silhouetted in the sudden light from the doorway. Then the door shut behind him. The man came slowly toward her bed, his hand outstretched. Terror-stricken but still in control, Maggie waited. If she screamed now, she would scare him away. She had to wait until he was close enough to grab.

He came closer, walking slowly as if he were feeling his way across the floor. There was something different about the man tonight, she thought, frantically trying to figure out what it was. As he neared her bedside she realized that this man wasn't wearing white. He was dressed in street clothes.

"Maggie? Are you awake? It's Joshua."

She felt faint with relief. As she took a deep breath she realized that her lungs were starving for oxygen. She took another breath and another as she sat up, hugging her knees with her arms to keep her body from flying into a million pieces. "Is this some new form of shock therapy?" she finally asked, her voice low and shaking. "How dare you sneak into my room after what happened last night!" Anger replaced relief. "Did you want to prove that I'd scream at any provocation?"

Joshua had known that it was the worst possible way to approach her. He had also known that it was the only way. He had no time now to soothe her. "Be quiet, Maggie, and listen to me."

"I'm available tomorrow between nine and ten o'clock for polite conversation. Now get out of my room!"

"If you don't keep your voice down I'm going to have to put my hand over your mouth."

Maggie opened her mouth to defy him and saw the quick, upward motion of his arm. She was silenced instantly.

"Maggie, don't make me do this. Promise me you'll just whisper your abuse and I'll take my hand away."

She struggled for a moment and then when she realized that Joshua was not going to let her go without a promise, she reluctantly nodded. When she was free again, she whispered with fury, "There's a nice padded room down the hall for crazy people, Joshua!"

"We don't have time for clever conversation. I've decided to try to help you get out of here." In the near darkness he could still see that her eyes were wide, blue pools of unbelief.

"Why would you do that?" Her anger, challenged by this new information, disintegrated. All her defenses went with it. "You don't even believe someone tried to murder me. Why would you want to help me escape?"

Joshua took the time to shoot her a warm smile. "Because I care what happens to you. You don't need to go to the state hospital, and I'm betting heavily on the fact that the chief of psychiatry here, Dr. Nelson, will agree. Unfortunately he's out of town and can't be reached, so he'll be no help before the hearing. I want to get you out of here until he comes back. Then we can have you discharged officially."

"You're going to get into deep trouble over this, aren't you?"

As frightened as she was about her own future, Joshua could see that her first concern was for him. That fact was enough to banish his lingering doubts about helping her. "Desperate circumstances cry out for desperate measures."

"I can't let you take the chance." Big tears welled up in her eyes, and she extended a hand to cover one of his. "Joshua, your willingness to do this will help me find the strength I need to face the hearing."

As always, just her casual touch infused him with warmth. He tried not think about how much of his decision had been based on his attraction to her. "You're not going to face anything. In five minutes you and I are going to walk out of this hospital together."

Maggie examined the stern expression on Joshua's face. It was a face that she knew by heart. At night as she closed her eyes, Joshua would come sharply into focus. She had used it as a talisman to help ward off her nightmares. Maggie knew all Joshua's expressions. She knew the one that he used when he tried to distance himself from her in order to be objective about her problems. Tonight his face was calm, but his eyes shone with a warmth and concern that tore through her own deep depression like a searchlight in the fog.

"I can't let you."

"You don't have a choice."

She was torn between her acute need to leave the hospital for her own safety, and her need to protect him from the consequences of his act. Her hesitation was the only answer Joshua needed. It was evidence that she would cooperate.

"Maggie, if we don't get out of here in a few minutes, we won't have a chance to make this work." He realized that if he gave her any more time to think, she might refuse to come. Standing, he gestured for her to stand, too.

She was wearing only her hospital gown, and she clutched it together behind her. "I think I have another one to use as a robe on the chair over there."

"You're not going to need it." Joshua started for the door.

"I can't go outside like this!"

"Trust me. You won't have to." He turned and saw the rigidity of her stance. With two steps he was back at her side. He laid his hands gently on her shoulders and pulled her close for a quick hug. Briefly he wondered how anyone so small and so delicate could stir such powerful feelings inside him. "I have everything taken care of. Just do what I tell you to, and you'll be safe. Can you do that?"

She nodded against his chest. "You're not going to leave me, are you?"

"I'll be with you the whole time. Ready?"

Maggie straightened her shoulders and stepped away from him. She knew very little about Joshua Martane, who he was or what he felt for her. But she was certain of one thing. He wouldn't harm her. And at that moment he was the only person in the world that she could say that about.

"Lead the way," she said quietly.

Chapter 4

The lights in the hallway had been turned down for the night. At the moment, all was quiet, but there was never a guarantee that the silence would last. Joshua measured the possibilities of success as he surveyed the long stretch to the stairwell door.

"I want you to walk in front of me," he whispered to Maggie. "Stay to the side of the hallway where it's a little darker. Walk as quietly as you can. I'll be right behind you. When we get to the exit door, step aside and I'll unlock it. If we're stopped, let me do the talking."

Letting Joshua do the talking would be easy, Maggie decided. Her own heart had lodged firmly in her throat, cutting off the possibilities of speech. At his nod, she stepped in front of him, took one last look down the hallway herself and began her escape.

She was barefoot. The only shoes she owned were paper slippers that the hospital had issued her, and they always flapped loudly when she walked. Barefoot she could walk undetected, but it made her feel strangely vulnerable. She was escaping from the hospital with no shoes and a gown that was only held together by two flimsy bows. Even now, with her future dependent on the success or failure of this attempt, she was still acutely conscious of the picture she must be presenting to Joshua behind her.

There was a sharp pressure at her waist, and Maggie felt herself being shoved toward a partially opened door. She stumbled and barely kept herself from crying out. When Joshua didn't follow her inside, she flattened herself against the wall beside the door and took stock of her surroundings. There were two beds in the room, only one of which was occupied. The old man in it was sleeping soundly. With her back still firmly against the wall, Maggie slid farther from the door and waited.

"Joshua, did you find what you were looking for?"

Maggie recognized the voice of one of the night nurses. It sounded as if she were coming down the hallway.

"No, but I remember now that I left it in the staff lounge. I was just on my way to look there."

"Do you need any help?" The nurse's voice was closer, as if she had come to join Joshua.

"I don't think so. Things are pretty quiet tonight, aren't they?" Maggie could almost see the casual smile that would accompany Joshua's words.

"After last night, we deserve the quiet." The nurse gave a wry laugh. "I'm going to go check on the patients in 815 right now. I don't want a repeat of all that screaming."

Maggie shut her eyes in defeat. The escape was a failure.

"I already checked." Joshua's voice was slightly sheepish. "I'll have to confess, that's part of the reason I came back tonight. I was worried about Maggie. Both she and Mrs. Tryon are sleeping soundly. You don't have to worry."

"Well, good. I won't bother, then. I sure don't want to take a chance of waking either of them up. Why don't you come have some coffee after you're done?"

"Thanks. I might, or I might just let myself out and go up to the roof for a while. It's a beautiful night." Joshua's voice became fainter, as though he were walking away.

Maggie shut her eyes and waited, praying that the old man wouldn't wake up and find her standing there. It seemed like an eternity, although she knew it was only a minute or two before the door creaked open and Joshua came in and motioned for her.

This time they made it to the end of the hall and through the exit door without being detected. Standing under the bright lights of the stairwell, Maggie knew that she was visibly shaking. Taking her hand in his, Joshua led her down to the next landing. "Put these on quickly." He leaned over and pulled a small shopping bag out of the corner.

Inside Maggie found a belted raincoat, a pair of white nurses' shoes and a triangular paisley scarf. "Where did this come from?"

"Lost and found."

"You have this so well planned!" She couldn't help it. Her voice was a whispered wail.

"Remind me to tell you about my adolescence." Joshua flashed her a quick grin that quickly turned into a frown when he realized that she hadn't moved. "Get going, Maggie."

She clasped the raincoat around her, slipped on the shoes and tied the scarf under her chin. Everything except the scarf was sizes too large. Maggie knew that she looked like a refugee, not a nurse who was on her way home.

Joshua talked softly as she dressed. "We're going to walk down the eight flights. The hospital staff rarely uses the stairs except for trips to adjacent floors. The next floor down is surgery, so we probably won't meet anyone until we get a flight or two beyond that." He examined Maggie and then smiled slightly. "I almost forgot." He pulled a pair of lightly tinted glasses out of his pants pocket. "Your eyes are unforgettable. This should help."

Maggie was surprised by the husky warmth in his voice. Instinctively she knew that it hadn't been put there to comfort her. She slipped on the glasses, which instantly slid to the tip of her nose. She pushed them up and tilted her head to keep them on. Her vision was slightly blurred.

Joshua linked his arm through hers, beginning to help her down the long flight of stairs. "If we meet anybody, smile and keep going," he said softly.

"My face is frozen."

"Freeze it in a smile, then, for Pete's sake. Don't look so forlorn. Somebody's going to get suspicious."

"What a perfect time to think of that," she muttered, as she concentrated on navigating the steps without losing her shoes.

Twice they passed other staff members, who, as Joshua had predicted, were traveling between adjacent floors. Once Joshua smiled and called a young nurse by name, the other time they just hurried on their way.

Maggie's knees were shaking from the unaccustomed exercise and the challenge of the escape. Finally they paused for a moment at the first floor exit. "The hospital has a parking garage," Joshua told her. "My car is there. We're going to go through this door, turn right and walk through the front waiting room. Then we're going to turn left, walk down a long corridor and out into the garage. Once there, we'll take an elevator to the third floor. My car is a dark blue Dodge Colt. If we get separated, wait for me there."

Separated? She shut her eyes. "I can't . . ."

"Yes, you can. Now I want you to link your arm through mine and look like you're enjoying my company."

"I should be good at that," she tried to joke. "I've been told I used to do it for a living." Maggie could feel herself descending into panic. She wasn't sure if she could move at all. She knew that Joshua could feel her trembling.

"Stop it, Maggie. Take a deep breath and get ready." Before she could respond, Joshua pulled the door open and pushed her through it.

The man rubbed his hand over his reddish whiskers and waited for the couple to continue their descent down the stairs. Another romantic meeting on the stairwell. He muttered a string of curses, which did nothing to alleviate his anger. He had been forced to wait for long minutes while the man in blue jeans and the young nurse took their time strolling down the stairs and past the sixth floor. Now he didn't have any time to waste.

He had never been lucky. He had been born unlucky. It wasn't fair. No matter how hard he tried, something always went wrong. The night before he'd thought his luck was changing. Another minute and the girl would have been dead. And then the old lady had begun to yell. It had ruined his chance.

Well, maybe not quite. Listening to the commotion as he hid in the bathroom next door to 815, he had discovered that no one had believed the girl's story. Tonight he would do everything the same way, but this time he'd be luckier. Tonight he knew exactly where to go and which bed to find her in. Tonight he'd finish what he'd started.

The couple on the stairs might have slowed him down, but they hadn't stopped him. He was ready now. His luck was about to change.

Maggie and Joshua made it through the waiting room without incident. They were halfway through the wide corridor when a man's voice came toward them. "Joshua? What are you doing here this time of night?"

Bearing down on them from the opposite end of the hall was the stern masculine figure of Sergeant Sam Long. Joshua bent toward Maggie and brushed a casual kiss across her cheek, his mouth lingering against her ear. "Turn your head when you pass this man. He's seen you before. Continue down the corridor and into the garage. Take the elevator to the third floor. Blue Dodge Colt parked somewhere in the middle. Now, Maggie."

She couldn't move. Joshua lifted his hand to her shoulder and gave it a painful squeeze. "Now, Maggie!"

Like a sleepwalker she turned and started down the hallway. Maggie didn't see Sam's curious glance as, intently, she followed Joshua's orders. Expecting to be stopped at any moment, she moved toward her destination, repeating the directions until they were burned into her brain.

Joshua waited for Sam. Out of the corner of his eye he noted with satisfaction that Maggie had reached the door and gone through it into the garage. "What are you doing here?"

"We just brought another girl in. Only this one was DOA. Damn." Sam's usually dispassionate expression was clouded with anger. "We came this close to catching the murderer. This close." He held his thumb and forefinger a scant inch apart.

Joshua felt as though someone had punched him in the stomach. "Are you on his trail or was it a fluke?"

"Oh, we're hot on his tail. We know his blood type, his hair color and general build, the kind of places he hangs out, his preferences in women. We know everything except his name and phone number. And I'll have that before he kills again." Sam stopped and examined Joshua. "You didn't say why you were here so late."

"I was meeting somebody."

"The girl you were with?"

"That's right."

A tiny smile softened Sam's features. "It's about time, don't you think? Hurricane Daphne's been married and divorced again already, and you've just been quietly licking your wounds."

"Spoken like a confirmed bachelor," Joshua responded, surprised to find that Sam's casual mention of his ex-wife left him with no feeling except surprise at the reminder. "You should try getting close to a woman yourself."

"The only person I want to get close to right now is the bastard who's committing these murders. I'm going to interview Jane Doe this week, amnesia or not." Sam raised his hand at Joshua's protest. "Yeah, I know what you think—you think I'll traumatize the little darling. Frankly, Josh, I don't care. I want whatever information I can get, trauma or not. There are lives at stake."

Joshua shrugged. He was in no position to argue about the patient who was sitting outside in the parking garage waiting for Joshua to help her escape. "We'll see," he said. "God knows, I want you to catch this guy, too."

"I'm going to catch him." With a nod, Sam was gone.

On the third floor of the poorly lighted garage, Joshua walked swiftly to his car, searching for the paisley scarf. He found Maggie perched sadly on the rear bumper of the blue Dodge. "The worst is over now," he said softly, sitting beside her for a moment with his arm around her shoulder. "We'll be out of here in a minute."

"Joshua, this is crazy."

"No, it's not. It's exactly the right thing to do, Maggie. Trust me, won't you?"

She nodded slowly. "But I'm worried about you."

"I can handle whatever happens."

He pulled her up, and with his arm still stretched behind her for comfort, he guided her to the passenger side of the car. "Here you go," he said after he'd unlocked the door and helped her in.

They drove out through the employees' exit, reaching the street with no incident. Once they were in the familiar New Orleans traffic, Joshua allowed himself a sigh of relief. "Well, we made it."

Maggie stripped the scarf off her head and ruffled her short curls. She was mesmerized by the sight and sounds of the traffic outside her window. She was out of the hospital. For the moment she was safe. She wondered if she would be able to sleep. "What happens now?"

"Now I take you somewhere for the night."

"Where?"

"I had planned to take you home."

"Home?"

"My home." He caught her incredulous look and smiled in response. "You'd be safe there."

"But wouldn't your family mind?"

"I have no family. I live alone, unless you count the world's nosiest landlady. After thinking about it, though, I realized that if the hospital notifies the police, my house will be the first place they'll look."

"Oh, no."

"Afraid so."

"Why have you involved yourself this way, Joshua?"

"Because you're worth it," he said simply. "I chose to help you; I was completely aware of the consequences."

"I wasn't. I didn't think it through."

"You didn't have time. But to answer your question, I'm taking you to stay with a friend of mine. The section of town isn't the best, but Skeeter can be trusted."

"Skeeter?"

"Skeeter and I grew up together. He's an artist... among other things."

"But we'll be involving him."

"He'll love it. I'm afraid it'll be one of the lesser crimes he's been involved in."

"Are you going to leave me alone?" Maggie knew that her voice reflected the utter and complete failure of her courage. Whatever surge of adrenaline had gotten her this far had finally worn off. She was out of the hospital, but essentially she was on her own. And she wasn't strong enough for that yet.

Joshua wanted to stop the car and soothe her fears. He understood her dilemma. "No," he promised softly. "I'm going to stay with you until this thing is settled and we can find you a decent place to live and a decent job."

"Why?"

The answer was too strange and too painful. He wasn't sure that he wanted to acknowledge it, even to himself. "Because I care what happens to you," he said instead. It was a watered-down version of the truth.

"Thank you, Joshua."

"You're welcome, Maggie."

Both of them were suddenly aware that the journey away from the hospital was also a journey into a new relationship. No longer patient and therapist, they were man and woman thrown together by circumstances beyond their control. Where they would go from here was as much a mystery as what had brought them together in the first place.

Skeeter's neighborhood was not the best. In fact, it was one of the worst. New Orleans, like other big cities throughout the United States, had tried to cure the problems of its urban poor by housing them in huge projects that stretched for miles, creating a veritable wasteland of squalor and crime. Skeeter did not live in one of the projects, but his neighborhood bordered on one of the most infamous.

It was one of the more ironic aspects of New Orleans life that when the housing projects had been sprinkled through the city, they often had been set down in the midst of an otherwise upper-class neighborhood. Mansions sat only blocks away from the rows of dilapidated brick buildings. Symbolically, Skeeter's house sat somewhere between the two worlds, just as Skeeter himself did.

Joshua parked his car in front of the fading salmon wood-frame house and behind the light blue van that was Skeeter's pride and joy. "Watch your step on the front porch," he cautioned Maggie as he came around the car to help her out. He had already scanned the street, checking carefully for any signs of suspicious movement. There were residents sitting, shirts unbuttoned, on nearby front stoops to catch the breeze, but tonight there was nothing out of the ordinary. Joshua knew that this was not always the case.

Together they skirted the gaping hole on the porch left by a missing board. Skeeter refused to repair the obstacle. He claimed that it discouraged intruders. At night he turned off his front light and dared any trespasser to survive an encounter with his porch. It was cheaper than a burglar alarm, more efficient than a watchdog. It was typical Skeeter.

Joshua knocked, waited and knocked again. Finally he opened the wheezing screen door and banged directly on the wooden one behind it. "Skeeter, it's Josh."

"Maybe he's not home." Maggie was so tired that she could hardly stand up, and her voice reflected her exhaustion. Joshua pulled her to stand in the crook of his arm, banging harder on the door.

"Most likely he's asleep," he explained.

The door opened suddenly, just as Joshua raised his fist to pound on it again.

"Persistent, aren't you?" A wiry man of average height stood in the doorway, scratching his bare chest with one hand as he tried unsuccessfully to cover a yawn with his other. The man was dark-skinned with straight black hair that fell to his shoulders in a shining pageboy and had a handlebar mustache that spread out almost wide enough to touch his earlobes.

"Aren't you going to ask us in?"

Skeeter stood back, making a sweeping gesture with his hand.

His arm still around Maggie, Joshua tugged her into the house. Once inside, he steered her to a newspaper-covered sofa and pushed her gently on to it, deftly piling the papers on the floor as he did.

"I'd have cleaned up if I'd known that the Right Reverend and his lady friend were coming for a social call." Skeeter grinned at Joshua, punching him lightly on the arm. "What's the occasion, Josh?"

"I need your help."

Skeeter's eyes narrowed, turning from his friend to examine the young woman on his sofa. Maggie had shut her eyes, the weariness of two nights of missed sleep claiming her totally. It was apparent to both men that she would be asleep in a minute. Skeeter lowered his voice. "What's wrong?"

"Maggie's been a patient at City. I smuggled her out of the hospital tonight."

Skeeter whistled softly. "Didn't you take a vow of obedience or something? I thought you gave up your life of crime years ago."

"Maggie was about to be committed to the state hospital. It was senseless and cruel. She's as sane as you or me. Saner than you, in fact."

Skeeter smiled, the corners of his mouth obscured by the drooping mustache. "And you rescued her."

Joshua nodded. "Can she stay here for a few days? I think I can have her officially released when the chief of psychiatry comes back into town. Until then, she needs to stay out of the way."

"No place could be more out of the way. No one with any intelligence at all will come looking for her here," Skeeter agreed. "Sure, she can stay." His eyes traveled over Maggie's sleeping figure. "I might even enjoy her company."

"I come with the deal," Joshua said firmly. "The hospital will know how she escaped and with whom. I have to stay out of the way, too. And Maggie is off limits, Skeeter. Understand?"

"That's too bad. I can understand how you got involved. She's something."

Joshua silently agreed. The tired lines around Maggie's eyes had not yet disappeared with the onset of sleep. Her short curls were still rumpled from their encounter with the paisley scarf, and they framed her face like a smoky cloud. Her long, curling eyelashes touched the ivory skin of her cheek. She looked enticingly female and totally defeated. "Where can I put her?" Joshua asked Skeeter. "Do you have an extra room or shall I try to make her comfortable here?"

"I have an extra room. You can both sleep in there." He laughed at Joshua's lifted eyebrow. "Don't go thinking I'm suggesting any untoward behavior. It's got a couple of single beds in it."

"Fine. I appreciate it, Skeeter."

"I may even have clean sheets."

"Remarkable."

Together the two men entered the bedroom, by unspoken agreement pushing the two single beds against separate walls. Skeeter found the sheets, and in a few minutes the room was ready to be occupied. "I'm going to get Maggie settled," Joshua told Skeeter. "Go back to sleep, if you want."

Skeeter squinted at an alarm clock sitting on one of the two Formica-covered dressers. "Nah, I've got to get going. I'm sketching portraits at one of the courtyard bars down on Bourbon Street tonight. I was just catching a few hours' sleep before I had to be there."

"Are you still doing portraits at Jackson Square?"

"About three days a week." Jackson Square was a park located in the section of old New Orleans known as the French Quarter or the Vieux Carré. One of its attractions was the artists who clustered on the sidewalk doing charcoal or pastel portraits for tourists willing to pay their prices. Skeeter was one of the best, capturing entire personalities with a few strokes of his pencil. It was the only time that he allowed his remarkable insight into human nature to show.

"I won't ask what else you're doing."

"Good." Skeeter clapped Joshua on the back. "It's better that you keep your nose out of my affairs. That way, what you don't know can only hurt me."

"Just don't bring the law down on your head while I'm here. That's all I need."

"My sins are so petty that no one is particularly interested. I haven't kidnapped anybody recently—unlike you, my old boyhood pal."

Joshua just smiled a tired smile and went to get Maggie. She was sound asleep, her hand thrown across her eyes to block the light. He didn't have the heart to waken her. Instead he slipped his arms under her inert body and lifted her off the sofa. She hardly weighed more than a child, but she didn't feel like a child in his arms. She felt like a woman, the softness of her breasts brushing his chest, the smooth skin at the back of her thighs sliding against his wrists.

In the bedroom he unbuttoned the khaki raincoat, slipped it over her arms and out from under her still-sleeping body. He removed the heavy shoes. The skimpy hospital gown left little to his imagination. Quickly he tucked a sheet and blanket over her, turned off the light and closed the door behind him.

Skeeter had dressed in a pair of disreputable jeans and a blue T-shirt advertising a popular Bourbon Street strip show. His hair was neatly pulled back into a low ponytail revealing one gold hoop earring. "There's probably something to eat in the refrigerator," he told Joshua. "I'll be back tomorrow morning sometime."

Joshua nodded. "Thanks, Skeeter."

"Think nothing of it. You have no idea what this does for my ego."

This time Joshua laughed. Everyone needed a friend like Skeeter to make them take themselves less seriously. One dose of Skeeter was all the humbling anyone could stand. Joshua locked the door after Skeeter's van pulled away from the house and rummaged in the refrigerator for a cold can of beer. Half a can later he made his phone call to the hospital.

The head nurse on the eighth floor was irate, as she had every right to be. Joshua explained the circumstances behind Maggie's removal and assured her that he would emphasize to Dr. Nelson that no one else on staff had been aware of his actions.

"You're going to be fired," she warned him.

"I know."

There was a long silence, and finally, "If you bring her back right away, I can cover for you."

Joshua was grateful that the nurse was concerned about him. "Thank you, but I did what had to be done. I haven't changed my mind. Just pass the word that I'll be in to talk to Dr. Nelson when he returns." With that, he hung up.

"Here's to you, Bashir," he said, toasting the empty room with his remaining beer. But there was no pleasure in knowing that he had bested the psychiatrist. Unlike Dr. Bashir, Joshua did not see the situation with Maggie as a personal vendetta. He would gladly have let the oily little physician win if it would have helped Maggie. Now that the drastic step of removal from the hospital had been taken, Joshua was beginning to understand that he would do almost anything to help her. There was very little of his own ego involved in this conflict. What he had done, he had done for her.

For a long time he sat on the sofa, his beer forgotten, and stared at the cracked plaster wall on the other side of the room.

"No. No...please!"

Joshua sprang from the sofa and covered the distance to the bedroom door in a dead run. Snapping the hall light on, he threw the door open and covered the distance to Maggie's side in three rapid steps. She was tossing back and forth, moaning in the throes of a nightmare.

"Maggie!"

She sat upright, her hands thrust in front of her. "Go away! Please don't hurt me!"

"It's Joshua, Maggie. It's Joshua." He leaned toward her, talking softly to reassure her.

But Maggie was responding to some inner vision. She shrank back against the pillow and covered her face with her hands. "Not again. Please!"

Joshua was afraid to touch her. He understood that she might interpret it as a new and more horrifying threat. "Maggie, wake up. Wake up, sweetheart. It's Joshua. You're safe."

Her moans softened. Carefully Joshua sat on the edge of her bed. "I'm right here, Maggie. Nothing is going to hurt you. You're safe."

"I don't...please...don't..." Her voice trailed off into a sobbing hiccup.

"Maggie, it's Joshua. Take your hands down and look at me."

Behind her hands she shook her head.

"It's really me," he reassured her. "I'm right here, sweetheart. You're all right."

Carefully he reached for her hands, talking to her quietly as he did. "I'm going to cover your hands with mine, and then, very slowly you're going to let me pull them back to your lap. Ready?"

She was immobilized.

He covered her hands with his own and gently pulled them from her face. "Open your eyes, Maggie. Now, sweetheart."

Finally she obeyed; her eyes, even in the dim light, were terror filled, tempered only by an impossible courage. Joshua knew that she had expected someone else.

"Who did you think you were going to see?" he asked her softly.

"My persecutor."

He nodded. "Tell me about it."

The vision was fading as it always did with the light. "It was the same dream I always have. Only this time he had a pillow in his hands."

"What else?"

She shook her head, searching Joshua's face for clues. Was she truly insane? Were the visions hallucinations as Dr. Bashir had informed her in his clipped, cold voice? Was this dream no different from the one of the night before that she had thought was real?

"Maggie, you've been through enough to give anyone nightmares." Joshua could sense her insecurity, and he tried to reassure her.

"Maybe . . . maybe they're not nightmares at all. Maybe I really am crazy." She covered her face with her hands, this time to blot out the horrible vision of her own insanity.

Joshua understood. Sliding closer to her, he took her in his arms, not allowing her to pull away. "You're not crazy, sweetheart. You've been through a very bad time. You suffered a severe head injury; you're frightened and very unsure of yourself."

She was trying to control herself, and the effort showed in her voice. "I'm awake now. I'm all right." She said the words to convince herself as much as to convince Joshua, but as soon as she said them, she knew that they were true. "I know that I was only dreaming." The terror of the dream was evaporating. Last night's terror would never completely die; she knew the difference. "Last night was real. I couldn't wake up because I wasn't asleep."

Joshua was silent. There was nothing that he could say about her conviction that someone had actually tried to murder her again. He just continued to hold her.

Maggie was silent for long moments, too. Then finally she said, "I wish you believed me, but I'm grateful that you're not pretending to, just to make me feel better."

"What I believe is that whatever happened last night seemed very, very real to you. Real enough to make you defy everybody else's opinion."

She let his voice soothe her pain. Tentatively she put her own arms around his waist and rested her head against his chest. Joshua had held her before, but she had never held him. She was suddenly very aware of him as a man. Joshua was large, strong and in the peak of physical condition. Her arms contacted hard muscles and firm skin under his shirt. He felt marvelous, a rock to hold on to in a world too chaotic to cope with, an anchor.

His fingers were stroking her hair, playing gently with the short curling strands. Neither of them could speak. Neither of them could break the dangerous contact. They just sat on the bed, holding each other, both trying not to think about how impossible their relationship was.

"You're so good to me," she said finally, trying to find the strength to draw away.

"I'm not going to let anything hurt you." Inch by reluctant inch, he loosened his hold on her. "We're going to find out why you're so frightened, Maggie, and we'll deal with it together."

She wanted to believe him; she wanted to believe that Joshua would be there for her, with her, when she needed him. But it wasn't fair to him. Already, she might have cost him his job. "I'm getting stronger," she said. "I'm going to stand on my own two feet."

"I know. But even on two feet, you'll need a friend."

Maggie understood, with perfect clarity, that Joshua would never be just a friend. In her own heart, he was already much, much more. "I feel as though I've always known you," she said. "I'm sure it's just what you've done for me. Dr. Bashir says it's trans . . ."

"Transference." It was a term used for the strong feelings that a patient develops for his or her therapist. Dealing with those feelings could be a breakthrough in a patient's entire way of relating to important people in his life. In this case it was much too simple an explanation.

"Maggie," Joshua said carefully, "don't try to categorize what has happened, what is happening." He pulled away and smiled at her, wiping a lone tear from her cheek with his thumb. "We've never had a typical therapist-patient relationship. Dr. Bashir filled that need for you."

Maggie wrinkled her slightly crooked nose. "Dr. Bashir talked, and I nodded my head. Is that supposed to be typical?"

Joshua laughed, bending to kiss her on the forehead before he stood. "Not really. Can you go back to sleep now?"

"Where are you going to sleep?"

He pointed to the other side of the room. "Skeeter doesn't have luxurious accommodations. I can sleep there or out in the living room if it bothers you to have me in here."

"Please stay here." The words came too quickly. She tried to modify them. "I mean, I want you to be comfortable."

"And you'd like to have someone close by if you get frightened."

Not someone. Joshua. "Yes."

"There's no reason to be ashamed of that. I'll be right here." He stepped out into the hall and flicked off the light, coming back in the bedroom to his own bed. Sitting on the edge, he began to undress. Moonlight filtered in through half-drawn shades, and Maggie turned on her side away from him to give him privacy.

"Joshua?"

"What?"

"Why do you care so much about what happens to me?"

I'm paid well to care what happens to my patients? You need me more than anyone ever has? I'm falling in love with you?

"Because you're Maggie," he said quietly.

"Maybe I'm not," she murmured sleepily. "Maybe I'm not who anyone thinks I am. Maybe I'm not *what* anyone thinks I am."

Joshua lay down with his hands behind his head and thought of a recent conversation with Sam Long. The two friends had sat together over drinks at a French Quarter bar near Joshua's apartment. "I don't think Maggie was ever a prostitute," Joshua had said after telling Sam about her return to consciousness and her subsequent amnesia.

"Any hooker on Bourbon Street could proposition you and you'd find something good to say about her. Not everyone is a little lost lamb, Josh."

"You don't know her."

The blond police officer had inclined his head toward two expensively dressed women in the corner. "See those two young ladies over there?"

Joshua turned slightly to examine the women in question. Both were fashionable, wearing modest designer clothing and subtle makeup. Joshua smiled and turned back to Sam. "What's your point?"

"One of those young ladies...isn't. The sweet young thing on the left is a man. He's been down at the station twice for soliciting. His partner there is a female. She goes under a variety of names. Last time I picked her up it was for forging one of them on somebody else's check."

"So?"

"The papers are full of stories about people like them. An airport terrorist shoots six people; a man kidnaps an heiress in Florida and gets her killed in the getaway chase; three illegal aliens are arrested for smuggling enough heroin into the country to addict the population of New York City."

"I don't have time to read the papers."

"You should."

"Why? I'm not stupid, Sam. I was raised on the streets, too. Remember?"

"Then think again. This Maggie was picked up, half dead, in a vacant lot. God only knows what she'd been through, but one thing was for sure. The man who tried to kill her was sure she was a prostitute. She was dressed like one and that area of town is crawling with hookers. If she was somebody's sweet little girl, she'd have been identified right away."

"But nobody recognized her. Not even the pimps you paraded through her room."

"You gonna trust a pack of pimps? Besides, she could have been a loner, a new girl in town. Who knows?"

"You don't know her."

"I don't want to. I know her type." Sam's voice was heavy with cynicism. "She can look at you with those big brown or green or blue eyes and take you for all you're worth. Don't give her an inch."

Now, Joshua had given her much more than an inch. He had given Maggie his support and his help in escaping from the hospital. And he was on the verge of giving her more, much more.

Once before there had been a woman who had taken what he had to give. There had never been any question about Daphne's identity. That time Joshua had known from the beginning what he was getting himself into, and he had entered that relationship with his eyes wide open. That love, that marriage, hadn't lasted. From it he had learned to be careful, to give his attention, his friendship, but never his heart. Evidently the lesson hadn't quite taken.

"Joshua?"

"Yes, Maggie."

"I'm glad you're here."

"So am I."

"Good night." Her voice was beguilingly husky and filled with sincerity.

Joshua wanted to believe, more than anything, that he was not in the presence of a first-rate con artist.

At first, Joshua slept fitfully, expecting a recurrence of Maggie's nightmare. When hours passed and she still slept quietly, he let himself drift into a deeper sleep. When the light of late morning woke him he was surprised at how renewed and rested he felt. Turning toward Maggie's bed, he discovered that she was no longer there. He could hear the sounds of voices from the other room, and he rose and dressed to go in search of her.

Maggie and Skeeter were sitting companionably at Skeeter's kitchen table. She was wearing the khaki coat, buttoned as a bathrobe, her feet bare on the scarred linoleum floor. Skeeter, dressed as he had been the night before, was listening in fascination as Maggie told him what she knew of her own story.

"Do I smell coffee?"

Maggie's face brightened. "Joshua, sit down. I'll get it for you."

He allowed her the small pleasure. She was obviously delighted to be able to do something for him. "Thank you," he said, cradling the hot cup in his hands. "Did you sleep well?"

"Very." She didn't add that for the first time since she had once again become aware of her surroundings, she had felt safe enough to allow herself the luxury of deep sleep. She had awakened feeling refreshed. She had awakened knowing that Joshua was sleeping in the next bed.

She had opened her eyes to find him facing her, his dark hair brushing his forehead. In sleep he looked younger, less formidable. He looked as if he might have needs and dreams of his own. He was less the caregiver, more the man. She had been stirred by this new image, and she had wondered how it would feel to be held by this different Joshua Martane, not as a therapist holds a patient or even as a friend holds a friend. But as a man holds a woman.

"Maggie was just telling me about herself." Skeeter was eating a bowl of sugar-coated children's cereal. Maggie turned from Joshua and watched with fascinated awe as Skeeter shoveled spoon after spoon under his mustache. "Did you ever think about getting Sam on her case?" he asked Joshua.

"He is."

"Who's Sam?" Maggie sipped her coffee, the first decent cup she had tasted since waking up in the hospital.

"Sam's the man I stopped to talk to in the corridor last night," Joshua answered. "He was one of the policemen who brought you to the emergency room."

Maggie made a face and set her cup on the table.

Skeeter shot her a sympathetic smile. "Hasn't Joshua ever told you about his boyhood?"

Maggie shook her head.

Skeeter finished the last bite of his cereal, holding the box out to Joshua, who shook his head in distaste. Shrugging, Skeeter turned to Maggie. "Joshua, Sam and I were the three musketeers. All for one and one for all. Sam became a policeman, you've seen how Joshua turned out, and then there was me."

"Let's not elaborate on how you turned out," Joshua said, only half joking.

"Joshua and Sam are still trying to reform me," Skeeter explained to Maggie.

"I think you're very nice," she said.

"So does my parole officer. Anyway, when we were growing up we were three of a kind. Joshua, the model citizen you see before you, was actually just a young punk. And Sam? Well, Sam had been in more fights, dodged more arrests and made more contacts in the New Orleans underworld than any sixteen-year-old boy in the city."

"And now he's a policeman?"

"A damn good one. The best. I hope I never have to tangle with him."

Maggie turned to Joshua. "What made the change in you and in Sam?"

Joshua glossed over his own rebirth. "I got involved in a church. Sam's parents finally scraped together enough money to send him down to the bayous to live with an uncle. The uncle was as strong willed as he was. Sam came back completely changed."

"I wonder why he came back at all."

"Sam says he loves the country, but he belongs in the city, on the right side of the law. In his own way, I think he's trying to do for others what his uncle did for him."

"Nobody reformed you, Skeeter?" Maggie turned back to their host.

"Jail reformed me. At least a little. I keep my nose clean...cleaner, anyway."

"I like your paintings." Maggie gestured to a series of small watercolors of New Orleans life fastened in crooked disarray to the wall above their table.

"How did you know they were mine?"

She tried to think of an answer. Finally she lifted her shoulders in defeat. "They look like you. Dark, tough outlines, with dreamy, abstract interiors. It's unusual using watercolors for such stark subjects, too." Most of the paintings were scenes of life in a New Orleans housing project. One was an old man, his head in his hands, sitting on a front porch. "You're very good, but they say a lot about you, don't they?"

Skeeter and Joshua just stared at her. Finally Skeeter turned to his friend. "I can see why you smuggled her out of that place."

"Yes."

Maggie smiled tentatively, trying to decide exactly what the two men meant. Joshua patted her hand. "You need to eat," he told her firmly.

"There's plenty of food in the refrigerator. I shopped on my way home." Skeeter got up and opened the refrigerator door, gesturing inside. "Help yourselves. I'm going to bed."

"Skeeter?"

He turned at the door and smiled at the young woman who had instantly seen into his soul.

"I hate to ask, but I was wondering if you had any clothes I might be able to borrow? I'll wash them if they need it, but..."

"I'll get you some things to choose from. You're so tiny I'm afraid everything's going to hang, but at least they'll be better than that coat."

"It's probably perfectly safe to take you shopping over on the West Bank, across the river somewhere," Joshua said in apology after Skeeter had left the room. "We could go this morning."

"I'd rather not take the chance. Not until I know they can't snatch me off the street and toss me into the state hospital."

Skeeter came back with an armful of jeans and T-shirts. "There's a pair of pants here with an elastic waist that might not be too bad if you roll up the cuffs and a couple of shirts that have shrunk since I bought them."

Maggie felt as though she were being given a wardrobe of designer originals. "Thank you. It'll be so good to get out of this hospital gown. Excuse me." Carrying the stack of clothes, she left for the bedroom.

"Now why didn't I realize that she'd be tired of those awful hospital clothes? I could have brought her something different to wear last week," Joshua muttered to Skeeter.

"Maybe you've been trying not to see her as anything other than one of your patients." Skeeter examined his friend. "You've been fighting a losing battle, though, haven't you?" Whistling, he left to catch up on his sleep, leaving Joshua to contemplate his coffee cup.

Chapter 5

I think we can safely say that I wasn't an artist." Maggie squinted at the watercolor in front of her. Pools of color ran in unattractive rivulets toward the middle of her paper, destroying her depiction of the magnolia tree in Skeeter's backyard.

"At least we can say that watercolor wasn't your medium." Skeeter leaned over her shoulder and examined her painting. "No, I think your first statement was correct." He ruffled Maggie's curls. "Is that supposed to be a tree or a telephone pole with algae growing on it?"

"Maybe I play the piano." Maggie crumpled her painting and tossed it into a nearby trash can.

"I have a harmonica. You wanna try it?"

"Does it have a keyboard?" She laughed at the look of dismay on Skeeter's face. "I remember what a harmonica is, Skeeter. I was just kidding. But I think I've delved into my past enough tonight." She stood and stretched. "What I'd really like to do is go for a walk."

"We don't 'go for walks' in this neighborhood. Jogging's okay if you can do a four-minute mile and outrun the muggers."

"Is the backyard safe?" She looked at the tiny plot of land surrounded on all sides by a six-foot wooden fence.

"I keep my pet mosquitoes out there."

"I think I'll go get acquainted with them." She gave him a friendly pat on the shoulder. "Thanks for entertaining me tonight."

"My pleasure."

Outside, the night was warm and humid, and Skeeter's magnolia was perfuming the air with its sweet, lemony fragrance. Maggie sat on a wooden bench beneath the tree and listened to the sounds of a distant bird mix with rock music from a neighbor's radio. She shut her eyes and tried to clear her mind. She had discovered that the harder she tried to remember details of her life, the more confused she became. When she just let her mind drift, not pushing it where it didn't want to go, she felt as if she were moving closer to her past. Sometimes she felt as if she were only inches away from remembering.

The heavy air felt right somehow. Even the occasional mosquito that buzzed near her ear seemed right. But there was something missing. The air was too still; the bird singing in the distance was too melodic.

"Maggie?"

"I didn't know you were back." Maggie opened her eyes and patted the wooden bench in invitation to Joshua, who was standing beside her. He had gone out earlier to pick up a few things at a nearby drugstore. Despite telling herself that she should get used to being without him, Maggie had missed him.

"What were you doing?"

She hesitated. "Experiencing the night," she said finally.

Joshua understood her answer and her hesitation. "Was it familiar?"

"Yes and no." She moved a little so that Joshua would have more room. The bench was small, and he brushed against her as he sat. There didn't seem to be any place for Maggie to put her arms. Had it been Skeeter, they would have entwined them companionably and Maggie would have teased him about trying to push her off her seat. That kind of easy playfulness was impossible with Joshua. Her breath caught in her throat, and each of her movements felt curiously strained. Nothing felt natural. Nothing flowed.

"Do you want to talk about it?"

Her thoughts had gone so far afield that she didn't know what he was asking. "About what?"

"About the night. About what's familiar and what isn't."

She didn't want to talk about her memories or lack of them. She wanted to sit there under the New Orleans misty night sky and feel Joshua's arms around her. She wanted to mold her body to his and feel his lips moving over hers. She wanted to know what it was like to have his hands explore the curves of her body. She did not want therapy; she wanted the therapist. Restlessly she stood and moved to lean against the tree. "Talking won't help."

Joshua felt her withdrawal. "Is anything the matter?"

"I just don't feel like explorations into my psyche tonight."

"Is that what we were doing?"

"Do you know how often you answer me by asking a question?" she snapped.

Joshua grinned, and Maggie was struck by how appealing he was when he relaxed. "It's a professional hazard. I'm sorry."

"You like making me angry, don't you?" She forced a smile to prove that he hadn't succeeded.

"It's another professional hazard."

"When do you let down your guard? Does the real Joshua Martane ever come out to play?"

"The real Joshua Martane kidnapped you from the hospital two nights ago." He watched her eyes get larger and more luminous.

"I'm sorry. I didn't mean . . ."

"Yes, you did. It's okay. Does it help to know that I'm in the same boat you are? That I'm trying to feel my way, too?"

His question was a mine field waiting for her to tread carelessly and explode the tensions just under the surface. Instead she leaned against the tree and watched him in the moonlight. In the two days since she had been out of the hospital they had spent very little time alone together. The demands of her physical recovery had taken precedence.

She had slept for long periods of time, dreamless hours that were hastening the healing process of body and mind. When she was awake, Skeeter was there for casual conversation and laughter. Outside the parameters of hospital life, her relationship with Joshua seemed strained and unpredictable. Maggie suspected that the desire to avoid this kind of intimacy had been mutual.

"What am I going to do about you, Maggie?"

She pretended to misunderstand. "Hopefully before long you won't have to do anything. I'll be on my own."

Joshua considered her answer and was surprised at the hollow feeling it gave him. There hadn't been time before helping her leave the hospital to think about all the ramifications of his act. But since then he'd had the time. More time than he needed or wanted. Time to watch her cheeks tint with more color, time to watch the blue-gray shadows underneath her eyes begin to disappear, time to watch the easy affection she had developed for Skeeter. There'd even been enough time to face the fact that if she disappeared from his life, she'd be taking a part of him with her.

"Besides," she added, "don't you think you've done enough?"

No, he hadn't done enough. His body reminded him every time he looked at her that he hadn't done enough. His head reminded him that such yearnings were dangerous. "You're not ready to face the world alone yet," he said, with no trace of the inner conflict that raged through him.

"Is that all?" She tried to keep her voice light. "Just because I don't have a place to live or a job or any money you jump to the conclusion that I'm not ready to be on my own."

"You must feel frightened."

She wondered if the other things she felt were as obvious. "Sometimes. But I've proved I'm a survivor."

Skeeter opened the back door and stuck his head out. "*Citizen Kane*'s on Channel 12. The first person to tell me who Rosebud was gets to make the popcorn."

"His sled," Maggie and Joshua said together.

Joshua stood and held out his hand to Maggie. It was a casual gesture but one he had never made before. "Now tell me where you were the last time you saw this movie."

She shut her eyes and put her fingertips to her forehead as if she were in deepest thought. "I'm sure. Yes, I'm absolutely sure of it." She opened her eyes and smiled. "I was sitting in front of a television set."

"Well, you may not remember who you are," Joshua said, grasping Maggie's hand and pulling her toward him, "but if we ever play Trivial Pursuit, I want you on my team."

"Add totally sentimental to your list," Skeeter said two hours later as he flicked off the television set. On the way back to the sofa he reached for a tissue and gave it to Maggie, who was wiping away the last of her tears. "Blow hard and get it over with." She complied with a watery smile.

"What list is this?" Joshua watched the easy camaraderie that flowed between the two of them. He felt an odd stab of pain.

"A list of everything we know about Maggie. Everyone's been so busy telling her what they think they know or trying to get her to remember for herself that no one's bothered to try and total up what we're sure of." Skeeter watched Joshua with a tiny smile. Skeeter could tell his friend a few things that he had observed about him, too, but the time wasn't right for that.

"Such as?" Joshua heard the note of arrogance in his own voice. It surprised him. It had obviously surprised Maggie, too, because she was frowning at him.

Skeeter's smile broadened. "Well, tonight's a good example." He began to twirl his mustache. "Tonight's an absolute treasure trove of information."

"You're enjoying this, aren't you?" Maggie asked, poking Skeeter with her elbow. "Get on with it. I'm dying to find out what we know."

"For one thing, we know you've never popped corn before. Exhibit A." Skeeter held up the bowl filled with hard kernels and blackened remnants of the corn that had popped.

"Actually I don't think I've cooked much at all," she admitted. "Your kitchen feels like the land of Oz." They all thought back to the spaghetti that Maggie had insisted on preparing for supper. Simultaneously all three heads nodded.

"What else?" she asked.

"You're used to mosquitoes."

Maggie nodded.

"And you didn't shriek and run out of the room when that chameleon came inside to pay a call earlier."

"He was cute. And familiar."

"You're well educated. Look at your taste in movies and your speech patterns." Skeeter turned to Maggie and bowed in mock salute. "A regular Princess Di."

"If I was well educated, why was I out walking the streets?"

"Maybe you weren't."

"What good does this do?" Joshua asked. Suddenly the room seemed too small for all of them. He stood and quietly began to pace. "It's not going to tell us the essential facts."

"It could be very helpful," Skeeter began.

"No, Skeeter. I'll handle this." Maggie stood, too. She could no longer ignore the irritation in Joshua's voice. There were a few things he needed to understand. "Maybe it's not important to you, Joshua, but I want to know everything I can about myself. You have no idea what it's like being me. I'm a blank. A nothing.'' She waved aside his protests. ''For all practical purposes I don't even exist, and yet somebody, somewhere, has tried twice to kill me. I'm willing to grasp at straws even if you think putting my life back together piece by piece is just an exercise in futility.'' She stopped and took a deep breath. ''I'm going to bed. Good night.''

Joshua stood very still and watched her walk from the room.

''You don't like it when somebody else tries to help her, do you?'' Skeeter watched his friend trying to regain the perspective he had lost weeks before. He knew that Joshua was already defeated. He also knew that Joshua hadn't yet admitted it.

''I don't want her more confused.'' Joshua faced Skeeter. ''I don't want her indulging in a lot of denial of reality.''

''Denial of reality. I like that phrase.'' Skeeter looked at his watch. ''It's time for me to go.'' He stood. ''Denial. That's a word to meditate on, Dr. Martane.'' At the doorway he raised his hand in a goodbye wave. ''I'll see you tomorrow.''

Joshua bit back the angry words that threatened to spew out. When the door closed behind Skeeter, he began to pace the floor again.

Maggie lay awake and listened to the angry sound of Joshua's footsteps. Their relationship had become so complex that she could no longer fathom where it was going. One moment Joshua was warm and considerate, the next he was irritated. She knew that the possibility of losing his job was eating away at him. But there was more to his irritability than that. It had to do with her. Joshua seemed to be as confused about their relationship as she was.

Obviously he felt something more for her than compassion or even friendship. She had no name for the feeling, however. She wasn't foolish enough to hope for love. Joshua would not love easily, although when he did it would be with no reserves. But if he gave his love it would be to a woman he trusted, not to a woman with a shaded, mysterious past.

She wasn't even sure she loved him. She couldn't be sure that what she felt wasn't just a mixture of gratitude and physical attraction. But she knew she wanted him. Some traitorous part of her that refused to respond to her common sense longed for him with a primitive intensity that threatened to make her its prisoner.

The footsteps stopped and then started again, coming down the hall to the bedroom door. The door creaked and Joshua was in the doorway.

"Are you awake?" he asked softly.

"Yes. Turn on the light if you need it."

He left the room in darkness and moved to sit on his bed. He began to take off his shoes. "I'm sorry," he said. He didn't elaborate; he knew Maggie understood his apology.

"All right."

"I just don't want you to get your hopes up. Finding out who you are might take a long time." He began to take off his shirt. Maggie refused to turn on her side, and she watched him in the dim moonlight through the open curtain.

"What you don't want is for me to begin hoping that I'm something I'm not." She delivered the words with no expression.

Joshua stood and pulled the sheet back. He began to slide off his jeans. "I just want you to be realistic."

Maggie's breath caught in her throat. Joshua was so gloriously male, so perfectly constructed. She had an acute longing to stand up and go to him, to fit her body to his and explore the differences between them. Perhaps it would clear the air between them in a way that talking never would. And then again, perhaps it would prove to him that she was exactly what he thought she was. She armed herself against her own painful desire and concentrated on responding to his words.

"Realistic? What you really mean is that I have to face the fact that I was a prostitute. That I walked the streets and slept with any man who wanted me as long as he had the cash." This time her tone challenged him.

"You can't discount the possibility."

"Don't play games. You don't think it's a possibility. You're convinced it's true. And no matter what you say to the contrary, it affects your opinion of me. I'm surprised you can even bear to sleep in the same room I'm sleeping in."

"Add overly dramatic to your list." Joshua slid between the sheets and folded his arms under his head. "I've told you before, it's what you become, not where you come from, that's important."

"And you want to be the one to play Professor Henry Higgins to my Eliza Doolittle." Maggie turned on her side away from Joshua.

"I don't want to transform you, Maggie."

"What do you want, then?"

It was fairly simple, really. He wanted to get out of his bed and crawl into hers. He wanted to pull her into his arms and absorb every particle of her into his being. He wanted to hold her until she melted into him, never to be separated again. He wanted to keep her safe, keep her happy, keep her with him always. It was fairly simple and fatally complicated.

"I don't know. But I don't want to hurt you."

Maggie shut her eyes. "Haven't you figured out by now that both of us are going to get hurt no matter what we do?"

Joshua continued to stare at the ceiling. He had no answer. The sound of Maggie's slow, even breathing filled the room long before Joshua was finally able to shut his own eyes.

The next evening Skeeter stood in the kitchen doorway with his arms folded and watched Maggie on her hands and knees scrubbing the black-and-white tile. "The floor doesn't have to be clean enough to eat off it. Did they invent the mop while you were in the hospital, babe?"

Maggie stopped and wiped the perspiration off her forehead with the hem of her T-shirt. "Doing it this way is better for everybody. Your floor gets cleaner, my arms get stronger...."

"And I get to watch your cute little rump swish back and forth."

"A dubious pleasure." Maggie sat back on her feet.

"Well, the house is shining. I'd call it quits for tonight." Skeeter extended a hand to help her up. "If you felt you had to pay me back for my hospitality, you were wrong."

"I'll always be grateful." Maggie stood and squeezed Skeeter's hand as a prelude to dropping it.

"Well, as long as you're feeling grateful, anyway, I've got something for you." Skeeter left the room and came back with a bag. "As cute as you look in my obscene T-shirts, it can't be too much fun sleeping in one. I got this for you."

Maggie opened the bag to find a pale pink cotton nightgown. It was full-length, not provocative at all, but to Maggie it looked like femininity personified. She wrapped her arms around Skeeter's neck and kissed him on the cheek. "You're such a nice person," she said. "Thank you, Skeeter."

"There's some underwear in there, too, and a blouse and a pair of jogging shorts that looked like they'd fit you."

"I'm very lucky."

Skeeter thought that nothing could have been further from the truth, but he didn't want to remind her. After an experience that didn't bear thinking about, the fact that Maggie could characterize herself as lucky was a complete testimony to her resilience and basic optimism. Standing in the kitchen watching her hold the nightgown up against her slender body, Skeeter wished, not for the first time, that he had discovered her before Joshua had.

"A fashion show?" Joshua was leaning against the doorframe watching them.

Maggie turned and flashed him a pixie grin. "Skeeter bought me some clothes."

Skeeter watched the expression on Joshua's face. It didn't change. Joshua was determined not to show Maggie what his feelings were. It was only because of her acute sensitivity that she was ever able to discern any of his emotions. With a sigh, Skeeter squeezed Maggie's arm. "Enjoy them, babe." With a nod to Joshua, he was on his way to work.

"Skeeter's very special, isn't he?" Maggie smiled at Joshua, wondering why he looked so stern.

"Maggie, Skeeter is off limits."

She wasn't sure she had heard him correctly. "Pardon me?"

Pardon me? It was the finishing school graduate again. Joshua shut his eyes. He couldn't deal with the cold feeling in his stomach. It had formed like an icy knot when he had seen Maggie hugging Skeeter, then holding the nightgown up against her lovely body for him to admire. No, that wasn't true. It had been building for three days. Every time Maggie looked at Skeeter or touched him or teased him. Every time she was in the same room with him. Joshua shook his head and opened his eyes. "I said, Skeeter is off limits."

She still didn't understand. "How can he be off limits? He lives right here…eats his…" Suddenly she understood. Her eyes widened, becoming vulnerable, bruised reflections of the inner woman. "I see." She couldn't move, she couldn't break their eye contact. She continued to stare helplessly at the man who had dared to think such a thing about her. The man she trusted completely.

Joshua saw the pain he had inflicted. He wanted to call back his words, but they were between them now. Stark, cold syllables destroying the affection and warmth that had been there before them.

"I'm sorry," he said, moving toward her.

She stepped back, her hand unconsciously clutching the nightgown in front of her. She took another step back, finding she was against the sink. "I'm going to bed."

"Maggie."

"Good night." She sidestepped, moving slowly around him and through the doorway. Safely in the bathroom she closed the door firmly behind her and turned on the shower. It was only later, when she was in bed defiantly dressed in the pink nightgown, that she gave way to bitter, angry tears.

Joshua sat in the living room, gazing out the window at a street lamp. He had never been more ashamed of himself. He was too good a psychologist to pretend that he didn't understand the feelings that had prompted his stinging insult. He had been jealous. Totally, blindly jealous. But more than that, he had been reacting to his fears that Maggie was not what she seemed. No matter what else he felt for her, unqualified trust was not one of his feelings. Too many things just didn't add up.

But tonight he had been unfair. Skeeter could be trusted completely. The scene in the kitchen had been innocent. Joshua had let himself react with a deep emotion that was a revelation. He had not felt this burning jealousy since he had discovered, at age twenty-seven, that his wife was being consistently unfaithful to him. Even then he had not experienced the gut-wrenching betrayal that had caused him to lash out at the fragile young woman who was trying to sleep in the other room.

God, the look in her eyes when she had finally understood his meaning. No one, no one could pretend to be that hurt. Her pain had been genuine. Completely genuine. And he had been its cause.

It seemed too late to make amends. She hadn't even wanted to hear his apology. With a few words, Joshua had destroyed her trust. She had been blooming with a delicate beauty, unfolding with the attention she received. Now she would withdraw to protect herself again. Joshua stood and began to pace the floor.

"Joshua?"

Joshua stopped and turned to face Maggie. She was standing in the doorway.

"Joshua, I didn't deserve your insult." She stepped out of the hallway, into the soft light of the living room. Covered from shoulder to toe in pale pink cotton, she was a feminine vision. The light just outlined the slight curves of her body, and she looked stricken and miserable. But she held herself with an innate pride that even his words had not erased. He shut his eyes in despair.

"No. You didn't. You didn't do anything. It was my problem, not yours."

"I wanted to hear your apology. We both need that much." She raised the back of her hand to her cheek then to her eye to rub it. "It wasn't fair not to give you a chance to explain."

"I'm sorry. Very, very sorry." He moved toward her, and she stood quietly as he approached. "You've given me no reason to say anything like that."

"You have all the reason in the world." Maggie's voice was calm, resigned. "We both know why you said what you did. You don't know what I'm capable of, do you? It's understandable that you wouldn't trust me."

Joshua stood in front of her, a scant inch from pulling her into his arms. To see his face, she would have to tip her head. She didn't bother. "I was jealous," he said, knowing that the truth was the only thing that might ease the pain he had caused.

She laughed. It emerged as a broken sound, a whimper encased in splintering glass. "How can you say that?"

He put his arms around her, stepping closer to hold her against his chest. "It's the truth. I was jealous."

The implications were too many for her to deal with. Her objectivity had been used up when she forced herself to face him again. "I don't understand. But could you just hold me for a few minutes, anyway?"

He tightened his arms around her and let one hand begin a slow journey over her back. At first she held herself stiffly against him, absorbing his warmth, his smell, the curious spell of his hand. Inch by inch she could feel her body respond to his, each muscle group relaxing, finding its counterpart in his body.

She slid her hands around Joshua's hips, coming to rest on his lower back. The smooth denim fabric of his jeans tantalized her fingers, and she longed for the feel of his skin. Slowly her fingers feathered up and then under his shirt to contact the heat of his body. The small intimacy hadn't gone unnoticed. He pulled her yet closer, and she could feel his lips against her hair. The moment went on until finally Joshua lifted her carefully, cradling her against his chest.

In their bedroom, he ignored the light, setting her down on her bed like the fragile object he believed her to be. Then, still fully clothed, he lay down beside her, pulling her to rest in his arms again. His chin brushed her hair, his arms held her close. "Go to sleep, sweetheart," he whispered.

Maggie shut her eyes and let her exhaustion take hold. She had no strength to examine what had happened between them. She had no strength to defend herself against this new twist in their relationship. She could only accept what was happening and trust that it wouldn't destroy either of them. Carefully she let herself snuggle closer. Joshua's arms surrounding her were stronger, better than her impossible fantasies. She let her hurt drain away as sleep overcame her. There was nothing that she couldn't forgive Joshua Martane. Nor was there anything she wouldn't give him if he asked. Her body, her heart, her soul were his for the taking.

She was completely unaware that if she had turned to him and told him her thoughts, nothing could have stopped him from giving her the same.

Maggie awoke the next morning alone. Sometime during the night she had felt Joshua slip across the room to his own bed, and although she had fallen back asleep soon afterward she had not slept as soundly. Now she turned over to find that his bed was empty.

She passed Skeeter in the hallway as she went in search of Joshua. "You're up early," she teased.

Skeeter looked at his watch. "You're up late. I'm just on my way out. Will you be all right here by yourself for a while?"

"Where's Joshua?"

"He called the hospital this morning and they asked him to come in at ten o'clock for a staff meeting."

Maggie knew a moment of utter desolation. "I bet I know what they want to talk about."

"It'll be all right. You've never seen Joshua go to bat for anyone before. He never loses."

"I wish I were as sure as you are."

"Trust me, babe."

By twelve noon, Maggie had worn a path pacing back and forth on Skeeter's living room rug as she waited for Joshua to return from the hospital. She was a solid mass of nervous energy, quickly using up her returning strength as she restlessly hiked the length of the room and back again.

When the navy blue Dodge Colt finally pulled up in front of Skeeter's house, Maggie forced herself to sit on the sofa and wait for the news that she was certain she didn't want to hear.

The day after her escape from the hospital, Maggie and Joshua had talked about his eventual meeting with Dr. Nelson. He had asked her if she would allow Dr. Nelson to make the decision about her future as well as Joshua's. "I trust Jim Nelson," Joshua had reassured her. "I know he won't send you to Mandeville, but he may want you back at City for a while. Will you be willing to go if he does?"

Stark white corridors, patients with dull eyes and insurmountable problems, screams in the night, mesh-covered windows. And a man who no one else believed was trying to kill her. Maggie had shut her eyes, fighting the fear of being imprisoned in the hospital again. "I don't know," she had answered truthfully. "I hope it won't come to that."

"We'll see."

Now Joshua had been to his meeting, and he was back.

"Maggie?" Joshua came in the front door and stood watching her. It was a warm afternoon. She was dressed in white jogging shorts and a sky-blue pullover that Skeeter had bought for her. Except for the stark pallor of her face, she was the picture of young American womanhood.

She forced herself to smile. "I've been waiting for you."

"So I see." Joshua crossed the room and sat carefully beside her. At that moment she looked so fragile that he was afraid she would crumble if he touched her. "Everything is fine, Maggie. It went much better than I had hoped."

"Tell me."

"You've been discharged from the hospital. You're free to begin a new life."

She blinked, waiting for the rest of it. "And you?"

He was surprised that she had glossed over her own good news. "I wasn't fired. I was suspended for three months. At the end of that time I'll probably be completely reinstated."

She couldn't understand the acceptance in Joshua's voice. "Three months? I never should have let you help me."

Joshua didn't know what to say. He just stared at her, watching the remorse build in her blue eyes. "Maggie," he said finally, too sharply, "don't prove me wrong and act like a crazy person now, for God's sake. They could have fired me, should have, in fact. But they didn't because they knew I had justifiable cause for my actions, and they respected me for it."

His anger stopped her retreat as his sympathy never would have. Unconsciously Maggie straightened her shoulders. "Damn you, Joshua," she said with spirit. "I am not a crazy person. And if I want to feel bad about what this has done to you, then I will. And if you don't like it, that's just too bad because I'm not under your care anymore."

Joshua smiled, the stern lines of his face softening with pleasure. "You're developing a temper to go with your name."

"You just wait until my strength comes back!"

"I'm trembling in my shoes." He put his arm around her shoulder and pulled her to rest against him. "Maggie, it's going to be all right now. I can use the time off. I've been working around the clock without any substantial free time for years. Only a few people know what I did. The hospital staff is going to be told that I'm on extended leave, and that's exactly how I'm going to look at it.''

She heard the genuine timbre of his voice, and she began to relax a little, letting her own good news take precedence. "And I'm free."

"You're on your own, sweetheart. Dr. Nelson agreed that you didn't need to be hospitalized any longer."

The meeting had gone better than Joshua had dared hope. He had received a rap on the knuckles when he had deserved to lose his job. Every staff member who had been involved in Maggie's case had been present to give their side of the story. In the end Jim Nelson had listened and used his own good judgment. Joshua had been suspended because no matter how pure his motivation was, he had still gone against hospital policy. In addition, however, Dr. Bashir had been reprimanded for allowing his personal feelings to interfere with the handling of a case.

Perhaps the best news of all had been that Maggie was now free. The authorities had never been notified of her removal from the hospital; the commitment hearing had been canceled with no plan to reschedule. And because Joshua assured Dr. Nelson that Maggie was doing well away from the hospital, the staff, with the exception of Dr. Bashir, agreed that there would be no point in readmitting her. Joshua was to arrange suitable therapy for her until she regained her memory.

Afterward Betty had walked Joshua to the door. "What do you plan to do about Maggie?" she had asked.

With all its ramifications, it was the most important question anyone could ask him. Joshua chose to ignore the more complicated dimensions. Instead he had answered simply, "I'm going to find her a place to live and help her build a life for herself."

"And your relationship to her?" Betty had never been fooled by Joshua's professionalism with the young woman whose life was such a mystery.

"My relationship with her is fraught with difficulties," Joshua had admitted. "Bashir is right about one thing. I've lost all my objectivity. She'll need a new therapist. It's one case I can't handle."

"You do realize with the kind of background she has, she's probably a master at twistin' people around her little finger."

"I know."

Betty had smiled wryly, realizing that her warning was coming much too late. "Just step carefully."

Now with Maggie sitting beside him and their futures unshadowed for the first time, Joshua wondered if "stepping carefully" was even in the realm of possibility.

Maggie had been quietly trying to put the news in perspective. The impact of her newly won freedom was just beginning to settle over her. She was on her own, but she had no place to go, no money and no strength to look for a job. Freedom was wonderful, but the problems that came with it were not.

Her first problem was immediate. Turning slightly to see Joshua's face, she asked, "Will Skeeter mind if I stay here until tomorrow morning? Then I can start looking for another place to stay."

Joshua tried to think how he could best approach Maggie with his plan for her life. He had had three days to consider all the possibilities. He had a solution that he thought would be best, but he was no longer in a position of insisting that she do things his way. "Maggie, I know you want to stand on your own two feet, and you will soon, I promise. But right now, you're not strong enough to work."

"I'm going to look for a job in a store."

"You wouldn't make it through a day," he said gently. "Standing up for hours would wear you out immediately. You're still recovering from your injuries and all those weeks in bed. Will you let me tell you what I think you should do?"

"I could go back to my old job. I doubt if I'd need to stand up too often." She had tried to joke, but her bitterness emerged instead.

"Are you going to listen to me?"

She let her head fall against the arm that encircled her and nodded slightly.

"I have a two-bedroom apartment. I want you to move in with me. You'll have all the privacy you need, but I'll be there to help if you need me."

"I'm already much too deeply in your debt."

He ignored her. "Then when it's safe, and you're strong enough, you can find a job."

"Safe?"

Without thinking about what he was doing, Joshua pulled her closer, wanting to shelter her. "The man who tried to murder you is still at large. The police won't want you to make yourself available as a target again." He could feel her shudder. "Maggie, I'll protect you. Sam assures me that the police are closing in on this guy. Hopefully it'll only be a matter of weeks before they find him. By then you'll be strong enough to hold down a job. In the meantime you'll have to stay indoors when I'm not with you. New Orleans is a big city, but if you ran into this maniac and he recognized you . . ."

"Oh, I don't think there's any question that he'd recognize me." Maggie realized that Joshua's concerns came from the initial attempt on her life. "He even recognized me in a dark hospital room."

Joshua was silent.

"I know," she said with resignation. "You still think I was living through a nightmare."

"I don't think we can take any chances one way or the other," he said carefully. "As extra protection I'm going to ask Sam to issue a statement to the newspaper that you've been sent to a convalescent hospital somewhere in northern Louisiana."

"The newspaper?"

"There was a lot of press coverage back in November. Anything this guy does is news. Reporters still call the hospital from time to time asking about you."

She tried to think of a way to release Joshua from the obligation to her that he so obviously felt. "Doesn't the state have programs to take care of people like me? Why are you stuck with it?"

"Because I want to be." He turned, pulling her with him as he did so that they were face-to-face. Carefully he brushed the soft curls off her forehead. "We've come this far. Do you think I want to be cheated out of the chance to see you make a full recovery?"

"Is that it, or are you afraid that if you let me out of your sight, I'll start walking the streets again?" The question had been between them for a long time. It took all Maggie's effort to ask it with Joshua's fingers caressing her face.

He saw the pain, heard the slight catch in her voice. He wanted to reassure her, but if they were going to be almost constantly in each other's company, there was no room for lies between them. "I wouldn't be honest if I said that didn't worry me."

"Well, it's good to know where I stand." She tried to pull away.

"I don't know where you stand, Maggie. How can you? I only know I care about you, I worry about you, and I want, more than anything, to make sure you're going to be all right before you face the world by yourself again."

Maggie shut her eyes as Joshua bent his head. His mouth on hers was a surprise. She had expected another brotherly kiss on the forehead. Instead, what had probably been planned as a kiss of consoling affection rapidly developed into something else. She caught her breath as his lips brushed hers, tasting, sampling their texture. Afraid to move, afraid to respond because she knew he would pull away, Maggie lay in Joshua's arms and let him kiss her. It was a gentle kiss, but there was promise in it.

When his tongue began to stroke her lower lip, inviting her to open for him, she tentatively put her arms around his neck, expecting at any moment to have him pull away. Instead the kiss deepened, catching fire, and suddenly there was no room for control, for fear. She let herself respond with all the passion that she had repressed. Joshua was kissing Maggie. For one blessed moment the confused roles that separated them had been discarded.

Willingly, she opened her mouth, receiving his tongue, shivering as he pulled her harder against him. Her fingers threaded through the curls at the nape of his neck, and she sighed in pleasure at the feelings flooding her body. He broke the kiss to begin another, and his hands began to travel the delicate curves of her torso. Her own excitement mounted with each new intimacy. She accepted it all, knowing that there was nothing she would ever deny Joshua. She was already his, no ceremony, no ritual of consummation could make it more official. She belonged to Joshua Martane, and somehow she knew that she had never belonged to anyone that way before.

"Maggie." Joshua pulled away carefully. Her arms were still around his neck, and he could feel her fingers massaging the sudden tension there. "I'm sorry," he said roughly. "I didn't plan for that to happen."

"Why didn't you?"

She looked so vulnerable. Under the circumstances, how could she look as if she had just been kissed for the first time and was still struggling in the throes of discovery? He shook his head. Words were impossible.

Maggie saw Joshua's defenses drop neatly into place. "I see," she said, carefully removing her hands to pull away. "The therapist doesn't kiss the patient. The minister doesn't kiss a lady of the night. Joshua doesn't kiss Maggie." She stood, her legs threatening to withdraw their support. She tilted her head back and confronted him with the sorrow in her eyes.

"I'll be ready to go when you are, Joshua. And I'll do what you ask. But just as soon as I'm able, I'm stepping out of your life. Eve's going to disappear and take the apple with her. Then you won't have to worry about temptation at all.'' Head erect, body swaying gracefully, she left the room.

Chapter 6

Joshua's apartment was one of four carved out of an old mansion on Esplanade Avenue near the French Quarter. Joshua had five rooms and a bath. The ceilings were twelve feet high, the woodwork ornate walnut, the floors a polished masterpiece of craftsmanship, the furniture antique. Because the neighborhood was transient and the house itself in a state of semidisrepair, Joshua paid an affordable rent.

That afternoon Maggie walked through the apartment and admired everything she saw. Compared with a sterile hospital room, it was paradise.

The spare bedroom was open and airy with two windows looking out on the avenue. Both windows had wrought-iron balconies that could be reached by stepping over the low windowsills. "Up until the turn of this century," Joshua told Maggie, coming to stand with her on one of the balconies, "Esplanade was considered the 'Promenade Publique.' The Creole dandies promenaded here every afternoon and flirted with the chaperoned Creole beauties. I imagine many a young girl stood on this balcony and fluttered her eyelashes at the men parading below."

Maggie watched the traffic zipping past and tried to imagine a quieter, gentler time. "It's a beautiful street. I feel like I'm on a movie set."

"Wait until Mardi Gras." Joshua stopped. Mardi Gras was almost a year away. He couldn't assume that Maggie would even be in the city then.

"When is that?"

"Right before Lent. February or March."

She refrained from reminding him that she would not be living with him then. Instead she turned and stepped over the sill into the room that was to be hers. Joshua followed her and began to move a pile of books off the dresser.

"I've been using this room for storage," he apologized. "It'll only take a few minutes to clear it out."

"Don't bother." Maggie put her hand on Joshua's arm. "Leave it the way it is. I'm not going to be staying long."

"You can't predict that. In the meantime I want you to be comfortable."

Maggie thought that "comfortable" was a peculiar word choice. She was sure she had never been more uncomfortable in her life. "I'm not going to stay at all if you insist on putting yourself out for me."

Joshua had been careful not to touch her since the kiss that had rocked his foundations earlier in the afternoon. Now he settled his hands firmly on her shoulders. He wanted to shake her for her obstinacy. He wanted to ask her for her forgiveness. He wanted to kiss her again.

"Look, I know you're confused and angry. I'm confused, too. But there's one thing I'm not confused about. I want you here. I'm very, very sure of that. The kiss didn't change that; your bullheaded obstinacy doesn't change that. Can we please call a truce?"

"I don't like being an obligation to anyone. I may not know much about myself, but I do know that." Maggie met his eyes defiantly.

"I want you here, but I'm not going to beg you to stay. It's your decision."

Some of the fight went out of her. The situation was full of complications, but even if she'd had another place to go, Maggie knew that she'd still choose to stay with Joshua. "I want to earn my keep."

"What are you proposing?"

"I'll keep house and cook while I'm here."

Joshua squeezed her shoulders and then dropped his hands. "It's a deal."

"Were you expecting another kind of offer?"

For once Joshua let his guard drop. His anger at her question was plainly visible on his face. He took a step closer. "Stop it, Maggie."

It had been a childish, spiteful question coming out of the painful knowledge that Joshua didn't trust her. She wished that she could call it back. "This isn't going to be easy, is it?" she asked softly. "I'm sorry."

"Let's not punish each other." Joshua raised his hand to her hair and brushed the soft tendrils off her face. For a moment they stared into each other's eyes, and then each took a step backward.

"We'll go grocery shopping tomorrow," Joshua said finally. "Let me take you out to dinner tonight."

Maggie nodded, resigned to her temporary dependency.

"Right now I'm going to take you shopping for some clothes."

This time she shut her eyes, and her shoulders slumped in defeat. "I hate this."

"You can pay me back later if you feel you have to. But I like doing things for you."

"You've already done too much. Now I feel like I'm your personal charity."

"I know you do. I wish you could understand that I'm doing it just because I want to."

"Someday you'll have to explain that to me."

Shopping at a department store, Joshua had to insist that Maggie at least buy the bare essentials of a wardrobe. As fast as he pulled extra items off the racks, she put them back. It became a test of wills, and as they made their way back to their apartment, it was difficult to say who had won.

Joshua's therapist's eye kept track of Maggie's reactions to the crowds around her, to the rigors of shopping and the trip through the busy city. She had weathered the storm admirably, paying scant attention to the entire experience. When the time came to reenter the world by herself, it looked as though it wouldn't be too frightening.

"How did it feel to be back out in the world?"

Maggie considered his question. She hadn't even thought about the fact that shopping was something she hadn't done in a long time. "It felt perfectly normal." She looked out her window at the passing scenery. "Driving on the interstate seems perfectly normal."

"Do any of your surroundings seem familiar?"

She squinted, as if seeing everything from a slightly skewed vantage point would help. "Yes and no."

"Tell me about the yes."

"Well, it doesn't seem strange. The landscape is comforting, somehow." She gestured to the rows of one-story homes they were passing. "I think I've seen lots of places like those."

"That's pretty typical of most cities."

"I guess so." She brightened a little. "The water seems familiar, too." They were passing over a winding bayou.

"That's good. What do you think about when you see the water?"

Maggie considered his question. She shut her eyes and tried to form a mental picture. "Lots of it. Blue and sparkling. And waves." She frowned after another minute and opened her eyes. "That's it."

"That was a good start."

"How am I going to make it all come back?"

Joshua decided that her question was as good a lead-in as he was going to get. He had been charged by the hospital staff with the responsibility of seeing that Maggie stayed in therapy until her memory returned. "You need someone to talk to, someone who can help you reassemble the pieces of your life.''

''What about you?''

''I've become one of those pieces.''

Maggie nodded. ''In other words I need somebody I can talk to without any constraints.''

''I have a friend, a woman, Antoinette Deveraux, who does therapy privately. She's agreed to see you if you're willing.''

''Do you think it'll help?''

''It can't hurt.''

Maggie turned and watched the passing scenery again. ''I'll do anything I can to find out who I am. I'll be glad to see her.''

''So you're Maggie.'' Antoinette Deveraux examined the young woman who was sitting in a comfortable armchair in front of her desk.

''Probably not.'' Maggie looked around the small office, admiring the tasteful, unobtrusive furnishings.

''I've never heard two words used more effectively.'' Antoinette sat back and watched her new client. She could understand immediately why Joshua had risked so much and been so captivated by the beautiful young woman sitting in front of her desk.

Maggie turned her attention back to Antoinette. She had expected someone older and more maternal. She had not expected such a stunning combination of grace and intelligence. Maggie wondered about Antoinette's connection to Joshua. The two psychologists would suit each other. There were no mysteries, no shaded pasts to overcome. ''Have you ever had a case like mine?'' she asked.

''No.''

Maggie smiled. ''Are you in the mood for a challenge, then?''

''Always.'' Antoinette smiled, too.

"Do you think you can help?" Maggie tried not to make the question sound too important, but as soon as she heard her own voice, she knew that she had failed.

"Do you want me to help?"

"Of course." Maggie thought about her answer. Antoinette seemed to understand that she wasn't finished, and she waited quietly. "I don't know," Maggie amended, after a long pause.

Antoinette nodded. "Let's talk about why you may not want to remember your past."

"That's not very difficult. I may not like what I discover."

"I can guarantee that you won't like all of it."

"I'm not talking about childhood pranks or failing college algebra."

"You're talking about prostitution."

Maggie lifted her shoulders. "I don't know what I'm talking about. I only know that my past terrifies me."

"Then part of what we're going to do together is try to help you peel off the layers, one at a time, until you feel strong enough to face all of it."

"But I don't have that much time." Maggie lifted her chin and Antoinette could see the determination in her delicate features. "I have to know so that I can get on with my life."

"You can't push a river. Things happen at their own good speed."

"Can't you hypnotize me and make me remember?"

Antoinette considered Maggie's question. "Hypnosis might help you later. Right now it's not appropriate."

"I'll tell you what's not appropriate. It's not appropriate for me to live off Joshua while I sit around and wait for my memory to return. And it's not appropriate to stay in a city where a man has tried twice to kill me." Maggie managed to keep her voice calm although she felt like ranting and raving.

"It's all right to be angry in here, Maggie. You don't have to work so hard to hide it."

Antoinette's gentle statement completely dissolved Maggie's suppressed resentment. She took a deep breath and let it out slowly. "I'm going to like working with you," she said, looking Antoinette straight in the eye. "But I'm not going to be nearly as patient as you want me to be."

"I just want you to go at your own pace. I promise I can keep up."

Maggie nodded. "Then let me tell you everything I think I know about myself."

Antoinette settled back and waited.

The intimacy that had always characterized Maggie and Joshua's relationship seemed to disappear with the increased intimacy of their living situation. It was as if the dangerous attraction continually kindling under the surface of their interactions had forced them both into a guarded politeness.

Maggie was grateful for everything that Joshua did for her. She kept the apartment clean and taught herself to cook with a determination that even she found humorous. She made a habit of staying out of his way, retreating to her room when she thought he needed privacy. She rarely initiated conversations or asked anything of him.

Joshua was thrust into the position of having to guess what she might need. He gave her books to read, bought her a radio to listen to in her room, offered to accompany her anywhere that she might want to go. But there the relationship came to an abrupt halt. Although he made attempts to find out what she was feeling, Maggie remained remote. On the surface everything was as it was supposed to be. Underneath, he had no idea what was happening to her.

A week passed and then two. Physically Maggie was blooming. They took evening walks into the French Quarter and each night, the walks grew longer and longer. She was gaining weight and sleeping less during the day. Although the nightmare still came with some frequency, its impact was less shattering. For the first time since she had awakened from her long slumber, Maggie felt that she was really getting well.

What she wasn't getting was any closer to solving the riddle of her past. She didn't talk to Joshua about her sessions with Antoinette, but she was becoming more and more aware that it would be a long time before she knew who she had been. Antoinette was helping her probe the depths of her memory, but the small bits of information they uncovered only tantalized her. Antoinette said that they were helping Maggie get ready to remember; when the time came, Maggie would be better able to face it. But Maggie found that as she improved physically she was becoming increasingly impatient.

Almost three weeks after Maggie's escape from the hospital, Joshua came home one afternoon after a visit to the police station to talk about Maggie's case. Lounging at his desk amid clattering typewriters and ringing telephones, Sam had given Joshua more assurance that the prostitute murderer was about to be apprehended. "No thanks to your Maggie," Sam had added.

A week before, Sam had finally been granted his chance to interview Maggie. He had come to Joshua's apartment and asked cryptic, loaded questions that Maggie had not been able to begin to answer. She had stood up well under Sam's probing, but she had added nothing to his information. The night of her near-death remained a mystery.

Sam was obviously not convinced that she was telling the truth about her amnesia. Now, ready to close in on the murderer, he warned Joshua again about not taking Maggie at face value. "I've seen a thousand just like her," he told Joshua. "When this guy is off the streets, send her back."

Joshua had swallowed his anger and shaken his head at his friend. "You just take care of finding this maniac; I'll take care of my own life."

Regardless of Sam's attitude, Joshua felt that he was bringing good news home with him. Soon Maggie would be as safe as anyone else was in New Orleans. But there was

Take 4 Books
–an Umbrella & Mystery Gift–
FREE

And preview exciting new Silhouette Intimate Moments
novels every month — as soon as they're published!

Silhouette Intimate Moments®

Yes...Get 4
Silhouette Intimate Moments
novels (a $10.00 value), a
Folding Umbrella & Mystery Gift FREE!

Catherine Coulter's AFTERSHOCKS.
When Dr. Elliot Mallory met
Georgina, everything between them
seemed so right. Yet, Georgina was
just beginning a promising career, and
a life with him would cheat her out of
so many things. Elliot was determined
to let her go, but Georgina had a way
of lingering in his heart.

Nora Roberts' DUAL IMAGE. Actress
Ariel Kirkwood wanted desperately to
play the scheming wife in Booth De
Witt's brilliant script. As Ariel the
actress, she awoke the ghosts of
Booth's past. As Ariel the woman, she
awoke Booth's long-repressed
emotions...and tempted him to love
again.

**Diana Holdsworth's SHINING
MOMENT.** Derek Langley had been
smuggled out of Russia as a small
child. Now, with the help of an acting
troupe, and its lovely leading lady,
Kate, he had a chance to go back and
rescue his father. But when he fell in
love with Kate, he knew he might
never be able to tell her.

**Barbara Faith's ISLANDS IN
TURQUOISE.** When Marisa Perret
saved Michael Novak's life during a
raging storm, it gave her a chance to
save her own life, too. Yet, she felt she
had to return to a husband who did
not love her. Which is worse? A love
with no future, or a future with no
love?

SLIP AWAY FOR AWHILE...Let Silhouette Intimate Moments draw you
into a world that promises you romantic fantasy...dynamic,
contemporary characters...involving stories...intense sensuality...and
stirring passion. It is a world of real passion and complete fulfillment.

EVERY BOOK AN ORIGINAL...Every Silhouette Intimate Moments novel
is a full-length story, never before in print, written for those who want a
more intense, passionate reading experience. Start with these 4 Silhouette
Intimate Moments novels—a $10.00 value—FREE with the attached
coupon. Along with your Folding Umbrella and Mystery Gift, they are a
present from us to you, with no obligation to buy anything now or ever.

NO OBLIGATION...Each month we'll send you 4 brand-new Silhouette
Intimate Moments novels. Your books will be sent to you as soon as they

are published, without obligation. If not enchanted, simply return them within 15 days and owe nothing. Or keep them and pay just $9.00 (a $10.00 value). And there's never any additional charge for shipping and handling.

SPECIAL EXTRAS FOR HOME SUBSCRIBERS ONLY... When you take advantage of this offer and become a home subscriber, we'll also send you the Silhouette Books Newsletter FREE with each book shipment. Every informative issue features news about upcoming titles, interviews with your favorite authors, even their favorite recipes.

So send in the postage-paid card today, and take your fantasies further than they've ever been. The trip will do you good!

CLIP AND MAIL THIS POSTPAID CARD TODAY!

NO POSTAGE
NECESSARY
IF MAILED
IN THE
UNITED STATES

BUSINESS REPLY MAIL
FIRST CLASS PERMIT NO. 194 CLIFTON, N.J.

Postage will be paid by addressee

Silhouette Books
120 Brighton Road
P.O. Box 5084
Clifton, NJ 07015-9956

Take your fantasies further than they've ever been. Get 4 Silhouette Intimate Moments novels (a $10.00 value) plus a Folding Umbrella & Mystery Gift FREE!

Then preview future novels for 15 days—
FREE and without obligation. Details inside.

Your happy endings begin right here.

CLIP AND MAIL THIS POSTPAID CARD TODAY!

Silhouette Intimate Moments®

Silhouette Books, 120 Brighton Rd., P.O. Box 5084, Clifton, NJ 07015-9956

☐ **YES!** Please send me my four SILHOUETTE INTIMATE MOMENTS novels FREE, along with my FREE Folding Umbrella and Mystery Gift, as explained in this insert. I understand that I am under no obligation to purchase any books.

NAME _____
                    (please print)

ADDRESS _____

CITY _____ STATE _____ ZIP _____

Terms and prices subject to change.
Your enrollment is subject to acceptance by Silhouette Books.

Silhouette Intimate Moments is a registered trademark.

CTM076

another aspect of the killer's apprehension that was just as important. With luck the man would be able to give the police details about Maggie that would help them trace her identity.

At home Maggie was not in the living room or kitchen. Calling out to reassure her, Joshua went to his room first. He changed his clothes and crossed the hall to tap on Maggie's door. There was no answer.

Since she sometimes spent time at their landlady's first-floor apartment, Joshua fixed lunch and waited. When Maggie didn't come back after an hour, he finally went to Mrs. LeGrand's to check on her.

Mrs. LeGrand insisted that he come in. She was an older woman, lap-dog friendly, who gauged the success of her days by how much gossiping she got to do. Joshua was fond of his landlady, but he avoided her as much as possible. Only Maggie seemed to have the patience to listen for hours on end to her stories.

"Ain't seen her all afternoon," Mrs. LeGrand said with a shake of her head. "Last time I saw her she was heading down Esplanade."

"When was that?"

"Early sometime. I was getting the mail."

Joshua excused himself in the middle of one of Mrs. LeGrand's longer sentences and sprinted to his car. Searching for Maggie along the city streets was like looking for the proverbial needle in a haystack. To complicate matters, an afternoon thunderstorm pelted Joshua's windshield with silver blankets of rain, further obscuring his vision. He drove for an hour, covering a two-mile radius from the apartment. Finally he turned his car around, realizing the hopelessness of the situation.

Trying to be calm, Joshua told himself that the chance Maggie would come to harm was very remote. The possibility of running into the man who had tried to murder her was a small one. Although that still worried him, other things worried him more. Maggie could wander into a rough neighborhood, thereby inviting new violence. Perhaps her

memories had returned and she was looking for old ac-
quaintances, or perhaps she was not as stable as Joshua had
thought and was having a relapse. He knew that it wasn't
uncommon for a patient to have periods of confusion after
an injury to the brain. The more he thought, the more
Joshua became convinced that Maggie was in serious danger.

Joshua considered calling Sam, but there was nothing that
the police could do. Maggie was not in protective custody.
There was no way that anyone could enforce her imprison-
ment on Esplanade Avenue. She had every right to leave the
apartment.

He parked his car and climbed the steps. Inside he
knocked on Maggie's bedroom door once again. There was
still no answer. Standing in the living room, Joshua knew
that he was helpless. When the rain stopped he would go
back out and search for her. Until then he could only change
out of his wet clothes and wait.

Even the long evening walks with Joshua had not prepared Maggie for the miles she had to cover to get to Hootie Barn's Tavern. She had looked up the address in the
telephone book and once outside the apartment she had
asked directions several times. Now she stood in front of the
flamboyantly painted bar, watching men come and go as she
tried to make her memory respond to the sight.

"I was here. I was found here," she whispered as if the
words, spoken out loud, would trigger a reaction. "I was
lying in that lot over there."

With acute distaste she picked her way around the building, stepping over broken glass, around old tires and other
assorted debris. The vacant lot was no more inspiring than
any other piece of wasted urban space would have been.
There were no answering echoes in her head, no charges of
excitement.

Her memories were imprisoned just as surely as she had
been imprisoned in the hospital and now in the Esplanade

apartment. She had nothing. No past, no future, and the present? Well, the present was especially painful.

She had been trying for weeks to adjust to the reality that Joshua would never be a part of her life. And why should he be? He had already given more than she had a right to expect. Wanting his love, his unqualified acceptance and trust was asking for the moon and the stars, too. She had no right to expect so much. Not when she had so little to give in return.

Knowing this, she had distanced herself from him, maintaining a friendly facade that did nothing to soothe the ache inside her. Until today. This morning something inside her had snapped. The enforced patience caused by her lack of strength and her lingering uncertainty about the future were finally all used up.

She had to know who she was. Somewhere in her past there might be someone who cared about her, someone who could forgive and accept her. A parent, a brother or sister, a former lover. Someone, somewhere who could explain to her why she had become a prostitute. Someone, somewhere, who could love her.

She could feel the plodding progression of her days. The loneliness of being a perpetual stranger was closing in on her. When she had awakened that morning she had realized for the first time that she didn't care who she had been. Whatever her past, she was ready to face it. What she couldn't face was the waiting.

Maggie felt tiny raindrops begin to sting the exposed skin of her arms and neck. On the sidewalk in front of Hootie Barn's Tavern, men called to her, offering invitations that she hardly heard. When several of them started toward her, she turned and began to follow a path around the other side of the building back to the front sidewalk. It was only then that she began to notice how unsavory her surroundings were.

She had been so busy examining every house, every street she had walked along, that she had not computed just how rough the section of town was. She had been searching for

her identity. Along the way she had forgotten about her
safety. Luckily the men who had come after her abandoned
their halfhearted chase, owing, she was sure, to the increas-
ing tempo of the rain.

The day had been warm, but the rain was cool against her
skin. As Maggie hurried away from Basin Street, she cursed
her lingering weakness. She was exhausted and discouraged. She was also lost.

As the rain increased, so did her confusion. She had not
paid enough attention to the directions that had gotten her
to the tavern. She began to wander along side streets, losing
her way further. There was no one to ask since everyone
with any sense was inside in what had now become a typical New Orleans thunderstorm. The small businesses she
passed were not the kinds of places to stop and wait out the
rain. Instinctively she knew that she was better off in the
storm than she would be inside.

Maggie made a right and then a left, becoming more and
more bewildered by the tangle of streets. She ended up in
what looked like a poor residential section, its houses bleak
and unpainted with sagging front porches and yards that
were nothing more than clumps of overgrown tropical foli-
age. Under the dubious shelter of a massive live oak tree, she
stopped and waited for a few minutes, hoping that the rain
would let up before she was forced to move on.

The neighborhood might be poor and run-down, but at
least its inhabitants were inside, safe and warm. For a moment she was tempted to cross the street, knock on the
nearest door and ask for shelter. She could call Joshua and
ask him to pick her up. Then she could be home and dry in
a matter of minutes.

On closer examination, however, she decided to move on.
She didn't like the looks of the house. Compared to its
neighbors, it was more dilapidated, more unkempt, with
garbage strewn over the yard and the rusting hulk of an old
automobile in the driveway. No, she didn't want to go inside. She shuddered and began to walk swiftly down the
sidewalk. Suddenly she felt as though she couldn't put

enough distance between herself and the house. Between herself and the street of houses similar to the one she had examined.

She tried to convince herself that the near panic she felt was a normal response, an instinct built in to protect herself in a strange city. No one with any sense depended on strangers in an urban setting such as New Orleans. But searching her limited memory, she had to admit to herself that this surge of fear was different from anything she had felt since leaving the hospital. There was no time to explore her feelings further. She was becoming increasingly lost.

At the end of the street she made a turn and then another. The rain made it difficult to see. Drops caught in her eyelashes, nearly blinding her. The sky was getting progressively darker, illuminated only occasionally by the flashes of lightning.

Joshua had explained to Maggie about the rows and rows of brick buildings that housed so many of New Orleans' poorest citizens. When she came around the corner and found herself in front of one of the housing projects, she turned and tried to retrace her steps, hopelessly mired in the maze of streets.

At the point of total exhaustion she leaned against a sign on a street corner, too tired to take another step. Through the haze of rain and fatigue she looked up to see a white bus decorated with purple, green and gold stripes splashing its way toward her. She could just make out the sign proclaiming Esplanade Avenue.

Maggie stepped off the curb, and the bus pulled to a stop. She was a nickel short, but the driver waved her to the back without a word. She collapsed on a seat and ignored the curious stares of the other riders.

On the front porch of the Esplanade mansion, after a ten-minute bus ride, she tried to wring as much water as she could out of the loose blouse she was wearing with her only pair of jeans. Satisfied that she had done the best she could, she opened the front door and climbed the stairs.

"Maggie, where in the hell have you been?" The door to Joshua's apartment flew open, and he stomped out into the hallway in his bare feet.

Maggie shivered at the anger in his eyes and the cool indoor air against her wet skin. Snapping herself out of a near trance, she finally turned, ignoring his question, and pushed past him to get through the door. He followed close behind.

"Just a minute, you're going to answer my question." Joshua was standing in her doorway towering over her like a furious prison warden.

Too miserable to respond, she turned again and found her way to her bedroom where she pulled the shorts and blouse that Skeeter had given her out of her dresser. She was much too cold to wear shorts, but the only pair of jeans she owned were clinging to her shivering body. Switching on the bathroom light, she closed the door and locked it, starting the hot water in the big, claw-footed tub. She soaked for long minutes, adding more hot water as the temperature cooled until she was finally warm all over. Only then did she pull herself out, dress in the shorts and blouse and come out of the bathroom to face Joshua.

"It's too cool to wear shorts."

She ignored him, going back into her room to pull a folded blanket off the bed to wrap herself in as she flopped down on top of the bed covers. "Go away," she mumbled, closing her eyes.

Joshua could see the absolute, unremitting fatigue that had etched thin lines around her eyes. For once, it did not touch him. "If you're tired," he said, his voice as cold as Maggie's body had been, "it's your own damn fault. What were you doing out there? I told you not to go out without me. Not ever."

"I went to Hootie Barn's Tavern. It's one of my favorite hangouts, remember?" With great effort she opened her eyes. "That's what you expected to hear, wasn't it, Joshua? Well, it's true."

Her eyes had drifted shut again when she felt Joshua's hands gripping her shoulders. She went limper under the insistent pressure.

"Maggie, you could have been killed. For God's sake, open your eyes."

Something in his voice surprised her enough to make her look at him.

"Maggie, sweetheart, why did you go back there? Did you realize how dangerous it was?"

"I went back to find myself," she murmured, her eyes beginning to close again.

"And did you?"

"No. I wasn't there. I was never there."

She was drained. Joshua watched as sleep claimed her.

He couldn't make himself leave. He pulled a straight-backed chair beside the bed and sat restlessly on the edge. Maggie slept on, completely unaware of the man at her bedside.

Chapter 7

The apartment was dark with evening's approach when Maggie opened her eyes. As always, waking from a deep sleep confused her, flooding her body with helpless dread. Staring at the wall beside her bed, she talked sense to herself with the courage of a little girl whistling in the dark to scare away the monster in her closet. There was nothing to be afraid of in this apartment. No, she didn't remember anything about her life previous to the hospital, but yes, all her memories from that time on were crystal clear.

"Maggie?"

Joshua startled her. She had forgotten that he had been in the room when she'd fallen asleep. Turning toward his voice, she propped herself on one elbow. "Hello."

He had been standing by the window, and he crossed the room to stand beside her bed. "I wasn't sure that you were awake."

"I didn't know you were still here."

"I was worried about you."

"You're going to need someone else to worry about from now on."

"And why is that?"

"Because I'm going to be just fine." Maggie sat up, hugging her knees, her chin resting on the blanket covering them. "For the first time, I know I'm going to be fine."

Joshua had not expected this response. He had watched her for hours as she'd slept the exhausted sleep of the weary pilgrim, and he had wondered how he was going to tell her his thoughts when she awoke. Now she was sitting up, her eyes bright and unclouded, her cheeks once again tinted with color. It was another rebirth.

Maggie smiled and gestured for him to sit beside her. "Don't look so serious. I feel good."

"Why?" Instantly he hated his question, but Maggie didn't seem annoyed by it. She extended her hand and pulled him down on the edge of the bed.

"Because I'm recovering."

"Are you remembering anything?"

She shook her head. "Just tiny flashes. Enough to whet my appetite, nothing more. But I think eventually it will come back to me. And when it does, I can face it. I proved that to myself today."

He had been so angry at her for leaving the apartment that he hadn't paused to consider the fact that her experience might prove valuable. His brows drew together in the semblance of a frown as he thought about her words.

"Do you know that you're wearing your therapist's face right now?" Maggie swung her legs over the bed and turned slightly to face him. "When you're trying to puzzle something out, trying to figure out just how you should respond, you get that frown on your face. It's fascinating to watch, but I'd rather you just told me what you thought."

"I was trying to figure out how today could have been helpful."

"I faced a piece of my past, and I survived. Surviving is a talent I seem to have, and I'm proud of myself for it. I'm tired of feeling guilty about my life. Whatever I did, whatever I was, I did it because I had to do it. I'm not going to spend any more of God's precious time feeling ashamed of something I don't even remember.''

This time Joshua smiled. "Good for you."

"I also realized today that I can't push the river." She smiled a little. "That's Antoinette's phrase, not mine. But it's true. I can't force myself to remember anything. I tried today and I failed. I'm going to have to settle for just getting on with my life."

"I wish it could be easier."

She nodded. "And finally, I'm tired of taking. It's weighing me down. With or without your permission, I'm going to look for a job."

"Just a minute..."

"Nope. It's my decision." She moved closer, placing one delicate hand on his knee in a gesture of intimacy. "We can't go on like this anymore. You have a life, too, but you spend all your time taking care of me. Don't you think I see what that's done to you? I know there must be places you want to go, women you want to be with. It's time for you to forget me." She successfully kept the pain from her voice. She was doing the right thing, but every word was a tiny wound inside her.

"As if I could." Joshua covered her hand with his. "Do you think you're just a millstone around my neck that I can't wait to be rid of?"

Maggie tried to smile. "No. I think I'm a patient that you got in over your head with, and you don't know how to back off gracefully. I'm telling you not to worry."

He couldn't believe that she was asking him to leave her alone. Joshua tried to examine the emptiness that her words evoked. His therapist's eye was tightly shut against his inner self. He was bewildered and angry. "What do you plan to do to make money?"

"Not what you're thinking," she said with a toss of her head.

"Stop that!" Joshua gripped her shoulders. "How dare you try to read my mind! The fact that you may have been a prostitute is way down on my list of things to think about as far as you're concerned. I'm tired of being punished because I once expressed doubts to you."

Maggie was shocked into total silence at Joshua's outburst. Eyes wide, she stared at him, her teeth sunk deeply into her lower lip.

He ignored her response. "I'm worried about your health and safety, not your morality. I care too much about you to let you jeopardize either. I care way too much."

"Do you?" she asked softly.

Joshua groaned, and his hands moved to her waist to bring her onto his lap. He settled her sideways, tipping her back to expose her face to the touch of his mouth. His lips were hungry, crushing hers with no thoughts of gentleness or caution. Joshua, who had given and given, was finally taking what he wanted. Maggie, who had taken and taken, was being allowed, finally, to give. "I care," he said between devouring onslaughts of kisses, one hand tangled in her hair. "I care more than is good for either of us."

She had no reply. Her emotions were being steadily assaulted; her body had completely succumbed to his touch. When his hands traveled beneath the blue knit blouse to discover that she wasn't wearing a bra, she trembled with him at the revelation. Holding her breath, she waited as he explored her softness. She was immobilized with longing, each feather-light touch an explosion inside her. The pleasure was unfamiliar, as so many things in her life were.

Alive with feeling, she arched her spine to bring herself in closer contact with him, her eyes tightly shut. There was a purring low in her throat, a sound of pure, unadulterated ecstasy.

"Maggie, you're so beautiful," Joshua said, his voice low and shaken. "I want you too much."

"Don't you know I'm yours?" she asked, opening her eyes to meet his. "Haven't you always known that?" With trembling fingers she began to unbutton his shirt. "You can't possibly want me too much."

But he did. He wanted her too much to be as careful, to be as gentle as her healing body deserved. He wanted her too much to do what was right for her. And the worst thing of all was that there was a rational part of him that still knew it. With Maggie curled up in his lap and the soft knit of her blouse caressing his naked chest, the pure sensual pleasure of the experience was laced with a thread of despair. He couldn't take her. Not like this. Not with so much still between them.

"We can't."

"I don't want to hear this." Maggie began to place nuzzling kisses along his neck. Joshua's hands were playing games with her spine, feathering out to caress the delicate skin along the sides of her breasts. She knew he was aroused, that stopping now was going to be as difficult as starting had been. She determined to make it even more difficult.

His voice was a groan. "Maggie, no more."

She ignored him, drunk with the knowledge that she could cause the torment apparent in his words. She had thought that he saw her only as an obligation. Now she realized just how wrong she had been. She was something much more to him, something much more special. And there was nothing that she wanted more in life than to be special to Joshua. If she could, she would gladly trade the return of her memories for one night of his love.

Maggie ran her fingertips over every inch of his chest, exploring the breadth of his shoulders, the hardness of his muscles. She rubbed her face over the sprinkling of hair, inhaling the good, clean smell of him. It was impossible to get enough of Joshua; five senses were too few. She wanted to possess him, to blend, to merge, not only in a sexual way but in a spiritual one, as well. Frustrated by the inadequacy of the human body to express what she was feeling, Maggie sighed and began to run her lips and tongue over him.

Joshua was possessed with a sweet fire that threatened to consume every cell in his body. He knew he should stop her, but his willpower was gone. There was an exuberance, a delightful lack of calculation in her touch and her kisses. She was totally engrossed in what she was doing, exploring him as though he were an uncharted island. She was a reverent seeker of new knowledge. They were both lost in her discoveries.

He had stopped his own explorations. He knew where they were leading. Her skin was so velvet soft, so completely touchable. She was lovelier to stroke than he had ever imagined, a delicate perfection that he had not believed possible. But Joshua knew he saw her through the eyes of his infatuation. Whatever imperfections there were, he was blind to them. The gift of rational insight, of logical analysis, completely disappeared in her presence. He was bewitched. For a few minutes he allowed himself the pleasure-pain of succumbing to her spell.

Maggie trailed soft, nipping kisses up Joshua's neck once more, exploring the tight skin with her tongue. She continued to his chin, feeling the slight rasp of whiskers against the smoothness of her lips. She found his mouth and pressed hers against it lightly, again and again, testing new angles, new amounts of pressure. And then, she was no longer in control; it had been taken from her by his response.

His mouth closed over hers, holding her a willing prisoner as his tongue sought the companionship of hers. She could feel the kiss all over her body as if she had become a finely tuned instrument completely sensitive to all pressures, all quivering, resounding vibrations. She knew a desire so acute that she could not think, could not breathe. At that moment she would have done anything to make Joshua hers.

"We can't."

She wondered how a rejection could be so firm and yet so poignantly gentle. Joshua had pulled his mouth from hers and turned his head. Maggie could see the regret engraved in deep lines on his face. She was struggling to catch her breath, watching him struggle to regain the control he was so rarely without. Both were shaking with their need for each other.

She wanted to protest, to let the passion just waiting to explode beneath the surface explode in anger instead. She could not. She could no longer retreat behind anger. She loved Joshua too much to punish him.

It took all her strength to accept his withdrawal. Finally she laid her head on his chest, and Joshua wrapped his arms around her back to shelter her there. Both of them were breathing audibly, and he was sure she could hear the walloping beat of his heart. "Maggie," he whispered finally, "you're still too fragile."

"No. You only think I am."

He had no answer.

"And you still don't know who I am."

He knew she was right, although not strictly in the sense she meant it. Sitting beside her bed waiting for her to awaken, Joshua had realized that no matter what they found to be true about Maggie's past, he wanted to accept it and move beyond it with her. But there was no way to put an end to a chapter of her life that they couldn't even read.

Then a new thought had crystallized. If the police were wrong and she had never been a prostitute, she still had a past. And that past might include a husband or a lover.

The thought was as shattering as the possibility of her prostitution. Somewhere there might be a man who had a prior claim on her love. Somewhere there might be a man whom she would want when she regained her memory. He was in the untenable position of not knowing which scenario of her past he wanted to be the real one.

An involuntary shudder went through his long frame at the thought of Maggie loving another man. Not loving him casually with her body, but with all of her, with the sweet intensity that flowed out of every word she spoke, out of every graceful movement she made. For the second time since she had come into his life he was shaken with jealousy. "We're going to have to find out. For both our sakes."

"What if you find out that the police were right, that my past reads like a criminal's record? Will you be able to touch me then?" With the palms of her hands firmly against his chest, she pushed away. Sick disappointment at his rejection surged through every cell.

It was time to speak his thoughts out loud, time to let her think about this new possibility. "Neither of us can know what we'll feel. Have you ever considered that there may be a man in your past that you'll want to go back to when your memory returns?"

He tried to pull her back, but she slipped off his lap to sit on the bed beside him. She shrugged off his suggestion with a lack of concern that confounded him. "Why do you assume that whatever I discover will wipe away the time we've spent together? Will you suddenly be less important to me?"

"That's entirely possible."

"I'd like to know who she was, Joshua."

He ran his fingers through the dark waves that had fallen over his brow. "What are you asking?"

"Who was the woman who's made you so desperately careful?"

"My past has nothing to do with this."

"I'm beginning to think that your past has more to do with this than mine does."

He refused to acknowledge the possibility that she was right. "Behind that locked door of your memory there may be someone waiting for you," he repeated.

With a sudden clarity Maggie understood that Joshua had his own locked doors, doors that he didn't even realize the significance of. Her doors might open with a single clue. Joshua's might never open to let another woman into his heart.

"And if no one is waiting for me, what excuse will you use then?"

Joshua was silent as though he were considering her question, but his answer destroyed her hope that he'd heard her. "It's understandable that you're impatient to have this resolved, Maggie. I'm impatient, too."

Maggie stood and straightened her clothes. Her hands were still trembling in frustration, but she struggled to lighten her voice. They had gone as far as they could go. She could not force Joshua to look at himself any more than he could force her memory to return. "I'd like to be alone now," she said, her body a statue sculpted of pride and regret.

Joshua knew that if he continued to stay, his good intentions would be worth nothing. "I'll make dinner."

Maggie had no appetite but she nodded her head. She would not let Joshua see how he had hurt her. "Thank you."

After a silent meal Joshua and Maggie stood in the living room watching each other. Neither wanted the evening to end despite the strain between them. Both knew that it should.

"Thank you for dinner," Maggie said, turning to go into her room.

"Would you like an Irish coffee before you go to bed?"

"Do you think that's a good idea?" She faced him, leaning against the wall. Joshua's own concerns were written across his features. Maggie wanted nothing more than to be with him, but the decision had to be his. From this point on, she realized, the decisions would all have to be his.

He didn't pretend to misunderstand. "I'm not sure what a good idea is anymore." He held out his hand. "Come on."

Maggie set out the cups and saucers and then wandered restlessly through the apartment as Joshua brewed the coffee. The dining room was on the side of the old house that fronted Esplanade Avenue, and there were tall windows with a view of a section of the French Quarter. Maggie stood at one, watching the traffic on the street below. Nighttime was as busy as day on Esplanade.

Everywhere she looked she saw weathered brick, shuttered windows and iron-lace balconies. There were huge live oak trees lining the street, and every one of the gracious old homes blended into a sympathetic portrait of New Orleans. "I was never here," she whispered. "Never." She shut her eyes and she was rewarded with an image of sparkling blue water. There was a boat, a cabin cruiser at a dock and in the background there was white stucco shining in bright sunlight.

"What is it?"

"Water," she said, opening her eyes to Joshua's face. "Lots of water and a big boat. And a stucco house. A white stucco house."

"Anything else?"

She shook her head as the image faded. Wrenching sadness gripped her; she tried desperately to hold on to the vision. It was gone, and her eyes filled with tears. "Nothing else," she said with a catch in her voice. "But I was happy there."

"Be glad, sweetheart." Joshua pulled her against him, intending to comfort her. "Be glad you were happy."

Maggie pressed her body against his and slipped her arms around his neck. "I don't want to go back. I just want to know."

"You may want to go back," he cautioned. "Don't destroy your options."

"I want you, Joshua. The only thing that can make me leave you is if you don't want me."

Abruptly he released her. "Let's have that drink."

They sat in silence sipping the whiskey-laced coffee. Tension permeated the room to fight a battle with the whiskey-induced languor. The atmosphere was as ambivalent as their feelings.

"I meant what I said about getting a job." Maggie saw the disapproval on Joshua's face, but she ignored it. "I'm going to begin looking for something tomorrow."

"What kind of job are you planning to look for?"

"I haven't gotten that far yet. Since I don't know anything about my training or education, I'll just have to take whatever I can get."

"Without a social security card, that could be a problem. Without a birth certificate, getting a social security card could be a problem."

"Without knowing where or when I was born, getting a birth certificate could be a problem." Maggie neatly completed his train of thought. "There must be a way around all of that."

"What would you like to do if we can find a way?"

She lowered her eyes to her cup. She had not missed his implied offer of help. "I'd like to work with children somehow, but I know that's impossible. Who would trust me with a child, considering . . . everything."

Joshua heard the sadness and the longing in her voice. "You like children?"

She nodded. "Yes. I'm sure I do. Sometimes I can remember what it feels like to hold a squirming little body up against me, feel a pair of strong little arms around my neck. . . ."

"Do you think you have a child somewhere?"

Maggie was startled by the question, and she raised her eyes to his. The thought had never occurred to her. She played with it like a cat worrying a mouse, but finally she shook her head. "No. I don't think so. I only feel good when I picture holding a child. If I had my own child and I was separated from him, surely I'd feel devastated with loss." She didn't miss the expression of approval in Joshua's gray eyes. "You must like children, too."

"Very much."

"Why haven't you married and had children of your own?" After all they had shared, the question seemed permissible.

He broke her gaze. "I was married once. My wife didn't want children."

Maggie couldn't imagine any woman not wanting Joshua's child. She wanted to hold him and reassure him that not all women were like that, that she would joyfully have his child. Instead she let the warmth of her voice communicate her understanding. "But you did, didn't you?"

He nodded. "I wanted children and a real family life. She wanted something very different."

Maggie guessed that telling her that small piece of his history was Joshua's own way of letting her know what she was up against. Somewhere deep inside him he understood the connection between his failed marriage and his distrust of her. She waited, but instead of more disclosures, he changed the subject.

"How would you like to work in a day care center?"

The idea was immensely appealing. "Where?"

"At the hospital. The wages will be low and the work demanding, but your employers would be understanding. We could classify it as therapy and probably not even have to set up a social security account for you."

"Tell me about the center." Maggie could feel her excitement building.

"It's very small, an experiment really. The children are offspring of hospital employees. If we had the money we'd have three times as many children as we do, but right now it's housed in an old wing of the hospital that's waiting to be remodeled."

"Would they want me, Joshua? With my history?"

"It's very hard to find good people to work there because the wages are so low. They'll be delighted, I'm sure. It means you'll have to face the hospital every day."

"I can do that as long as they don't lock me up again."

"Will you give me a few days to check it out?"

"Will you promise not to delay on purpose?"

Joshua smiled. "You're too insightful."

"Promise."

"All right."

"Josh?" A man's voice was accompanied by a loud rap on the door. "Josh, it's Sam."

Joshua set his cup down and got immediately to his feet. As close as he was to Sam Long, Sam rarely just dropped by. "I'm coming."

Sam stood in the doorway. His eyes swept the cozy intimacy of the scene, and his pupils narrowed. "Your landlady let me in downstairs." He nodded coolly to Maggie.

Joshua motioned to the sofa. "Come in and sit down."

"I don't have time. I need to take Maggie down to the station for a little while."

"What for?"

Maggie stood and held up her hand to silence Joshua. "Why do you need me?" she asked Sam.

"Because we have the maniac who tried to kill you behind bars right now. By tomorrow his picture will be spread over every newspaper in the state. I want you to identify him before that happens."

Joshua watched Maggie go pale. In a moment he was at her side, pulling her to rest against him. "It's all right, sweetheart," he reassured her.

She turned in Joshua's arms and faced Sam. She did not miss the expression of revulsion on his face at Joshua's display of affection. "Has he given you any details about the night he tried to murder me?"

Sam shook his head. "He insists he's innocent of everything. But we have enough evidence to prove beyond a shadow of a doubt that he's not."

"Then why do you need to drag Maggie through all this?" Joshua asked sharply.

"Don't speak for me. I want to do it," Maggie intervened.

Sam ignored her, speaking to Joshua. "We need her because it will be one more bar for this guy's jail cell. I can connect him directly to three of the seven murders. If Maggie can identify him, that's one more count against him."

"I don't want her traumatized...."

"Stop it!" Maggie listened to the blessed silence for a moment and then pulled herself out of Joshua's arms. "I'll be glad to go to the police station and try to identify him. Just let me change my clothes."

The two men watched her retreat down the hall.

"She doesn't remember her own name. How can you expect her to recognize the man who tried to murder her?" Joshua faced Sam.

"It's amazing what people can do when it serves their purpose."

"What's that supposed to mean? Have you taken up psychology now?"

"I understand the psychology of certain types of people, the types I put behind bars with regularity. I could give lectures on people like the maniac we picked up tonight. Do you know how we finally got him? We set up one of our policewomen as a lure. He went into the trap like a fly into a spiderweb."

"You don't understand Maggie."

"And you do?" Sam shook his head and for a moment compassion flickered over his strictly controlled features. "You didn't understand Daphne, either."

"If you try to bully Maggie tonight, I'm going to forget we're friends. I'm warning you." Joshua's face settled into hard, unforgiving lines.

"It's gone that far?"

"It's gone that far."

Maggie came back into the room and saw the tension between the two men. She knew immediately that she was its cause. "I'm ready," she said, coming to stand before them. She searched Joshua's face, wanting to tell him that she was sorry, that she had taken too much from him already, that she didn't want to separate him from his friends.

Joshua shook his head as if he understood her unspoken apology and wanted no part of it. "I'm going with you," he said quietly. "We'll do this together."

Maggie turned to Sam, but his face was expressionless. "Let's go," he said. She had no choice but to follow him out the door.

Hours later the heavy police station door closed firmly behind them. The night had turned cooler, and Joshua slipped his jacket off and placed it around Maggie's shoulders. But he knew that nothing could begin to take away the chill she must be feeling.

She didn't even seem to notice the jacket. "I really thought I'd recognize him. When they turned on the light and all those faces stared back at me, I was sure I'd know one of them."

"It doesn't matter. They've got an airtight case." His words were reassuring, but Joshua felt much of the disappointment that he knew Maggie was feeling. He had watched her face as she'd scanned the lineup. Her concentration had been total. She had willed her brain to react, to unlock the floodgate of memories. Instead she had been faced with another failure.

"The man in my nightmare is taller, different somehow."

"Sleep distorts the truth."

"I wanted to remember."

"You're safe now," he reminded her. "Even though you're disappointed that your memory didn't return, you're safe now. The man's been caught. If he does confess, he may be able to give us some details about you that can help us. In the meantime you can build a life without fear."

Maggie turned to face him. Joshua was right. Another door had been closed to her past, but her future was wide open. "Will you call about that job tomorrow?"

"I will. Now it's time for you to go home and get some sleep." With his arm around her, Joshua guided Maggie down the steps and past rows of blue-and-white police cars. "Tomorrow will be here soon enough."

"Not soon enough," she answered softly. "It can't come soon enough to suit me."

Chapter 8

Gray squirrel, gray squirrel, swish your bushy tail." Maggie and twelve four-year-olds were on their hands and knees in the center of the frayed area rug that covered one section of the largest day care center classroom. Every one of the four-year-olds was trying valiantly to swish an imaginary bushy tail as well as Maggie was swishing hers. The worn seat of her jeans was arched high, and her nose twitched in rhythm with her bottom. The nose was more the imitation of a rabbit than a squirrel, but the children thought it was perfect and more than one little set of nostrils was trying to twitch, too.

"Maggie, you're silly!" One little girl, a pale blond vision in a pristine party dress, hung back from the others as if she believed that the activity was beneath her.

"You're right," Maggie agreed, sitting now with the other children flopping on the carpet around her. "Sometimes it's fun to be silly." She held out her arms and the little girl came into them, sitting carefully on Maggie's lap and smoothing her dress down over her legs. "Does anyone else have a song they want to sing?"

"It's too hot to sing!" A little boy with chocolate skin and a shining Afro fanned himself with his hand. "It's too hot to do anything!"

Mid-June in New Orleans was summer fully launched. The air-conditioning system that had originally cooled the hospital wing where the day care center was located had long since given up the ghost. Since the wing was to be renovated someday, no money was available for repairing it. Instead all the windows were thrown open and fans set high on aluminum frames were placed around the room. Since Maggie had begun working at the center four weeks before, she had noticed this classroom growing hotter and hotter each day. By August it would be unbearable. Designed for air-conditioning, the windows were not plentiful enough or the fans adequate enough to effectively cool the room.

"Tomorrow morning we're going on a field trip to the French Quarter," Maggie promised them. "We'll walk along the river and it will be cool there. Then we'll buy milk and beignets and sit in the shade and eat them."

At the promise of the little French doughnuts liberally sprinkled with powdered sugar, the children quieted. Maggie was glad that she was going to be able to get them away from the depressing atmosphere of the day care center. In addition to the inadequate cooling system, the rooms were gloomy, too small and lacking in much of the furniture and equipment that Maggie thought they needed. But the staff was dedicated to doing the best they could, and the children were well taken care of, even if the environment wasn't as stimulating as Maggie thought it should be.

"Maggie?"

Maggie smiled at the white-haired woman who was in charge of the center. Millie Taffin had run a nursery school in her own home near the hospital for twenty-five years. Ready to retire, she had been asked by the hospital administration to administer their new day-care program. Millie had signed on for a year. In December she would turn the reins over to someone else, if indeed the center still existed by then. So far, attempts to find new funding had not been successful.

"Maggie, Helen isn't feeling well. I don't want her handling the babies if she's under the weather. All we need is an epidemic in this heat. Will you spend the rest of the day in there? Monica can handle the fours with my help."

Maggie gave the blond child in her lap a quick hug and a push as she stood. Monica, a slender, attractive woman who assisted anywhere she was needed, came in and immediately got the children involved in a new activity.

"I hope you don't mind," Millie said, wiping the perspiration off her forehead, "but the last time Monica took the babies, she was ready to quit her job by the end of the day."

"I'm glad for the chance," Maggie reassured her. "I rarely get to spend enough time with them."

"We'll see how you feel by the end of the day."

There were six babies to one worker. Maggie and the rest of the staff wanted to reduce the ratio to four to one, but at the moment, because of finances, that was impossible. Helen, the woman who usually handled the babies, was a small Hercules with the stamina of three normal women. Maggie, even with her steadily developing strength, was exhausted by midafternoon.

"Are they supposed to cry that much?" Maggie looked up to find Joshua standing in the doorway, surveying the bedlam of wailing children.

She had just finished diapering every child, and now she was in the process of feeding two babies simultaneously, a bottle in each tiny mouth as she sat on a blanket on the floor between them. Although she knew that Joshua had an appointment with Dr. Nelson that day, she had not really expected to see him. The sight of the tall, powerful body in the doorway gave her a new jolt of energy. "It's triage," she informed him. "All I can do is take care of the ones who need me most. It's a terrible shame."

Joshua strolled across the room and scooped up a crying infant from one crib, humming tunelessly in its tiny ear until it quieted. For a moment, the room was peaceful. One baby was sound asleep and two others in playpens stopped fretting as the infant in Joshua's arms quieted.

"Thanks, miracle man," Maggie joked. "You're always there when I need you." She examined him as he swayed back and forth comforting the baby who was finally falling asleep. He was dressed in new blue slacks and a short-sleeved dress shirt in a soft shade of blue that complemented his coloring. She had trimmed his hair the week before on one of the infrequent evenings they spent together, and the shorter waves emphasized his strong jaw and slashing brows. As always, she found him totally appealing. She was sure that would never be any different.

What was different was their relationship. There had been no more tempting nights in each other's arms. With the advent of Maggie's job, they had seen less of each other. Despite his protests, she had convinced Mrs. LeGrand to let her move into a one-room apartment across the hall from Joshua's. The room, which for years had only been used for storage, was cramped and time-scarred with a jumble of furniture that wasn't good enough for the other apartments. Still, it represented a step toward independence for Maggie, who could manage the modest rent on her own.

When she arrived home in the evening, she was usually exhausted. Since all she had was a hot plate, she still ate with Joshua who watched her struggle to stay awake with each mouthful. But more often than not, the rest of the evening included only a few minutes of quiet conversation before she went back to her own apartment so that she could sleep.

On weekends, they usually spent part of Saturday together. They did laundry, visited local places of interest and spent time relaxing in City Park, the largest city park in the United States. Saturday evening they often ate out, talking casually and enjoying each other's friendship. There was an unspoken pact between them to let things develop slowly. Their relationship had begun in a whirlwind, and now they were catching up, developing a solid base. Maggie had no idea where any of it was leading. She hoped Joshua was learning to trust her.

Maggie lived completely in the present. She didn't think about her past, although tantalizing bits of memory still appeared from time to time in her sessions with Antoinette. She didn't think about her future, either. She lived day to day, grateful for what she had, refusing to regret what she didn't. Her life was busy, and if it sometimes seemed incomplete without Joshua's arms around her, that was just the way it was.

Today, watching him rock the baby in his arms, so completely masculine and yet so nurturing, she tried to banish the ache inside her that demanded more from their relationship. "You do that like an accomplished father," she told him.

He bent over the crib, tenderly laying the baby down and covering its tiny legs with a receiving blanket. After retrieving a teething ring for one of the toddlers who had thrown it out of the playpen, he came to sit beside Maggie, gathering one of the babies on the floor in his arms to feed it as she took the other. "I've always thought that role would suit me." For a moment his features were softened by a poignant wistfulness. Before Maggie could comment, he continued. "Millie told me you're saving her life in here today."

"I love it. I just wish there were more people to help. None of these little sweeties should have to cry for anything."

"Spoiling them, are you?"

"Not at all. An infant needs total support. When they have a need, it should be met immediately. That way they grow up trusting the world to give them what they have to have, and they learn to be patient because they know they'll get what they want eventually."

Joshua watched her cuddle the baby she held, rubbing its back gently. She was rewarded with a loud burp. "Your knowledge of child development is astounding."

"I do know a lot," she agreed. "I think I must have had training somewhere along the line."

She settled the baby back in her arms and continued to feed it. She was the picture of maternal devotion, a madonna in blue jeans and a new mauve blouse that she had bought for herself out of her meager salary. Days at a nearby playground with the children had warmed her pale complexion to a golden beige, sprinkling light freckles across her slightly crooked nose. Her hair was longer, still tousled and curly, but softer and more feminine than before. Joshua found her lovelier every day.

Maggie looked up to find him watching her intently. She gave him a slow smile. "Do I have finger paint on my nose?"

"Freckles."

"The sun always does that. My father always said..." She stopped, stunned at the revelation. "Joshua! My father always said I looked like a dalmatian puppy after a summer in the sun!" Her face was wreathed in a grin that threatened to rival the Grand Canyon; her eyes were suspiciously moist. "I can almost hear him say it."

Joshua shared her joy. More and more often, glimmers of memory broke through the barrier walls that she had built against them. Soon she would remember everything. "Your father was special to you," he said. "That's not the first memory connected with him."

She shook her head. "No, it's not. If I could just remember his face."

"Or his name." There was irony in Joshua's voice.

"I never remember anything that helps, do I?" Maggie stood, careful not to wake the baby who had finished its bottle and gone promptly to sleep. She tucked it into one of the cribs and came back to sit beside Joshua, a toddler in her arms.

"It all helps, sweetheart."

She was thrilled at the endearment. "But it doesn't help Sam trace anything, does it?"

"He's still working." Joshua didn't add that although Sam still checked the missing persons reports that came in, the police were no longer actively involved in the case. Now that Maggie's attacker had been caught, they had done their job.

She decided to change the subject. "We're taking the fours to the French Market tomorrow. Would you like to come and help?"

"Tomorrow's my first day back at work."

"A whole month early?" Maggie's huge grin reappeared. "Why?"

"They're shorthanded. And Dr. Bashir resigned."

"That's good news." Maggie had run into the little psychiatrist twice since she had come back to the hospital to work. It had been two times too many.

"It's good news for this hospital, although I'm sorry to say he's going on to become chief psychiatrist at a small private facility out west somewhere. But with Bashir gone, Dr. Nelson has agreed to reinstate me."

Maggie leaned over and gave Joshua a congratulatory kiss. "You must know how glad this makes me."

"Why don't you prove it by staying awake long enough to have dinner with me tomorrow night?"

She liked the sound of his invitation. "Maybe I could take a quick nap first as insurance."

"We'll plan on leaving about seven, if that's all right." He smoothed her curls back from her forehead, and then he stood. "I'll be sure they serve seafood." Maggie had shown an insatiable appetite for New Orleans style fried seafood. She could never seem to get enough.

"Perfect."

Joshua put the baby he had been feeding back in its crib, adjusting a mobile for it to contemplate. Maggie had helped her four-year-olds construct the mobiles for the babies' room out of colorful plastic spoons, aluminum foil and bright bits of felt. Millie had confided to Joshua that without Maggie's ingenuity the center would be a bleak place indeed. When she retired the following December, Millie intended to try to have Maggie hired in her place. Unless Maggie's memory returned and her mysterious past was cleared up, however, there was no hope that Millie would succeed.

Maggie was lifting the other toddler out of the playpen now that there were no babies on the floor to run over. "Thank you, Joshua. I'll see you tomorrow night."

He watched as she became completely engrossed in the antics of the two toddlers. She handled the children with an expertise that was not accidental. He had mentioned this new twist to Sam who had shrugged his shoulders. "She could have worked in a day care center someplace else before she turned to prostitution. Maybe she's just from a large family. There's no way for me to check it out; it's too slim a lead."

More and more, Joshua was convinced that Maggie had never walked the streets, and he told Sam so. "You're not rational about this girl, Josh," Sam said in his tough police sergeant voice. "I've seen the way you look at her. You're going to wake up one morning and see things the way they really are, and it's going to be damned hard on you when you do."

Sam had been right. Joshua had awakened one morning, and with a sunburst of insight he had seen the way things were. He was in love with Maggie. It was not infatuation or protectiveness or sexual attraction, although all those things were present. And it was a love that he had never felt for Daphne or any other person in his life. He no longer accepted Sam's opinion about Maggie's past, but Sam had been right about one thing. Joshua's feelings for Maggie were damned hard to cope with. Nothing had really changed—only his feelings. Maggie was still an unknown quantity, and Joshua was fast reaching that dangerous point where he no longer cared.

"This is perfect. Thank you for bringing me here."

Joshua and Maggie were seated at a small table overlooking Lake Ponchartrain. The sun had just set, and the horizon was still tinged with gold and rose. An occasional gull flew overhead, and in the water right below them a trio of ducks was swimming in lazy circles.

"I couldn't find white stucco and cabin cruisers. You'll have to settle for the water and an occasional sailboat, although its too late for that, I guess."

Maggie reached across the table and squeezed Joshua's hand. "Whether I remember anything or not, it's still good to be here with you."

He covered her hand with his own, refusing to release it as they ordered huge seafood platters. "Tell me about your trip to the French Market," he said when their waitress had gone.

Maggie told him, trying to capture the excitement of the children in her words, but the whole time she was aware of his hand covering hers. Joshua had done no more than give her brief hugs or chaste kisses since the night, a month before, when they had almost made love. Now the prolonged contact was igniting a slow-burning desire throughout her body. "Each one of the children got to pick a vegetable to take back for lunch," she finished. "We ended up with one stalk of asparagus, an avocado, cauliflower, tomatoes, peppers and one wily little character got sugarcane. It was some lunch."

She listened to Joshua chuckle, and she wondered if she should tell him the most significant thing that had happened on the trip. Walking through the Quarter, guiding the children who were clinging to a long jumprope held on the other end by Monica, Maggie had looked up to find a man staring at her. He had been coming out of one of the bars along Decatur Street, near the French Market, and as they came closer, he had stepped back into the shadows as if afraid that he might be seen. As they passed, Maggie had looked in his direction, curious why he would be so interested.

His cap had been pulled down, shading his eyes with the brim. The rest of his face had been covered by a bushy red beard. Lounging in the doorway, he was no more sinister than any man who has spent too many hours in a bar. But for Maggie, seeing him had been terrifying. A cold chill had racked her body and her hands had begun to shake. It had taken every ounce of self-control she possessed to continue down the street. Each step had been torture.

Once past, she had turned in slow motion, as if in a nightmare, to get one more look at his face. He had disappeared.

It had taken almost an hour for her heart to begin beating normally and for her hands and legs to stop trembling. She had attended to the children, tried to share in their laughter, but inside she had continued to quake. Only the practice of the past months had allowed her to finally regain her composure.

Almost as frightening as seeing the stranger had been her own reaction. Maggie had finally convinced herself that her strength, both emotional and physical, was back to normal. Her abnormal reaction to the stranger seemed to belie that conviction. Apparently her recovery was not as complete as it had seemed. She still hovered in a twilight world where the slightest stimulation could set off inappropriate reactions within her.

Now she debated whether to tell Joshua of her experience. She recalled his reaction when she had tried to convince him that the night before he'd removed her from the hospital someone had tried to murder her. What would he think about her sanity now? He was holding her hand, talking in a husky, intimate voice that was threatening to take her insides apart and rearrange them. If she didn't ruin it with reports of her own neurotic behavior, the evening seemed to show great promise.

"You're deep in thought."

Maggie smiled, certain she was making the right decision. "I was just trying to remember if there was anything else interesting to tell you about. There wasn't."

"What shall we talk about, then?"

"You never talk about yourself. Will you tell me about growing up here?"

Joshua looked up to refuse and saw the intent expression on her face. Maggie was not asking him to make casual conversation. She was inviting him to share some of himself with her just as she had shared so much with him. He never talked about his past; indeed, he rarely thought about it. But tonight, he owed some of it to Maggie.

"Skeeter told you about my childhood. I literally spent most of it on the streets, running with a gang, skipping school. I was in trouble all the time."

"What about your family?"

"I was an only child, and my father died when I was small. My mother fell apart after that. Between working and drinking after work, she didn't have much time to raise a son. Especially one like me. Then when I was a teenager, I got involved in a local church."

Maggie shook her head. "I'm getting the *Reader's Digest* condensed version of this, aren't I? From the streets to a church is a long journey."

For the first time since he had started his story, Joshua smiled. "You have no problems going after what you want, do you?"

She wasn't sure he was right, but she shook her head anyway. "Add it to my list."

"The Irish Channel, where I was raised, and the Garden District, an exclusive section of the city, stand side by side. When I was growing up, there might as well have been a continent between them. Reverend Hank Carroll of the Garden District Community Church didn't like the invisible boundaries. His congregation was wealthy and they had built a magnificent church with a beautiful gym that stood empty most of the time. Hank decided to change that.

"He organized a basketball team of the teenagers who roamed the streets around the church. It was in the middle of a heat wave and the church was air conditioned. Hank passed the word around that there was an endless supply of soft drinks and popcorn for anyone who wanted to join the team. It was mid-August before I succumbed to the lure.

Skeeter was already on the team, and Sam never did set foot inside the church, but I finally made an appearance.''

"What kind of basketball player were you?'' Maggie was entranced by the faraway look in Joshua's eyes. She knew he was a man who didn't often turn his gaze to his roots.

"I was their star center. Hank was a real taskmaster. He was small, but incredibly tough. We all tried to wreak havoc, but nobody gave the Reverend Hank Carroll trouble for long. He liked me. He saw potential and determined to shape me in a new image. I was convinced to play on the church's own team, and before I knew it I was sitting in a pew every Sunday. The next year I was given a scholarship to the private school run by the church, and he tutored me so that I could keep up. When I graduated he helped me get a scholarship to college. Somehow there was always money when I needed it.''

Maggie knew something about Joshua's pride. "How did you feel about all that?''

"Different. I was the kid whose mother didn't show up for graduation because she couldn't afford a dress that was good enough.''

"Why did you put up with it, then?''

"By that time I had a goal. It was very simple. I wanted to be Hank Carroll.''

Maggie absorbed his words as the waitress returned and set plates heaped with fried shrimp, soft-shell crab and oysters on their table. With a small sound of pleasure she took a bite of the succulent crab. "And that's why you went into the ministry.''

"And that's why I got out of it.''

She shook her head. "I don't understand.''

"I discovered that putting on a clerical collar didn't change who I was. I was Joshua Martane. I hated writing sermons; I hated board meetings and church politics. I hated living my life under a microscope. I continued to struggle until one day I realized that there were different ways to serve. When I looked at the things I did really well, I realized that I could do much more good as a counselor or a psychologist than I could ever do as a minister."

"Was it hard to tell Reverend Carroll?" Maggie asked softly.

Her quiet concern made him drop all his defenses for a moment. "It was probably the most difficult thing I've ever done. But when I was all finished explaining, Hank looked me dead straight in the eyes and said, 'You've turned into just the kind of man I knew you would, son.'" Joshua was quiet for a moment. "I've never told anyone that. Hank died last year. I still miss him."

Maggie ached for the man across from her who gave so much and took so little. "He was right to be proud of you."

"And there you have the story of my life."

"You didn't tell me how you met your wife."

Joshua smiled and bit into an oyster. Without even discussing it, he and Maggie had traded their oysters and shrimp as he talked. Neither had even thought about the intimacy the act had shown. "You don't suppose you've had training in counseling, do you? You ask questions like a professional. A very tenacious professional." She just smiled, and he continued. "My wife was a member of Hank's church. Her father was one of my benefactors. Daphne saw me as a challenge. I was different from the kids she knew."

"She had good taste."

Joshua ignored her comment, determined to finish as soon as possible. "When I finished seminary I came back to the area to serve a small church out in Metairie. My mother was very ill and I wanted to be near her. She died a month later. I was feeling very lonely, and one day I went to Daphne's house to pay my respects to her father. Two months later I was standing in the Garden District Community Church with Hank in front of me and Daphne at my side."

Maggie waited quietly for him to continue. "It wasn't long before I realized that I could never give Daphne what she wanted. I had been a challenge, but once we were married, she wanted to go on to greener pastures. I tried. I thought if we had a child she might settle down, but Daphne didn't want my child. And if she had given birth to a baby, there would have been no guarantee it would have been mine.''

Maggie couldn't imagine anyone being given a chance to love Joshua and rejecting him so totally. She couldn't find the right words to comfort him.

Joshua continued, his voice carefully expressionless. ''Actually, her father had warned me. He told me that his daughter would never be happy married to me. He loved her but he knew what she was like. When we finally divorced, he remained my friend. I still see him occasionally. Daphne's been married twice since. The last time she married a millionaire, and I'm betting that the money will make up to her for whatever else is missing in their marriage.''

''I can't blame you for being bitter.''

''I don't think I'm bitter. It's been a long time.''

Maggie ate her last shrimp and thought about his words. He had been badly hurt, and as much as he denied it, the scars were obvious to her. It would take a very special woman to make him forget the pain he had suffered at the hands of the spoiled Daphne. ''You have so much to give,'' she said after she was finished. ''It's time you gave it to someone who could give it back to you.''

''Do you have someone in mind?'' Joshua reached across the table and took her hands, wiping them clean with a slow sensuous rotation of his napkin.

Maggie watched in fascination as the napkin moved over the palms of her hands and between her fingers. She couldn't tear her eyes from what he was doing. ''Why didn't we meet under different circumstances?'' she asked softly.

''Do you want me to say something comforting and theological? Or probing and psychological?''

She shook her head.

''Then truthfully, I don't know. Maybe we both needed a lesson on looking underneath the surface.''

Dropping the napkin, he laced his fingers through hers and lifted them to his mouth. Maggie shut her eyes as he kissed each one. Even after he released her hands, she sat with her eyes closed, inhaling the tangy aroma of seafood and savoring the feeling of Joshua's lips on her fingertips. When she finally opened her eyes it was to the warmth in Joshua's.

Outside the night was dark as they walked with arms around each other along the lakefront, watching the waves crash against the steps leading into the water. "I love this city," Maggie said. "But everything I see seems new."

"Well, you don't have a New Orleans accent. And when I suggested that you order the crawfish bisque tonight you turned that crooked little nose of yours up higher than I would have believed it could go."

"What sensible person eats crawfish?"

"Everyone in Louisiana eats crawfish."

"Then I'm not from Louisiana."

"Do you want to know what I think?" Joshua watched as Maggie tipped her head to look at him, her short curls brushing his shoulder. "I think you're from the South, but not the deep South. Your drawl isn't pronounced enough."

"Would it help if we knew that?"

"It might. It would be easier for Sam to investigate if we knew just a little more."

They stopped under a massive gnarled oak that blocked the light of the full moon. Joshua's arm tightened around her, and he pulled her around to face him. Maggie knew that if she tipped her head to his again that Joshua would kiss her. But she had decided a month before that she would never offer herself to him. It had to be Joshua's choice. He had to trust her enough to believe that she was a person who would only give him good things.

"Look at me." Joshua rested his fingertips under her chin and tilted her head. Their noses were almost touching. "Nothing's changed. We still don't know who you are or how your past will affect you once you remember it. And yet everything in my life is different. Before I met you, I thought I had everything I needed. In the months I've known you, I've discovered just how wrong I was." He bent the tiny distance to take her mouth with his and Maggie responded with all the pent-up passion that a month without his caresses could engender.

They stood together for long minutes, exploring each other like lovers who have been long separated. "I haven't stopped wanting you," Joshua said in a low buzz against her ear.

"I'm very, very glad," she answered. Her arms tightened around his waist.

Joshua's laugh was husky and plaintive. "I've been trying for a month now to pretend it isn't true."

"You work so hard at denying yourself what you want. I won't hurt you. I want to give, not take."

"I'm only used to women who take." His mouth closed over hers, and his hands ran restlessly over her body as if, long denied, he was trying to make up for a lifetime of famine.

Maggie pulled away slightly and held her fingers out. The thumb and forefinger were almost touching. "Last month we were this close to being ready for each other, but you drew away from me. How close are we now?"

"You tell me," he said, watching her face.

She closed the gap until thumb and forefinger were no longer separated. "This close."

Joshua's gray eyes ignited with a smoky desire. "I want to be even closer."

The drive back to the apartment was silent as was the walk up the stairs. At Joshua's door he held her against him as he turned the key in the lock. He remembered the night a month before when he had almost taken her, almost given into the inevitable. He had stopped himself then, convinced that they would only hurt each other. Now he no longer cared. Nothing could hurt more than the constant disavowal of their feelings.

Fighting the part of himself that didn't want to give her a chance to refuse, fighting the part of himself that reverberated with the knowledge that under the circumstances they couldn't be sure that they weren't going to do each other irreparable damage, he found her ear with his lips. "Are you sure?"

"Completely."

The commitment was made. Without another word he pushed the door open. He found disaster.

The apartment had been ravaged. Drawers were flung open, some dumped upside down on the floor, some hanging only by a wedged corner in the bureau. Lamps, furniture and bookcases had been overturned; Joshua's desk had been searched, his papers scattered throughout the room. "Maggie, get back," he ordered quietly.

Maggie pulled at Joshua's arm, her eyes wide with fear. "Don't go in, Joshua. Come downstairs with me to call the police. Someone might still be there."

"You go," he said, giving her a slight push. "I'm going to see if anyone's here."

"No," she commanded in a hoarse whisper. "Please!" But Joshua had already gone inside.

Turning, she raced down the stairs to Mrs. LeGrand's apartment, knocking wildly on the door. Inside, she made the call to the police, told Mrs. LeGrand to watch for them and ran back upstairs. "Joshua?" Her heart was pounding in terror. "Joshua?"

"It's all right." Joshua came out of his bedroom. "Whoever left us this little surprise wanted to remain anonymous. He's gone."

"Thank God." She followed Joshua back into his bedroom, which was the scene of more devastation. "You shouldn't touch anything," she warned.

Joshua nodded. "I'm not, but it probably wouldn't matter. Even if they try to get fingerprints, it won't help. Do you know how many robberies the police have to investigate in a day?"

"Let's wait at my place. It won't do any good to stay here if you can't touch anything." Maggie slipped an arm through his. "Please?"

Joshua caught the faint pleading in her voice. The brush with the senseless crime had upset her more than she was letting on. It couldn't help but remind her of her own near death. "That's a good idea. Let's make some coffee."

Gratefully Maggie let Joshua guide her out the door. Her gratitude only lasted a minute. In the hallway, they both realized immediately that Joshua's apartment had not been the only one that had been broken into. "My door's been jimmied, too," she said, trying to keep panic out of her voice.

"Go downstairs and wait. Don't come back up until you hear me call or until the police come." Joshua's voice was stern.

"Please don't go in," she pleaded.

"Yeah, don't be heroic, Reverend." Sam Long's voice drifted up the stairs at the same time that they heard the door into the downstairs hallway creak shut. Maggie peered over the railing and watched as Mrs. LeGrand closed the door behind the two men. Sam and another man came up the stairs. Mrs. LeGrand remained at the bottom, her faded blue eyes big with excitement.

"This isn't your kind of case, is it?" Joshua greeted Sam.

"No, the regular team will be here in a few minutes. I just happened to hear the call and recognize the address. I was in the neighborhood." Sam drew his gun. "Now get out of my way, and get the girl downstairs."

Joshua firmly gripped Maggie's arm and led her down the steps. At the bottom, he handed her over to their landlady. "Both of you go inside. I'll come get you when everything's clear."

Maggie suffered Mrs. LeGrand's chatter until she thought she would scream from frustration. A knock on the door saved her from disgracing herself. "You can come up now." Sam stood in the doorway, his eyes impenetrable.

"Was the man gone?"

"Yeah."

There was much more she wanted to ask, but Sam's obvious dislike made her table her questions for later when she was alone with Joshua. She followed him out into the hallway.

"Any chance this could have been done by one of your friends?"

The question took Maggie by surprise. She hadn't expected Sam to say anything at all. "What friends?"

"The ones you claim to have forgotten."

Desolation settled over her. Although she had only rarely talked with Sam, she had known that he didn't trust her. But she had never suspected that his distrust was so deeply rooted. Even though she understood that Sam was a friend of Joshua's and protective of him, the scorn in his tone cut through her confidence like a razor.

"I know," she said carefully, "that you're afraid I'm trying to use Joshua. I can understand that. But have you ever thought how unfair it is to keep yourself on this case when you've already judged and found me unworthy of further consideration?" Successfully she kept her voice calm. She started up the stairs.

"Lady, as far as the police are concerned, your case is closed. Any investigating I do is on my own and strictly because I don't want Josh hurt. I'll find out your secrets, and when I do, he's going to be the first to know them."

"Good," she said fiercely. "That's what I want, too. We both have his best interests at heart."

Sam's answer was a snort.

Maggie was unprepared for the sight of her apartment. It had been totally and thoroughly ransacked. The few possessions she had managed to provide herself with were broken and scattered on the floor. Children's drawings that she had brought home from school were torn from the wall; sheets and towels had been ripped to shreds with a sharp object.

"Why?" She stood in the middle of the room, looking at the destruction around her. "I don't have anything anyone would want."

Joshua came up to stand behind her, putting his arms around her waist. "They didn't know that. Maybe they got mad when they discovered there was nothing to steal."

More policemen arrived, and in the flurry, Maggie didn't have time to consider his words. It was only after everyone departed, leaving her alone with Joshua, that she had time to think at all. Mechanically she wandered the room, straightening what could be straightened, throwing away everything that was beyond repair. "I just don't understand," she said, as if their conversation had never been interrupted.

"It was random violence, Maggie. It's impossible for anyone to understand." Joshua was setting furniture back in its place.

"But they didn't steal anything. Not from either apartment."

That had been the strangest thing of all. After fingerprints were lifted, Joshua had checked to find out what was missing. Nothing was. "The police think that the burglar started in your apartment, didn't find anything, came to my apartment and was in the process of collecting things to take when something scared him away."

"They're just guessing." There was little else that Maggie could do to repair the damage that had been done. The little apartment would show the effects of the night's work for a long time. "I think that's all we can do for now. Let's start on yours."

Joshua came over and put his arm around her shoulder. "We can tackle it tomorrow. You need your sleep."

The evening had shown such promise. Now the senseless acts of a stranger had spoiled that promise for both of them. Without discussing it, their decision was mutual. Intimacy would have to wait for a more appropriate time. "Where will you sleep?" she asked. "Your place is such a mess."

"I'll straighten a path to the bed. Will you be all right here? You can use the bolt at the top until we get your lock fixed. And Mrs. LeGrand has a locksmith putting a good lock on the front door right now. No one can get back in tonight."

Maggie nodded. "I'll be fine. I'm too tired to worry."

"Then I'll see you tomorrow." Joshua pulled her close for a kiss. "Try to get some sleep."

"I will." She watched Joshua disappear, and she followed him to shut and bolt the door. What should have been a landmark night in her life had turned into a dismal failure. Telling herself that there would be other, better nights, Maggie turned off the lights and went to bed.

The man wasn't surprised to see the cops come. He had done a real number on both apartments. He smiled a little, but his smile was hidden in the midst of the red beard that was now so thick and unruly that it obscured his mouth completely. He downed his beer and continued to watch from the window of the bar on the corner of Bourbon and Esplanade. How convenient that the girl was living so close to one of his favorite watering holes. But then New Orleans was good about that. There were bars everywhere. You never had to stay dry for long in New Orleans.

It was the only thing about the miserable city that he liked. He hated everything else about it; the miserable climate, the shabby little neighborhood he lived in, his job at the hospital. Just the day before he'd been ready to pack up and leave, forget the girl and what she knew about him. She was a vegetable, wasn't she? What could she tell the police? They had spirited her off to some convalescent hospital because she was no good to anyone, and besides, they'd caught the man they thought was responsible for her near murder.

He had almost convinced himself he could exit this hellhole. Of course there was still the nagging fear that she might regain her memory and tell her story. If she did, the law would move heaven and earth to find him. There was no place safe enough to hide, not considering who the girl was. But he'd almost taken the chance.

The man gave a low, squealing laugh. That had been yesterday. Today was a different story entirely. He felt good. Damn, he felt good. Here he'd almost given up hope of finding her again and now she was only scant yards away. And she'd been working at the hospital for a month. She hadn't been convalescing somewhere; she'd been working, right under his nose. He cackled at the irony, missing the disgusted glances of the men sitting at the bar behind him.

There she'd been today, towing a bunch of little kids through the Quarter. She'd looked right at him. She hadn't screamed, she hadn't gone for help. He'd watched her help the children into the van with New Orleans City Hospital emblazoned on the side, and he'd realized why she was there and where she was going. He hadn't even had to follow her. It had been easy after that to find out her new name and where she was living.

"Maggie Kelly." He tried the name out loud and then he cackled again. That was a good one. What would her father think of that? His precious daughter calling herself Maggie Kelly. There'd been nothing in her apartment to indicate that she had any idea who she was. No letters, no mementos. He was still safe. Soon he'd be safer. Soon he'd finish what he'd started.

He cackled again and downed the rest of his beer. "Bring me another," he called over his shoulder to no one in particular. He had a long wait ahead of him, but he was sure this time that it would pay off. And in the meantime he was going to enjoy every second of it.

Chapter 9

The dream started, as it always did, with Maggie lying on a hard cot in a tiny room. There were fingers of light coming from one small window above her head. She was confined, although she didn't know how. She only knew that unrestricted movement was impossible. Her eyes were focused on a door. Slowly, as she watched, the door was cracked and the figure of a man appeared in the doorway. He was dressed in black, and he had a cap pulled over his head to shade his eyes.

The diffuse light behind him made his body stand out in sharp relief, like a figure appearing from the fog. He was moving toward her. The closer he got, the more terrified Maggie became. "Don't hurt me," she pleaded. His response was a laugh and then his mouth opened to scourge her with hideous, degrading names.

Always before, she had awakened at this point. The dream had occurred so many times that Maggie had learned to pull herself from its clutches, to tell herself, even in her dreaming state, that what was happening was not real. Tonight, her will had no impact. The figure of the man continued to advance. He loomed over her bedside, peering down at her. Like a patron at a horror movie who knows she shouldn't look, Maggie found herself unable to resist the terror of staring into the man's face.

His eyes were brown, bloodshot and set too close together. The nose was bulbous and veined. The chin was covered with a sprinkling of red hair, as though he hadn't shaved for several days. As she watched him in fascinated horror, he came closer and closer.

With a small cry, Maggie woke up and sat upright, her hands clasping the one top sheet that hadn't been destroyed by whoever had vandalized her apartment. She was trembling all over. A total, unremitting fear gripped her body until she wasn't sure that she would ever be able to loosen its clutches. Fully awake, she scanned the room, now lit with the light of early morning. She was alone. The man had existed only in her imagination.

But as she tried to convince herself of that, she knew that it wasn't true. The man did exist. The man in her dream was the same man she had seen on Decatur Street. Except for the beard, which was now full and bushy, he looked exactly the same. She had taken his face and embellished her dream with it. No longer was the persecutor enshrouded by mist. Now he had an identity. And Maggie didn't know if she had created the identity for him or if there was some bizarre truth to her nightmare.

She only knew that sleeping any more that morning was going to be impossible.

When the terror of the dream had diminished to a manageable level, Maggie got up and showered, drying herself on the remains of a tattered bath towel. She dressed and found yogurt and orange juice in the refrigerator for breakfast. It was 6:30 A.M. and her body demanded an outlet for the vestiges of fear that still haunted her. Staying cooped up in the apartment seemed like an exercise in masochism. She needed activity. For lack of anything better to do so early in the morning, she decided to go to the all-night Laundromat to wash her clothes.

One of the ironies of the vandalism was that Maggie had been saving her laundry for a week, and a small mountain of dirty clothes had been piled in a basket at the very back of her closet. Although the intruder had dumped the few clothes in her dresser drawers on the floor and destroyed some of them, the dirty clothes in the laundry basket had been saved. At least she had something left to wear.

Knowing that Joshua would be worried if he found her gone, Maggie wrote him a note and slipped it under his door before she headed down Esplanade to the Laundromat where they often went together. She hoped that he would join her if he woke up in time.

As she had suspected, her timing was perfect. The late-night laundry crowd was home asleep, and the after-breakfast crowd had not yet straggled in. Congratulating herself on her farsightedness, Maggie made casual conversation with the old woman who gave out change and kept the floors clean.

"I can't figure why anyone would come here at night," the old woman said. "Been robbed more times than I can count. I stopped working that shift. Got tired of forking over money to hoodlums."

Maggie listened sympathetically. The old woman obviously found her job boring. What else was there to do besides chat with customers? "So this shift is safer?" she asked politely.

"Yeah. Nobody's ever bothered us this time of day. And now we've got a sign out front telling 'em we don't keep more than twenty dollars on the premises."

"That's good." Maggie busied herself measuring soap powder into the washer she was using. With her back to the door, she bent over to begin piling her clothes into the machine. "I'll have to remember that this is the perfect time to come. Safe and no crowds." The door opened and she felt a rush of air fan her legs.

"Get to the back of the room." A man's whiny voice sounded right behind her. Curiously Maggie turned, wondering why the voice was muffled. Standing in the doorway, a rubber gorilla mask pulled over his entire head, was a tall man dressed in jeans and a plain white T-shirt. More alarming than the mask was the gun that was pointed directly at Maggie's chest. "Now!" he commanded.

Maggie couldn't move. She leaned against the washing machine and stared at the gorilla mask. A dreamlike lassitude invaded her limbs, and although she was acutely conscious of everything unfolding around her, she could not make her body behave normally.

"It ain't Mardi Gras," the old woman said boldly. "Get out of here."

"Old woman," the voice behind the mask intoned, "shut up or you won't be making change tomorrow." He waved the gun in front of Maggie. "Do I have to show you I mean business, honey?"

Somehow she moved. The next thing she knew she was standing at the back of the room with rows of washing machines in front of her. The man with the gorilla mask was leaning on one of them. "That's better. Now give me your money."

Maggie hadn't even brought a purse with her, only some loose change for the washer and dryer. "All I have is change," she said, fishing in her pocket.

"That's too bad, honey. Too, too bad for you."

The old woman broke in. "Here, you can have all that I've got. About twenty dollars in quarters and dimes. It's in that little room in a locked drawer." She pointed and Maggie noticed that her hand was steady. The burglary was too commonplace to frighten her.

"We'll all go get it." With the gun the masked man motioned for Maggie and the old woman to walk in front of him. In a moment the woman was unlocking the drawer. "Here," she said. "You're lucky I had just emptied the machines."

"Yeah. Real lucky." The man pocketed the change. "Now ladies, lie down on the floor. If you do what I say, you won't get hurt."

Maggie's knees wouldn't bend. She stared helplessly at the gorilla-man. "Do you need some help, honey? I could kick them out from under you."

The voice, even muffled by the mask and an obvious attempt to disguise it, was nibbling at Maggie's memory. It was horrifyingly familiar. She wondered if she would wake up in a moment and find herself safely in bed.

"Do what he says, darlin'. He's got what he came for. Just get down on the floor and you won't get hurt." The old woman was already down on the floor, resigned to the indignity of her position.

Maggie's knees buckled and she felt herself float to the ground. The old woman pulled her the rest of the way. "Just stay calm," she said, "he'll be gone in a minute."

Maggie shut her eyes. The floor beneath her felt hard and real. Without a doubt she was not dreaming this. The man with the terrifyingly familiar voice was still standing above her. The room was quiet, and then there was a click that sounded like an explosion. Maggie knew that it was the sound of a gun being cocked.

Strangely she wasn't afraid anymore. She was just terribly sad. Her life was going to end on the dirty floor of a Laundromat. She would never know what it felt like to be held in Joshua's arms as he made love to her. She would never solve the riddle of her past. She would die, alone and unmourned, except, perhaps, by Joshua. And Joshua would soon forget.

When the shot sounded, she waited for an explosion of pain. There was nothing. She opened her eyes and discovered the reason. The gorilla-man's arm had been caught by a strong hand and the gun had been knocked to the floor, probably discharging on contact. Joshua stood behind the man and the two were locked in a fierce embrace.

Joshua's presence did nothing to shake Maggie from her dreamlike state. When she analyzed her actions later, she understood her trance for what it was: her body and mind's way of protecting her from understanding the danger she was in. Now, still buoyed by her sense of unreality, she scooted slowly across the floor and picked up the gun. It slithered through her hands: plastic and metal, a terrible, lethal weapon that told her of its conquests as she sat quietly and stared at it.

Above her, the two men tumbled to the ground, rolling over and over, out into the main part of the Laundromat. The old woman jumped up and ran to the pay phone. "He's got all my change," she wailed. Rising slowly, Maggie pointed the gun in front of her and followed the men.

Joshua was larger and stronger than the man with the mask. But the other man was fighting for his freedom, and it gave him a wildness that made them more equally matched. Maggie watched in awe as Joshua matched the other man's tactics with street-fighting wisdom of his own. His movements were instinctive; Maggie could see shadows of his past.

"Stop it or I'll shoot." The words came straight off the television screen. Maggie wondered what program she had lifted them from. Her voice reflected her own suspended emotions. It was calm, almost detached.

The two men ignored her. Joshua was sitting on top of the smaller man, his strong hands, so often used for healing and soothing, locked on the other man's shoulders, bouncing them against the black-and-white tile.

With a tremendous effort, the masked man turned to his side, spilling Joshua onto the floor. Joshua twisted and grabbed the leering gorilla mask, pulling it off in one motion as he attempted to tangle his fingers in the man's hair. The man leaped up, grabbing one of the portable metal laundry carts in the aisle, and rammed it at Joshua. In the split second of impact, he turned to run from the Laundromat. But not before Maggie got a good look at the red beard, the close-set, bloodshot eyes and the bulbous nose.

It was the man from her nightmare. Calmly, with educated precision, she cocked the gun and aimed it at the fleeing man. Assuming a marksman's stance, feet spread apart, both hands steadying the weapon, she followed his moving back. The trigger against her finger felt familiar; she caressed it lightly and waited for the sound of an explosion. There was nothing. She tried again. And again.

"For God's sake, Maggie, put that gun down."

In surprise she heard Joshua's voice. She blinked, and the room began to swirl around her. Carefully she lowered herself to the ground. The gun clattered at her feet. She could hardly believe it. She had taken careful, calculating aim at a defenseless man, and she had pulled the trigger. She had wanted to kill him.

Maggie lifted her head and watched Joshua advance toward her. He seemed to be miles away, and it felt like hours before he got to her side. She noticed a tiny cut on the side of his face, and a raw, red area that soon would be black and blue. His shirt was pulled out of his jeans and filthy from rolling around on the floor. He had never looked better to her.

"You saved my life." It was a statement of fact. Because she was still cushioned from the reality of the situation, her voice conveyed the message in the same tone she would have used to tell one of her four-year-olds, "It's time for a story."

Joshua knelt beside her and extended his arms. The feel of his body against hers was unreal. She could think of nothing to say.

"I got the cops. I finally remembered we've got a new emergency number you can call without money." The old woman came out of the back room. "You two all right?"

Joshua nodded his head. Maggie just shut her eyes and leaned against him.

It was only a few minutes before the police arrived. Maggie and the old woman told their stories; Joshua told his.

"Did any of you get a good look at the man?" one of the policeman asked.

"I did." Maggie's voice was barely audible. "I can give you a complete description."

"Are you sure?" Joshua was watching her, a puzzled expression on his face. "The mask was only off for a second or two before he turned and ran out the door."

"I've seen him before." Maggie couldn't meet Joshua's eyes. Instead she turned to the policeman. "This is a long story, but someone tried to murder me about seven months ago. I haven't been able to remember anything about it. Yesterday I saw a man in the French Quarter and I recognized him, although I didn't know from where. Just seeing him terrified me. It was the same man who tried to kill me today."

The policemen looked at each other in a silent message of disbelief. "Lady, this was a robbery, not an attempted murder."

"No." She wished they were right. It would be easier. "That's where you're wrong. He didn't want the money. He broke into my apartment last night and this morning he followed me here to kill me. He was cocking his gun to shoot me when Joshua grabbed him. That's why the gun discharged when it fell."

"Why would he want to kill you?"

"I don't know. I wish I did."

"That's why you tried to shoot him." Joshua's voice was emotionless.

"Tried to shoot him?"

Maggie winced at the interest in the policeman's voice. "I tried to shoot him when he fled. Evidently the gun had no more bullets in it."

The policeman shook his head. "I checked. It was loaded all right. It jammed. I guess if it hadn't, we'd have ourselves a mangled suspect right now."

"A dead suspect." Joshua's voice was cold. "Her aim was perfect."

"Where'd you learn to handle a gun, lady?"

"I don't know."

The two policemen exchanged glances. "I think you'd better come down to the station," one of them said finally. "We'll need a full report and description."

"Sergeant Long can fill you in on the whole story," Joshua interjected. "I'll bring her down to the station in a little while for details."

Maggie listened to Joshua negotiate with the two men. Finally they left, and Joshua turned to her. "Come on. I'm taking you home."

"I'll do your laundry and send it to you," the old woman said. "Just leave me your address."

"I couldn't let you do that—"

"Yes, you could," Joshua interrupted Maggie, pulling out a card and scribbling an address on it to give to the old woman. "Thank you. We appreciate it."

"Considering you saved our lives, it seems like little enough." The old woman raised her hand in farewell and headed into the back room.

"You did save our lives," Maggie said, meeting Joshua's gaze for the first time since she had told her story to the policemen. The expression in his eyes wilted what strength she had left. Anger blazed in them, turning their gray depths to silver ice.

"Come on." With a hand gripping her elbow, Joshua pulled her along behind him. "I'm sure that guy is clear across town by now, but stay close to me and don't stray."

Maggie put one foot in front of the other, plodding slightly behind Joshua until they reached his car. "You drove," she said inanely.

"Damn good thing I did or you'd be lying in a morgue right now."

"I guess you're mad."

"Nothing like it. I'm furious."

The drive back to the house was silent. Maggie opened the door to her apartment with unsteady hands. "I'd like to change my clothes before you grill me," she said.

"I'll wait."

She went into the bathroom, showered quickly and changed into the dress she had been wearing the night before. She came out of the bathroom brushing her mop of curls. "Go ahead," she said, flopping on the side of her bed. "Let's get this over with."

"Let's see if you can get the questions right without my help." Maggie could see the muscle jump in Joshua's jaw.

His mouth was a grim, straight line, and not one feature showed any compassion for her.

"You want to know why I didn't tell you about the man in the Quarter."

Joshua nodded.

"And you want to know why, after seeing the man and feeling afraid of him, I was stupid enough to go out by myself so early in the morning."

Joshua nodded again.

Maggie set the hairbrush down and folded her hands neatly in her lap. "I didn't think you'd believe me."

"Try again."

She lifted her eyes to his. "Just like you don't believe me now. No matter what else there is between us, you don't trust me, Joshua. I'm still the little streetwalker, scooped up out of a vacant lot, with no memory and nothing to recommend her. I knew that you'd think I was lying intentionally, or hallucinating, or—"

"Cut it out, Maggie!" Joshua jumped out of his chair and ran his fingers through his hair. His face showed weariness for the first time, and his hand massaged the back of his neck.

"You're never going to trust me."

Her words seemed to overcome the last barrier to his self-control. He jerked her off the bed, eyes blazing down at her. "You let your pride get the better of you and it almost killed you, you little fool."

"I let my love get the better of me." She refused to plead for mercy. "I wanted your love or what I could have of it. I thought if I told you, it would pull us farther apart."

Joshua held her a few inches from him. She saw the conflicts her words created.

"I'm very sorry," she said in a whisper. "I know now I was being foolish by trying to ignore my reactions to that man. I'll never forgive myself for endangering you."

"Endangering me?" His tone was incredulous. "You were almost killed and you're worried about endangering me?'' He laughed a soft, bitter laugh. "Maggie, what am I going to do with you?"

"I'll get out of your life. I'll leave New Orleans. Surely that will keep us both safe if I do."

Joshua's hands released her shoulders and slowly followed the soft skin of her neck to her face. He framed it gently, his thumbs caressing her cheekbones. "You don't understand, do you? I can't let you go. It may destroy us both, but it can't be changed."

As her eyes filled with tears, he dropped his hands, turned and walked to the door. "Rest for a few minutes while I'm gone, and be sure to bolt the door behind me. I'll be back to take you down to the police station after I change my clothes."

She stared at his retreating back. It was a long time before she could walk across the room to throw the bolt.

The same boards were missing from the porch floor; the screen door still creaked like the tin woodsman before Dorothy oiled his joints. Skeeter's house looked exactly the same as it had two months before. With a sense of déjà vu, Maggie stood beside Joshua as he knocked insistently on the front door. The one difference was that they were standing in bright daylight.

"Another visit?" Skeeter stood in the doorway, covering his yawn with a fist. With the other hand he gestured for them to come inside.

The trip to the police station had been frustrating in the extreme. Sam had listened to Maggie's story with a lifted eyebrow. "So you thought you recognized the man," he said. "I thought you had amnesia." The interview had gone quickly from bad to worse. There was no doubt in either Maggie or Joshua's mind as they finally left the police station that nothing she had said had made any impression on the police, especially Sam. They still regarded the scene at the Laundromat as a robbery, not an attempted murder. Even the experience of looking through books of mug shots had proved to be worthless.

"You can't go back home," Joshua said as he slid behind the wheel of his car. "Obviously this guy knows where you live."

Maggie had dropped her head into her hands, aware that the tentative security she had found, both in her job and her apartment, was now shattered. She could not go home; she could not go back to work. Any man who would track her to a public Laundromat and try to kill her was perfectly capable of attacking her in a room filled with small children. "I should leave town," she said, defeat in her voice.

"Sam may not believe you, but he's too good a cop not to follow up on this. If anyone can find this guy, it's Sam. We'll spend the night at Skeeter's."

Now they were back almost where they had started. Inside, Joshua told Skeeter about the events of the past twenty-four hours. Skeeter was suitably impressed. He sat next to Maggie on the sofa and draped his arm around her shoulders. "And you have no idea, do you, what this is all about."

It wasn't a question. It was a sympathetic statement. After Joshua's anger and Sam's disbelief, it was very welcome. "No. I wish I did."

"Do you think you could describe this guy for me? I could draw him and circulate his picture. I probably have as many contacts as friend Sam does."

Joshua was standing at the window, his back rigid. At Skeeter's words, he turned. "That's a good idea. I got a brief look at him, too, so I can help." He had not touched Maggie since their trip to the station. His own emotions were in such turmoil that he didn't trust himself. He was angry, suspicious, hurt and above all, confused. And now, watching the sympathetic by-play on the sofa, he was also fighting jealousy. His voice betrayed none of his feelings.

"I'll get my charcoals. If the picture turns out well, we'll photocopy it and I'll pass it around."

After Skeeter left, Maggie leaned her head back on the sofa and closed her eyes. But even with her eyes shut, the image of Joshua's rigid stance persisted. "I wonder if either of us will live long enough to laugh at this someday.'' The words had an ominous ring; she had not meant to refer to the third attempt at murder, only to the inherent melodrama of their situation.

''If I live to be a thousand, I won't be laughing.''

''Can't you talk to me, Joshua?'' Her eyes were still shut. ''Tell me how you feel. I'd rather know the worst than keep trying to second-guess you.''

''There are no words comprehensive enough.''

''I see.''

Skeeter came back, sketch pad in hand. ''Where do you want to do this? I can set up anywhere.''

''Right here will be fine.'' Joshua came over to sit next to Maggie so that they could both comment on Skeeter's efforts.

Forty-five minutes later, Skeeter held a portrait of Maggie's assailant in his hands. It was so frighteningly real that Maggie, after giving her approval, refused to look at it anymore.

''I'll take it out and have a hundred copies made to start with,'' Skeeter said. ''I'll spend the afternoon passing them around.''

''Sam ought to have a copy.''

Skeeter nodded. ''I'll take him one.'' He teased Maggie. ''You know what a sacrifice this is working on the right side of the law, don't you?''

She tried to smile in appreciation. ''Thank you.''

With Skeeter gone, Maggie was left alone with Joshua. She had made an attempt to understand his feelings; he had rejected her. She was too emotionally weary to try again. ''I'm sure I'll be fine here,'' she said, standing to stare out the window that Joshua had vacated. ''Why don't you go home?''

''I wouldn't leave you alone.''

''You already have.''

There was no answer from the sofa.

Maggie wandered through the house looking for something to occupy her. She had gone from living day to day to needing to live minute to minute. Skeeter's backyard fence was surrounded by a long-neglected border of perennials. She found a trowel and a small stool and spent the rest of the morning and part of the afternoon weeding.

Joshua watched the small figure perched on the edge of the footstool, digging weeds out of Skeeter's garden with the energy of an evangelist saving souls. She was still wearing a dress, and the fabric of the skirt billowed over the surrounding ground. The image was that of a young society matron preparing the soil for a prize rose garden. As he watched, Maggie lifted her arm to wipe the perspiration off her brow. Joshua knew that her determination to stay away from him was the only thing that kept her outside in the summer sun.

He wanted to go to her, to take her in his arms and whisper apologies for his suspicions. But no apologies could wipe away the distrust he still felt. Just the night before he had been ready to make love to her. Now he no longer trusted her. She had not told him about the man in the Quarter. She had, with professional skill, picked up a gun and aimed it at a defenseless man, and she had pulled the trigger. Over and over again. This was not the sweet, sensitive woman he had come to love. This was a stranger. A stranger with a mysterious past that hinted at crime and violence and a web of lies.

He was a psychologist, trained to objectivity and careful analysis, and yet he loved this woman with a passion that was unequaled by anything in his life. He loved her beyond his suspicions about her. And that was the part he could not change or accept.

"She's something, isn't she?"

Joshua had been so lost in thought that he hadn't even heard Skeeter unlock the door. Now his friend stood by his side. "She's something," Joshua agreed bitterly. "I just wish I knew what."

"You wear your halo well, Josh."

"What's that supposed to mean?"

"Only that you're about to sprout wings and leave the real world. When did you become so holy?"

"I've never claimed to be anything other than a man."

"Funny. I was beginning to wonder if you put your manhood in a sacred trust."

Joshua turned to sweep Skeeter with a cold stare. "What makes you think you have a right to criticize my life?"

"Are you beyond reproach?" Skeeter jammed his hands in his pockets, and for a moment, Joshua was transported back to the streets of the Irish Channel to stand on a street corner with Skeeter on one side, Sam on the other. The teenage Skeeter had stood just the way the adult Skeeter was standing. Joshua didn't love him any less today than he had two decades before. His anger faded.

"No. I'm not beyond reproach. Tell me what you see, Skeeter. I've lost the gift of insight."

"I see a man in love with a woman. I see a woman in love with a man. I see him keeping himself at arm's length because he's afraid to trust again, to give his love without doubts." He stopped as if he were loath to continue. "And I see his chance for happiness slipping away because the woman needs him now, not tomorrow. She needs him while the doubts exist, not when they've been cleared away."

Joshua couldn't think of an answer.

"I came home to change. I'm going to work at the Square for the rest of the day and at a bar tonight. I won't be home until early tomorrow morning. I'll see you then." Skeeter turned to leave.

"Skeeter?" Joshua faced his friend. "I am only a man."

"I'm glad to hear it. I'd hate to think that God chose the Irish Channel to launch His second coming." He smiled at Joshua's grimace.

When she could no longer stand the blazing sun, Maggie washed her face and hands under Skeeter's hose and went back inside. She was surprised to find Joshua in the kitchen preparing red beans. The beans, flavored with celery, onions and various spices, were a staple of the Louisiana diet.

Served over rice they were a healthy and cheap alternative to meat. Joshua's version smelled delicious.

"Your clothes arrived." Maggie was startled by Joshua's voice.

"You had them sent here?"

He came to the door, still holding the wooden spoon he had used to stir his creation. His hair was rumpled where his fingers had combed it, and the small scrape on his cheek was already turning black and blue. "I knew you wouldn't be able to stay at the apartment."

"That was thoughtful."

"I put them in our room. Why don't you shower and change and then have some lunch. I was just about ready to drag you inside."

Maggie sensed a subtle change in Joshua's manner. The tension, previously apparent in his face and voice, was gone. He was relaxed. There was warmth in his eyes when he looked at her. She erected her defenses. "You don't have to take care of me."

"I realize that. You're a very capable woman. Still, even capable people can get sunstroke." Somehow the words caressed her. She refused to respond to their power.

"I stayed in the shade."

Joshua walked toward her, raised his hand and stroked her face with his fingertips. "You have a sunburn. It's not a bad one, but I'd count on at least twenty-five new freckles."

Maggie stepped back to avoid his touch. "I'm going to take a shower. Because I want to. Then I'm going to change. Because I want to. Then I'm going to eat lunch."

"Because you want to. See? You are a very capable woman and an intelligent one, to boot."

Maggie turned and left the room before he could see how his playful warmth was affecting her. In the shower she tried to whip up a protective barrier of righteous anger. One minute Joshua was ready to make love to her and the next he was distrustful and distant. The dichotomy was destroying her. She tried to be critical of his suspicions, but her anger failed her.

She was in love with a man who would never be casual about love or commitment. Her anger slowly dissolved and with it the protection she had tried to build around her heart. Maggie knew she was still completely vulnerable as far as Joshua was concerned. She could only watch their story unfold and hope for a happy ending.

Later, clad in shorts and a cool tank top, she found him in the kitchen, fixing her lunch. "Is grilled cheese okay?" he asked.

She nodded. "I could fix my own."

"It's my pleasure."

She sat at the table, watching Joshua's sparing movements. "Have you ever wondered why you spend so much time taking care of people?"

"Sure. Sometimes it's an easy way to relate to others. It gives me a role to play."

She was astonished at his honesty. "Is that why you insist on taking care of me?"

He leaned against the stove, arms crossed in front of him. "No, Maggie. I take care of *you* because I love you."

The turmoil of the past twenty-four hours had been nothing compared to Joshua's simple statement. "How can you say that?" She tried to choke back the emotion that was threatening to overpower her speech.

"Because it's true."

"You don't know me!"

"I know everything I need to know. It's not you I haven't trusted. It's myself." He flicked off the burner and came to kneel in front of her. "I've been looking for excuses not to care. There are no excuses. I care. I love you no matter what."

"What if I was a prostitute?"

"It doesn't matter."

"I tried to kill a man."

"You had a reason."

"No reason could be good enough!"

"Not when you're sitting here philosophically discussing it. But the man tried to kill you. Reacting as you did made perfectly good sense at the time."

"I handled the gun like a professional."

"I'll admit I wouldn't want to meet you in a dark alley." Joshua held out his arms. "I love you, Maggie. I want to make love to you. No matter what."

Her laugh was shaky. "That could turn out to be dangerous." She ignored his outstretched arms. "What if we find that I'm already married, or have a lover?"

"Then we'll have to deal with it when the time comes." He leaned forward and wrapped his arms around her.

She was disappointed. There was no assurance that Joshua would fight for her no matter what. He was still protecting her and himself. "I don't want any more therapy from you, Joshua." She felt him stiffen against her. There was nothing more cruel that she could have said to him. But she had not said it to be cruel. She had meant every terrible word.

"Therapy?" His voice was hoarse.

"I don't want you to make love to me because you think it will be good for me." She tried to break away from him.

His fingers on her shoulders pinned her against him. "Good for you?"

"I'm not a confused little girl lying in a hospital bed. I'm a woman who needs to be loved, who needs to be trusted. You're telling me that you'll forgive me anything. I don't want your forgiveness. I want you to trust me enough to believe there's nothing to forgive. And I want you to want me enough to fight for me no matter what we find." She tried to wrench free.

"What I'm telling you is that I need you. I need what only you can give me, Maggie. Sweetheart, I'm giving you control over my heart."

She stopped her struggle and sat perfectly still. The tears she had refused to cry drifted slowly down her cheeks. He had laid it out for her, simply and with genuine emotion. He was offering himself to her but there were no guarantees that when the facts were in, he wouldn't step back out of the picture.

Still, it was more than he had ever offered. Instinctively she knew that this much of Joshua was more than any other woman had ever had. She knew she could not turn away. "Every time we've gotten this far," she said, her voice quavering, "you've withdrawn from me. What will come between us this time?"

"The only thing stopping me from carrying you into that bedroom is my lack of preparation," he admitted. "I don't want you to get pregnant."

"You've used up your excuses, then. That's not a problem right now." She waited for a new defense to spring up, but instead Joshua's eyes softened, and he brushed his lips across hers.

"Then there is nothing between us, Maggie, my love."

She buried her face in Joshua's shirt, breathing in great gulps of air as he held her tightly against him.

The last time Joshua had carried her into this bedroom, she had been dressed in a pale pink nightgown, and she had slept through the whole night in his arms. Today she wore shorts and a tank top, and sleep was the furthest thing from their minds. He set her on her feet in front of the twin beds that had been pulled side by side.

"Do you know," he said, his voice a husky whisper, "that late at night, almost every night, I wake up after dreaming about making love to you. I can feel your skin beneath my fingers, as soft and silky as a cloud. And just as ephemeral. You slip away, and I wake up. Do you know how hard it's been to keep myself from coming to you?"

"Do you know," she answered, "that late at night, almost every night, I wake up after dreaming that you come into my room and tell me that you love me and want to make love to me?"

He smiled, his features softening with tenderness. "And what do you say?"

"I say yes. And then you reach for me, and I can feel the roughness of your fingertips against my skin. And very slowly, you bend to kiss me."

"Like this?" Joshua stroked his fingers against the sunburned skin of her cheeks.

Maggie shut her eyes, letting the whisper-soft caress work its magic. "Yes." His fingers moved down her neck, patiently exploring every inch. As he reached her shoulders, he bent to take her mouth with his.

"And like this?" he whispered against her lips.

"Yes." His mouth proclaimed that they had all the time in the world to savor each other. He nibbled lightly at her bottom lip, sucking it gently, until she sighed and opened her mouth to his trespass.

There were few visible signs of the fragile Maggie who had existed months before. But as Joshua kissed her, he was aware of her hesitation, her uncertainty. "Come to me. Give to me," he coaxed her. "I want all of you."

She relaxed against him, her arms entwining around his neck. His chest was hard against hers and her breasts flattened against it. She searched for aloofness and found none. Joshua's body was alive next to hers. His need for her complete and real. She felt his arousal and knew the force of his desire. She also knew the first tremblings of fear.

Joshua could feel it, too. "Maggie," he whispered, his lips nuzzling her ear. "I'm not going to hurt you. Are you afraid?"

She could not pretend otherwise. She nodded.

"Do you know why?"

She didn't answer.

Joshua had not told Maggie of his other dream. She was not the only one who dreamed of her persecutor. In his dream, the nameless, faceless man stood over her body, a demonic laugh rending the air around him. Joshua tried to reach her, tried to save her from the man's attack, but he was unable to move. As the man bent over Maggie, Joshua always awoke, sweating and fighting to free himself from his paralysis. It almost destroyed him to know that once, Maggie had lived through the dream. Only for her, it had been a reality. If she was frightened now, there was a reason for it.

"You can stop me if I frighten you."

Her fingers crept up his neck to tunnel through the short curls at his nape. "You don't frighten me."

"Does making love frighten you?"

"I don't know if I've ever made love."

Never in a lifetime, in a millenium, would he have expected that response to his question. He stroked her back through the soft knit of the tank top. "I can see why you're afraid, then."

"You're going to be disappointed."

"Did you think I was expecting a professional performance?" His gentle tone took the bite out of his words.

"What are you expecting?" She lifted her eyes to his, waiting for his answer.

"I'm not expecting a virgin. I'm not expecting a pro. I'm expecting to hold the woman I love in my arms and seal my commitment to her. And I'm expecting the experience to be imperfect, full of risks and absolutely magnificent." His fingers traveled to the hem of her top and then to the smooth skin beneath. "What do you expect?"

"I expect to feel whole."

"Tell me you love me."

"I love you." She stood on tiptoe to claim his mouth.

"If you love me, you have nothing to be afraid of."

"There is no 'if.'" With hands that were steady and sure, Maggie began to undress him. Joshua stood still under the ministrations of her fingers as she adored his body with her hands and lips. The past months of her life had taught her nothing if they had not taught her that life was short and full of too many twists and turns to count on second chances.

She savored each part of him: the wide shoulders, wide enough to try to take on the burdens of the world; the hard chest that was such a perfect opposite to her own; the slim hips and firm buttocks; the throbbing evidence of his masculinity that already sought her femininity; the tapering, muscular thighs; the perfectly proportioned legs. Revealed to her, he was better than a fantasy. There was a scar from a childhood battle; there was a scattering of tiny imperfections. He was human, a man like many others, and completely special because of it.

When it was her turn, she watched the expression on Joshua's face as he discarded each item of clothing. Proudly she stood before him, welcoming his gaze. She felt her nipples harden beneath his hands, felt a warm gush of desire when he stood close to her, exploring her body with his.

Together they lay down on the bed, their arms seeking the comfort of each other. She expected him to make love to her, to give her the wholeness she craved. Instead his hands and lips began a slow, torturous expedition seeking the places that she hadn't known existed. She was afraid to breathe, afraid that the magic would disappear if she moved.

"Maggie, show me that you like what I'm doing."

His words set her free. She moaned and tangled her hands in his hair. "Yes, I do... Oh, Joshua." This time when the palm of his hand began a rhythmic kneading of her most intimate space, she moved with him.

"Maggie," he said, her name a rough groaning sound. "That's right, sweetheart."

Joshua could feel the heat radiating from her, the moistness that told him she was becoming ready for him. He watched her as, with eyes closed, she began to respond to his caresses. For just a moment he mourned the careless giving of her body that had taught her so little about her own needs. He knew he was teaching her the most fundamental aspects of her sexuality. Inside he cried for women everywhere who have known a man but never the pleasure a man can give.

"Joshua?" Maggie's eyes were open, and her expression conveyed all the love she felt for him. "Come to me." She gave with the same enthusiasm with which she had taken. Half sitting, she ran her nails over him lightly, following their path with her tongue. She tasted and teased, nibbling the smooth skin of his neck, sucking lightly on the sensitive places on his chest. His response was instant and passionate as he pulled her beneath him.

His hands followed the contours of her legs, smoothing them. He levered himself over her. Her eyes were wide and full of trust. It was only that trust, expressed so poignantly, that gave him the control he needed to enter her slowly.

She was hot, and wet, and very tight around him. He was not her first lover, but he knew instinctively there had not been many before him. She was very new. He wanted to weep with the discovery.

She was surprised, too. Joshua could see it proclaimed across every feature. The feel of a man inside her was unfamiliar. She shuddered and lay very still. "Maggie. Sweetheart." His voice was broken. "My love." He gathered her close, his arms around her back, his chest crushing hers. He hid his face in the brown curls that caressed her neck.

"Joshua, love me." Her voice was a plea. She seemed unsure of what to do, how to convince him that she still wanted him. She turned her head to kiss his neck; her hands traced feverish patterns on his back. Hesitantly she began to move beneath him, her body responding on its own in a way that she could not have predicted. "Please, Joshua."

It was all he could do to overcome the heartsick guilt that he felt. No matter how many disclaimers he had made about Maggie's past, he had never quite shaken the suspicion that she was what Sam believed her to be. But the woman lying beneath him, moving her hips so sweetly against his, had never been a prostitute. Her movements were untutored and innocent; her responses had been previously untapped. "Maggie, I'm so sorry I ever doubted you."

"Just love me now."

Joshua lifted himself above her, his eyes devouring the flushed, damp skin of her face, his body consumed by the feel of her softness beneath him. Maggie shut her eyes, closing off everything except the feel of Joshua against her. She willed her instincts to control her movements. Each thrust of his hips sent liquid fire dancing through her body, yet she found the sensations confusing. They were building to a conclusion, but without help from her they faded, far removed from the intensity that she desired. Frustrated with her own confusion, she moved restlessly, avoiding rather than prolonging true intimacy.

"Maggie?" Joshua held back, his body rigid with his effort to control himself. He wanted to bury himself in her, to move with abandon against her, taking his own release. He knew if he did, that she would understand; she would take true pleasure from giving so much to him. But he wanted more. He wanted everything for her. The pleasure of giving and the pleasure of taking, too.

He moved his hands beneath her. "Move with me, Maggie." When he thrust into her again, he lifted her hips to meet him. His reward was a soft gasp of appreciation. With a patience that bordered on the unearthly, he taught her to make love to him. Hesitant at first to trust her own body, at last she let herself be guided to a place where there was no turning back.

Finally, there could be no more lessons. Each thrust, each meeting of hips, each small cry, took them further toward the place where Maggie had never been. She wrapped her legs around Joshua, trying desperately to merge. She trembled with the force of the effort, calling his name and pleading with him until there were no more words.

With one final cry, she gave herself completely, all her trust, all her faith in Joshua's love for her. The series of explosions that rocked her body set off an earthquake in the man she adored, and wrapped tightly in his arms, she felt herself brought down to earth again. Safe.

Chapter 10

Joshua wouldn't let Maggie go. He turned to his side, with her body still entwined with his. He held her, and he thought of all the times he had almost lost her, all of the circumstances that could have been different so that he might never have met her. He wanted her again. Immediately. He wanted to fill her, join together again for those blissful seconds when they could truly be one. So fierce was his need that he held her too tightly, afraid that now he had finally found her she would be taken from him.

Maggie hid her face in his neck. The heat of their bodies wound so closely together was smothering in the New Orleans summer afternoon. Maggie didn't care. She wanted nothing to break the spell that their lovemaking had cast over her. She felt loved and treasured and completely secure. She felt reborn.

"I don't know what to say." Joshua spoke first.

"I do." Maggie nuzzled Joshua's neck with her lips, her voice husky. "Thank you."

Her gratitude embarrassed him. "If I tell you it was my pleasure, will that be too corny?"

"It will be perfect."

"It was my pleasure."

"I noticed."

He hugged her tightly, kissing her before he let her go to move slightly away. His hand came up to trace the flush of her cheeks and the freckles appearing in sharp relief on her nose. "It seems to me that it was your pleasure, too."

"Oh, yes."

They lay together, touching each other with the natural ease of lovers who have been completely lost in each other. Words were more difficult. And yet words had to be spoken. When he could put it off no longer, Joshua began.

"It seems, sweetheart, that we named you after the wrong Mary."

"I wasn't a virgin."

"Not quite." Joshua ran his hand along the curve of her arm. "Nor were you experienced."

"Perhaps I've forgotten."

"I think not." His hand traveled lightly over her breasts, and he felt her shiver. "I think that we have to look harder for answers."

"The man who tried to murder me must have believed I was a prostitute."

"I don't think it was the same man who tried to kill the others. Sam is sure the man they've locked up is responsible for at least three of the murders. Obviously the man who tried to kill you is still on the streets."

Maggie waited for Joshua to continue. She could almost see him trying to work out an answer.

"What if someone tried to murder you and wanted to cover up the evidence?"

"Isn't that where cement blocks and deep water come in?"

Joshua shuddered lightly at the thought, pulling her a little closer. "Suppose this somebody had a twisted sense of humor. He dresses you like a prostitute and leaves you for dead in a vacant lot with a scarf, just like all the other prostitute murders."

"Only I don't die." She thought about the possibility. "Wouldn't someone have reported me missing?"

That was a mystery. Joshua knew that Sam had thoroughly searched all the missing persons reports that came into the station. "I don't understand that part," Joshua admitted.

Maggie shut her eyes and willed herself to remember something new. Anything. She had trained herself to bring up an image of the white stucco house and blue, sparkling water. Her father's voice...a boat...the sound of guns firing. This was new, but there was no answering jolt of fear. She concentrated on the sound of guns. Rapid firing. No screaming. She drifted with the sound. It came from a room that was semidark because the walls were painted gray. It looked like a barn or a bowling alley. On the wall in front of her was the figure of a man; part of it was ripped to shreds by tiny holes, gathered in a circle. Bullet holes. She opened her eyes.

"A firing range. At some time I've been to a firing range."

"That would explain the professional way you handled that weapon."

"But why?"

"Maybe you needed training for a job?"

Maggie shook her head. "I'm certain that I worked with children."

"Self-defense?"

"But why?"

"Maybe you lived in a big city, in a bad section of town."

"No, I lived on the water in a white stucco house."

Joshua smiled. She was as sure of that small piece of information as she was of anything in the world. "As an adult?"

She nodded slowly. "Because of what I was told about myself, I thought perhaps I was remembering my childhood, but now I think it was more recent." She shut her eyes again. "The house is two story, and it has a red tile roof."

Her eyes flew open. "It's Spanish in design. Maybe I lived in New Mexico or Arizona."

"Probably not with all that water."

She shrugged. "When I imagine the house, I see lots of green shrubbery growing around it and a big yard that stretches to the water."

"What else?"

She shut her eyes again. "Sunshine and iron gates. Tall iron gates. Hibiscus and orange trees." Her eyes flew open. "Oranges! California."

"More likely Florida."

She sat up and clapped her hands. "Florida. I'll bet you're right, Joshua."

He sat up to join her. "The central or southern part of the state. Probably on one of the coasts."

"Florida." Maggie threw her arms around his neck.

He wanted to caution her. They still didn't know what she would find when her memory returned completely. He wanted to prepare her, to cushion her if the reality of her former life was painful. But he could do nothing. He could not dull the shining joy in her eyes with talk of keeping her feet on the ground. He could only be there to catch her if she fell. He hugged her, letting the soft breasts against his chest rekindle his desire. Ah Maggie, how much longer will you be mine?

They were so attuned that it was almost as if he had spoken the thought out loud. "Joshua, wherever I came from, whoever I am, it won't come between us. It can't." Her mouth sought his, her hands began to travel his body. "Love me again, Joshua. Let me show you what I've learned."

He pushed her back against the pillows, and this time there was no hesitation, no careful tutoring. They gave, they took, and for a long time they took pleasure in the moment with no thoughts of yesterday or tomorrow.

The sun set before Maggie and Joshua returned to the kitchen. Maggie's grilled cheese sandwich was cold rubber, but the red beans had cooked down to a creamy perfection. Joshua put rice on to steam, and Maggie made a salad. They sat across from each other at Skeeter's kitchen table as they waited for the rice. Neither of them needed to say a word.

Maggie noted the little things about Joshua that she loved: the way his dark hair grazed his forehead, the stern lines around his eyes that softened when he looked at her, the smooth, tanned cheeks that would be rough by early morning. Even now, satiated from their lovemaking, she wanted to reach across the table, take his hands and communicate wordlessly to him the startling depth of her desire.

Before she could, his hands had captured hers. "I've just had you, and yet, I want you still." He brought her fingertips to his mouth. "That's never going to change."

She wondered if that was enough, if wanting her even without trusting her enough to believe that she would stay with him was really enough. It didn't matter, though, because there was nothing she could do to change it. Joshua would have to be the one to take that final plunge. And he wasn't a man who indulged in blind faith.

"I hope you'll always want me," she said. "I know I'll always want you."

The timer went off, and reluctantly Joshua let go of Maggie's hands to turn off the stove. They dished up plates of rice, covering it with the red beans, and they added bowls of salad. When they finished, they cleaned up the kitchen, working together with the sensitivity of a couple who have been together for many years.

When they were finished, Maggie put her arms around Joshua's waist and rested her head on his chest. "How long do you think I'll have to stay here?"

"I don't know. Can you stand it for a little while?"

She shook her head. "I can't take time off from work without forfeiting my job. And the police don't believe my story. They may never catch the man who..."

Joshua gave her a fierce hug. "I'm going to call Sam and have a talk with him. If I don't get any assurances that they're really trying, I'm going to quit my own job and get you out of New Orleans."

"Where would we go?"

"Florida."

Joshua had already given up so much for her. Now he was volunteering to quit his job and undertake a wild-goose chase through an unfamiliar state just in case their theories were correct. Maggie couldn't let him. "No."

"Funny, I didn't think you'd be saying no to me to-night."

She laughed, but the sound was an audible tremble. "I won't allow you to sacrifice your job for me again. I'll go myself."

"I couldn't let you."

"I'd just be trying to put together the pieces of my life so that we can go on with our life together."

"You don't know what you'll find." Joshua cupped Maggie's chin in his hands and lifted her face to meet his.

"I have to find out who I am to put an end to this terror...."

"No, I mean you can't assume you'll want a life with me."

"You know I do."

"You do now, but, Maggie, you don't know what you'll want later. I don't want you feeling guilty because you're pulled between me and your past."

She stepped back and put distance between them. "Stop taking care of me. I don't need to be shielded from the real world. I know what I want. If you can't believe it, fine, but don't start trying to prepare me for leaving you. I won't have it!"

"And what will you have?" He put his hands on her shoulders and held her still. "Can you guarantee how you're going to feel? I can't."

"There are no guarantees that come with this life. There's only loving, and giving, and risking. We've come so far. Go the rest of the way with me. Can't you do that?"

"I'll go just as far as you want me to."

She heard the unspoken codicil. He would stay with her. But when the day came—as he knew it would—when she didn't want him anymore, he would leave. And in preparation for that moment he would keep a part of himself from her as protection.

She could only fill him with her love and hope that someday it would be enough. "I'll take what you can give me," she said, turning her head to kiss each of his hands. "No matter what you withhold, what you give is more than I ever expected to have."

Then, filled with dinner and with their need for each other, Joshua took Maggie by the hand and led her back to their room. And the evening passed much too quickly.

It was almost midnight when Joshua heard the key in the front door. He had been awake for some time, watching Maggie sleep beside him. She was lying on her side, her head pillowed on her hands and her face utterly composed, like a child who has never known sadness. Guilt had stirred deep within him for the depthless desire he had shown for her. No matter how many times they made love, he couldn't get enough of her, couldn't begin to touch the passion he felt. Tomorrow, she would know how inconsiderate he had been.

There had been no complaints from Maggie. She had come to him again and again, with the same need that he had shown. Now she was sleeping an exhausted sleep, pleasure shining on her face. Joshua was still filled with the emotions of the day and evening. At the sound of Skeeter's key in the front door, he got out of bed, pulled on his pants and went to see his friend. Maggie didn't even stir.

"I thought you weren't coming home until the wee small hours," he said in greeting.

"I was hoping you'd be up." Skeeter motioned for Joshua to follow him to the kitchen. "I've got a lead on Maggie's attacker."

Joshua was in the process of stretching when the news came. He stopped in midair. "No."

Skeeter cocked his head to one side, surprised by his friend's reaction.

It was too soon. Much, much too soon. No matter what he said, Joshua knew that letting Maggie go would be the hardest thing he had ever done. He had counted on more time with her than this. He had counted on building memories to last him a lifetime. He wanted to stop Skeeter, to scoop Maggie out of bed and take her far, far away before her past claimed her. There would be time later to deal with it. Now he needed her more than she needed to know who she was.

"Joshua?"

He knew it was already too late. Too soon and too late. He laughed bitterly at the irony. "Tell me," he said.

Skeeter was showing his flair for the dramatic. "Well, I kept the original sketch for myself. It was so well done, I decided to put it on my display board." In order to captivate potential customers, all the portrait artists that worked in Jackson Square put their best work on display beside the little stands where they worked. Often the portraits were of celebrities, but just as often they were well-done pictures of ordinary people.

"So?"

"I didn't get any comments on it while I was at the Square, but later, when I moved to the Jazztown bar on Bourbon Street, I put it up again. About an hour ago, this guy came up, almost falling-down drunk, and started staring at the picture. So I asked him if he knew the man. He said, 'Sure.' Then he started to wander off."

"Go on." Joshua pulled a chair out from the table and turned it to sit on.

"Well, I followed him. He was pretty easy to keep up with, he was so out of it. I told him that the guy had asked me to do his portrait and paid me, but that I had lost his address and couldn't deliver it."

"And he believed that?"

"He was so drunk I could have told him I was the president and he would have tried to snap to attention. He told me the guy's name is Stoney Cox, and he gave me directions to his place. Now get this. Cox lives over off of

Basin Street. About six blocks from Hootie Barn's Tavern.''

"God.''

Skeeter nodded at Joshua's stricken expression. "Trying to call out the troops? You're going to need them. The guy says that this Cox character is a real bad dude. Evidently he owed money to the guy I talked to, and when the guy tried to collect, Cox went after him with a knife. He said that Cox told him once that he was wanted in Florida for something real bad, but he's managed to keep his nose clean in Louisiana.''

"Why didn't this guy report him to the police?''

Skeeter clucked and shook his head. "Honor among thieves, Joshua. What would you expect? The guy I talked to was no saint himself.''

It was much, much too late to turn back. "We've got to call Sam.''

Skeeter leaned back in his chair, his hands behind the back of his head. "Can you identify the guy if you see him?''

Joshua tried to imagine the face of the man in the picture. He had only seen him for a few seconds, but the image was permanently engraved in his brain. "Yes.''

"I've already called Sam myself. There was no answer at home, and the woman I talked to at the station says he's not expected back until late tomorrow afternoon.''

They could wait. They could wait, the man could disappear and they might not ever discover Maggie's identity. Joshua shook his head. He could not deprive her of her past, no matter how much he wanted to. And by not acting on the information now, they might lose track of the man. Maggie's safety would be in permanent jeopardy.

"I don't want to wait for Sam.'' Joshua stood and began to pace. "What if this guy hears that someone is circulating his picture and decides to leave town?''

Skeeter nodded. "I think that first thing tomorrow morning, we should go to the guy's house. My van has tinted windows. We'll take it and you can stay inside. I'll go to the guy's door on some pretense or other, and when he comes out, you can get a good look. If it's the right guy, we can keep his house under surveillance until we can notify Sam."

"I don't want you near this guy. I'll do it."

"He's seen you. I'm a stranger."

Joshua knew that Skeeter was right. "Then we'll just watch his house until we can get hold of Sam. We can wait to identify him without risking your life."

"I don't think so."

"Why not?"

"Because Sam doesn't buy any of this. I saw him earlier today when I dropped off the sketch. He thinks Maggie is leading you down the primrose path. I want to confront him with as much evidence as possible. If we tell him you're sure it's the guy from the Laundromat he'll jump to attention. If I tell him it's just a guy who looks like a sketch I made using Maggie's description, he's not going to be impressed. He'd come eventually, but I don't think there's time to waste."

"Sam's the one who isn't being objective."

"He loves you. We both do."

Joshua smiled at his friend. "It's not just me you love, is it?"

Skeeter shook his head. "I know where Maggie belongs and with whom. But maybe she's made me believe a little."

Joshua understood.

"I don't think we should tell her until right before we leave tomorrow," Skeeter said, standing to head to his room. "She won't want us to go."

Joshua stood, too. "How can I say thanks enough?"

Skeeter was quiet for a moment. "Do you remember when I was arrested six years ago?"

Joshua waited. Skeeter rarely talked about his arrest for selling drugs to a narcotics officer. He had been one of many, cleaned off the streets in a drug sweep that shook the city. Dealing in drugs had been a sometime thing for him, and he had never dealt the hard stuff. But everyone's sentence had been stiff; Skeeter had been caught in the furor and given a harsh five-year sentence.

"You stood by me then, Josh. If it hadn't been for you and Sam, I don't think I would have lived through those years in jail. You both jeopardized your jobs for me. Thanks won't ever be needed between us."

The two stepped together and embraced. They had grown up on the streets, tough kids who had learned early that showing emotion only got them into serious trouble. Tonight, they trusted each other enough not to care.

"Well, what are you two staring at?" Maggie knew by the bright sunlight flooding Skeeter's kitchen that she had slept much too late. Skeeter and Joshua were both up, dressed as though they were ready to go out for the morning. She met Joshua's gaze, and she knew her face was awash in color. The memory of the night's passionate lovemaking was between them.

"It's not every day a beautiful woman steps into my kitchen," Skeeter teased. "You look lovelier than ever this morning, Maggie." She blushed again, tearing her eyes from Joshua's to smile at Skeeter.

"Thank you." She poured herself a cup of coffee and came to the table to sit beside Joshua. He didn't miss her wince as she lowered herself into the chair. His guilt was mixed with teasing affection.

"I told you one more time would be your undoing," he told her in a low voice as Skeeter went to the refrigerator to get the milk for her cereal.

"You told me? I think I told you.... Thank you, Skeeter." This time her cheeks were on fire.

"You look a little feverish this morning," Skeeter said, reaching over to put his hand to her forehead.

"Yes, I thought she was feverish last night," Joshua agreed politely.

"Will you two leave me alone to eat my breakfast, please?" Maggie slapped Skeeter's hand away. The two men just laughed.

Maggie noticed, halfway through her cereal, that no one else was eating. "Why am I the only one having breakfast?"

"We ate earlier. We have to go out in a few minutes."

Maggie was surprised, but it didn't take her long to understand that something was different. "It has something to do with me, doesn't it?"

"Maggie, we may have a lead. Skeeter and I are going to check it out his morning." Joshua's voice was calm, as though he had just announced that he was going to the corner store for a newspaper.

"What lead?" She put down her spoon and stared at him. Suddenly the cereal tasted like wood chips.

"Somebody identified the picture. We think we know where the guy lives."

"Where?" Maggie shut her eyes and clutched the edge of the table.

"About six blocks from Hootie Barn's Tavern." Joshua got up and knelt beside Maggie's rigid body. His arms crept around her. "Don't be afraid, sweetheart. It's going to be all right."

"Don't go, Joshua. Call the police. Let them do it."

"We know what we're doing. Sam's going to be at the station this afternoon. We'll call him then."

"Please don't go!" Her voice was a plea.

"Maggie. Sweetheart. We can't live our life together this way. Even if the guy doesn't provide any clues to your identity, he has to be caught. Even if all we can have him arrested for is the Laundromat robbery."

"Joshua, he must know who I am. What if we find out something terrible?"

"We won't." Joshua understood her sudden absence of courage. Everything was coming to a head much too quickly. Much too quickly for both of them. Unfortunately it couldn't be helped. They couldn't wait until they felt ready to face her past.

"You and Skeeter could be killed!"

"We won't be." Reluctantly he loosened his hold, brushing his fingers across the warm skin under the back of her blouse as he stood. "We're going now. Lock the door behind us. We'll be back before you know it."

There was no color in her cheeks now. She was white, and her blue eyes seemed to swallow her other features. "Please?" She tried one last time to keep him from leaving.

"No." Joshua helped her out of the chair and pulled her close. "One kiss," he ordered her. "Then lock the door."

With her lips and with her body she tried to tell him of her fears, but Joshua was steeled to her pleas. He broke away finally. "We'll be back as soon as this is taken care of." In a moment, he was gone.

Maggie stood on the front porch and watched Skeeter's van drive away. When it was out of sight, she went back into the house and closed and locked the door behind her. Her mind whirled with possible actions she could take. Nothing that came to mind made any sense. If she searched for Joshua's car keys and found them, she wasn't certain that she would be able to find the men. If she did, she wasn't certain that she could be any help. She had no friends that she could call; she had no resources of any kind.

She paced the living room floor, unconsciously following the same path that she had followed the day that Joshua had gone to the hospital staff meeting. Why had Skeeter and Joshua wanted to identify the man first? How would they get him outside to do it? The man had tried three times to kill her; he was not a safe person to engage in a game of cops and robbers. Joshua and Skeeter, as tough and streetwise as they were, would be no match for him.

But Sam would be. There was nothing that Maggie wanted less than to expose herself to Sam's ridicule again. She knew what the police sergeant thought of her. He was convinced she was a hooker, the lowest of low-life trying to sucker his best friend. If Sam could protect Joshua and Skeeter, however, his opinion of her was of no importance. Finding Sam was her only hope.

She hesitated only briefly. She shut her eyes, and the strongest vision she had ever had of her persecutor overwhelmed her. The man in the picture was leering at her, reaching for her with dirty, nicotine-stained hands. In the waistband of his pants was a gun. In one hand, a long scarf.

She was trembling all over when she opened her eyes and ran to the telephone.

It took long minutes for her to convince the policewoman receptionist at the station that getting hold of Sergeant Long was a life or death matter. Finally the woman promised to call a couple of numbers to try to locate him. There were no promises that even if she did, Sam would return Maggie's call.

Maggie waited, pacing a six-foot path in front of the telephone until she was certain the floor would have a permanent rut. When the telephone rang she grabbed it in the middle of the first ring. "What trouble are you in now?" Sam asked with no polite introduction. Maggie went weak with relief.

At first Sam was unimpressed with her pleas. He was about to play tennis with his partner; he didn't like having his morning off disturbed. Finally, however, something about her pleading seemed to get through to him. He insisted that she calm down; he didn't like hysterical women. Maggie told him that she didn't care if he liked her or not, she just wanted him to do his job. Then she repeated, desperately, that Joshua and Skeeter were in danger.

She told him what little they had shared with her. No, she didn't have the license number of Skeeter's van. No, she couldn't describe it. Yes, she would probably recognize it if she saw it, but she wasn't going to have the chance if he didn't get his big blond body in his car to come and get her. In a second there was a humming noise on the line, and she knew that she had finally done the impossible. She had gotten Sergeant Sam Long to listen to her.

The car that pulled up in front of Skeeter's house only fifteen minutes later was unmarked, and Sam and his partner were in shorts and casual shirts. Maggie was down the sidewalk, opening the back door before Sam had a chance to move. "I don't know what side of the tavern they're on," she said as she climbed into the back seat and slammed the door. "They were purposely vague, I'm sure."

"They both use a lot of energy protecting you."

"Yes, and I know you don't approve, and I couldn't care less," she said, almost shouting. "Just forget what you think of me for a moment and get going."

For the first time she saw something like a flicker of admiration cross Sam's handsome face. "The sweet little kitten has claws."

"If that's what it takes." She settled back against the seat, peering out the window as though she could practice for the task to come. "How do you plan to find them?"

"We're going to cruise the streets around the tavern, starting on a seven-block radius and work our way in. You keep your eyes open when I tell you to."

"I don't need you to tell me." She concentrated on the scenery. Her body was tense, every muscle ready for action if necessary. She was a tightly wound spring ready to react when she had to.

"Does any of this look familiar to you?" Sam's question lacked its usual sarcasm.

Maggie tried to think. "I don't know," she said finally, her voice echoing her defeat. "Something always stops me from knowing. It's like viewing everything through a billowing curtain. I get glimpses and then I'm blocked."

She expected him to snort, but he didn't.

Maggie felt as if she would explode. The terrible pressure of fear built inside her. At this moment, Joshua could be confronting her attacker. She was so frightened for him that all she could concentrate on was her terror. It was moving her toward a terrible gray place, a place with no light, no hope. Slowly, as if layer after layer was being peeled away, she began to see visions.

Joshua, at the mercy of a gunman. Joshua alone, trying to find her attacker. The scene was so vivid that she could see it in her mind. The man was wearing a mask...a gorilla mask. He was pointing a gun at Joshua. No! It wasn't Joshua. It was an older man. Medium height, heavyset, brown wavy hair. He was reaching out to her and she was trying to go to him. But she couldn't. The masked man held her, but his mask dissolved. It was not the man from the Laundromat. "Oh, no." She put her hands over her face. "No!"

Sam turned to watch her. "Maggie?"

She didn't hear him. The scene was changing. Now she saw the man from the Laundromat. She was tied to a bed, and he was taunting her. *All women are whores!* he was shouting. *You're no different!* Maggie cringed against the seat. "No!"

"Maggie, pull yourself together."

She ignored Sam's voice. It was too late to turn back. Images ran into images. The first man dragging her across a parking lot. The older man with wavy hair lying lifeless on the ground. Darkness. Terrible cramps all over her body and unbearably stale air. Then she was in a room. The man from the Laundromat was taunting her, hitting her; she was trying to resist. Darkness.

"Sam." Her voice was a plea.

"What is it, Maggie?"

"Sam, my father..." She couldn't put it together. The man on the ground was her father. He was dead. The first man was dragging her away. She was screaming. He hit her once, then again. Then darkness. And terrible cramps. Air she could barely breathe.

A woman. More taunting. *Please leave me alone.* It was her voice. *You've killed my father, no one will pay your ransom!*

Your father's not dead. But he was, she had seen him fall. *Go ahead and kill me!* Then darkness.

"Sam!"

"Go on, Maggie. You're safe here. What do you see?"

"I don't know. My father...the man killed him and dragged me away."

"The man that Joshua and Skeeter are trying to find?"

"No. Another man. And a woman was there, too." She pulled her hands from her face, tears streaming down it. "But, Sam, the man that Joshua is trying to find was there later. I was tied to a bed. He called me a whore. He tried to rape me." She shut her eyes and squeezed them tight. "He'll kill Joshua. Find him, Sam."

"Then open your eyes, Maggie." Sam turned in his seat and held his hand out to her. "Grab my hand, honey. You're fine. You're strong. You can handle this. But we have to have your help now. We have to find Skeeter and Joshua."

Sam's hand was light-years away, but Maggie reached across the incredible distance between them and grasped it. She was shaking so hard that he could barely hang on to her. "We're getting close to the right area now. Can you help us? You have to help us."

She nodded, tears still streaming down her face. "I still don't understand."

"You will. First we have to find Joshua."

Maggie held on to Sam's hand and stared out the window. The streets were unfamiliar.

"We're on the six-block radius now," Sam's partner told him.

"Okay, Maggie. Watch closely. Do you remember anything about the van at all?"

"It was light blue, with a wide chrome running board and a smashed fender in the back. Big windows in the side. It's a panel van that's been converted."

Sam grimaced. "I thought you couldn't describe it."

"I wanted to come. I had to come."

She expected Sam to be angry, but instead he squeezed her hand and dropped it. He opened the car's glove compartment and pulled out a pistol. "When we get there," he warned, "you will not set foot out of this car."

"Sam?" Sam's partner pointed to the next block. Parked on the side of the street was a van like the one Maggie had just described.

"Does this neighborhood look familiar?"

Maggie willed herself to remember. Nothing came. There were rows and rows of small shotgun houses, houses built one room behind the other to save space on the narrow lots. The neighborhood was shabby. It made Skeeter's neighborhood look like a ritzy New Orleans suburb. "I can't remember." And then she did.

She had seen it in the rain the day she had gone to Hootie Barn's Tavern to find her memory. But she had seen it before that, too. It had been dark. There hadn't even been the luxury of lamplight to guide her steps. She was running past houses like these. Trying to run. She could hardly move her legs because they were on fire with the return of her circulation. *You little whore.* The voice behind her was slurred. The man, her persecutor, was chasing her. She ran between houses and tried to hide in a yard, but a dog snarled at her and voices threatened her from the house.

She stumbled on, hiding against shrubbery. There was no one else on the dark streets, no one to turn to. She turned a corner, then another one. There were no lights. There was no moon. She stumbled on. The man was coming closer and closer. She was freezing cold and crying, trying not to make any noise for fear that he'd find her. It began to drizzle. In the distance she could see a street that was brightly lit. She headed toward it. She was trying to run. And then, mercifully, everything went black.

"There were no lights," she said with a sob. "No lights. And I was trying to run."

"The streetlights are hidden by tree branches." Sam's partner pointed to one of the few lamps on the street. It was shaded by the limbs of a tremendous live oak. "On a starless night, this place would be pitch dark."

They pulled into a parking space about a half block behind the van, and quietly, Sam radioed their location to the police station. Then he turned down the radio to avoid having it heard. "Where in the hell are Skeeter and Josh?" he muttered. "Are they having tea with the guy?"

"No!"

"Hush, Maggie." He nodded to his partner. "Want to make a guess which house they're in?"

A movement from one of the houses on the other side of the street caught their attention before the policeman could answer. With a sinking heart, Maggie recognized it as the house she had stood in front of the day of the thunderstorm. A door opened, and Skeeter came out, laughing and talking as if he was with an old friend. Following him was the man with the red beard. Skeeter was shrugging, as if he had made a mistake.

"What in the hell?" Sam turned slightly toward Maggie. "Is that the guy?"

Maggie wanted to scream. "Yes," she choked out. "Oh, yes!"

"This is going to be very simple, then. As soon as Skeeter gets back inside the van, I'll knock on his door and we'll arrest him. You will stay put. Do you understand?"

Maggie was immobilized with fear. At the same moment that Sam had turned to her to give her his instructions, the door to Skeeter's van had been flung open. Joshua now stood on the sidewalk. The man with the red beard saw him at the same instant Maggie did. "Joshua!"

There was no time for thought, no time to calculate her actions. All Maggie knew was that Joshua was in danger. She was out in the street before she knew that she had moved. "Joshua! He'll kill you."

Joshua turned toward her. "Maggie!"

The sunlight glinted off a shining object on the front porch. There was a sound like a small explosion. Maggie was knocked to the ground. Another explosion. "He's been hit."

"Joshua!" Then there was silence. And darkness. Another void. She drifted. *Maggie, darling, don't run down the stairs. I won't, Daddy. I never do. Mommy told me not to.*

She was in a monstrous white castle and she was crying. *Why did Mommy have to die, Daddy? Maggie, darling, we don't understand. Don't call me that, Daddy. Mommy wouldn't like it.*

She drifted. She was on a patio, a man put his arm around her back. She felt suddenly sad. Why? *James, stop it. I'm not ready for marriage.*

There were guns firing. She held one in her hand and murdered a paper target. Over and over again. Then a man was grabbing her. *No!* Her father was trying to save her. *Daddy!* Her father was lying at her feet.

She drifted. There was no reason not to drift. Joshua was dead. She could feel his hands caress her, his lips on hers. Joshua was dead. She was destined to lose, and lose, and lose.

"Maggie?"

She stirred restlessly.

"Maggie. Sweetheart. It's Joshua."

It was funny how the mind could play tricks on you. She knew that when she opened her eyes, she would find herself alone in a hospital bed. The old woman would be rocking next to her. Surely Jane Doe was as insane as anyone could possibly be.

"Maggie. Open your eyes."

She wanted to die. But to die, she must first live again. Where she existed now was neither life nor death. It was the void between. She had faced so much—surely she could face this, too. She had to live in order to die. It was a paradox, but then life was nothing but a paradox.

"Maggie!"

Slowly she felt her eyelids flutter open. Joshua was kneeling above her. In the background she heard the sound of police sirens. She blinked, trying to bring the scene into focus.

"Oh, Maggie." Joshua scooped her up against him.

"I told you not to move her. I'm not sure if she hit her head when I knocked her down." She recognized Sam's voice.

Tentatively Maggie reached to stroke Joshua's cheek. His flesh was warm to her touch. He felt startlingly real. "Joshua, you're alive."

His laugh was shaky. "Just."

"Skeeter?"

"I'm here, Maggie."

She lifted her eyes and saw his outline above her. "Sam?"

Joshua answered. "Sam killed Stoney Cox before he could get off another shot. His first one missed me."

"Stoney Cox. Yes, that was his name." She rested against Joshua's chest. "I'm glad he's dead."

Joshua rocked her slowly. "He can't hurt you now, sweetheart. The worst is over, Maggie."

She listened to her name roll so sweetly off his tongue. It seemed like a shame to correct him. Still, he had to be told. She drifted with his rocking body, gathering her strength.

"Maggie?"

"Joshua, Maggie will do just fine, but for the record, my real name is Mary Margaret O'Hanlon."

Chapter 11

Joshua's arms tightened around Maggie's back as her words penetrated his concern for her. "Mary Margaret O'Hanlon?"

"Lately of Palm Beach... I guess not so lately." She stirred in his arms. "Daughter of the late Chester Gilbert O'Hanlon who was murdered by a man I knew as Bob Claiborne." Joshua could hear the tears in her voice.

"Hush, sweetheart. You don't have to tell it all now."

They heard Sam talking to some of the other police officers who had just arrived. Maggie lay in Joshua's arms as if unable to rouse herself sufficiently to get up. Joshua stroked her hair, wondering at her words. "Mary Margaret O'Hanlon." He tried the name on his tongue. Somehow it fitted perfectly.

"My father called me Maggie when I was a little girl. My mother hated it. She was very proper. She thought that little girls should be called by their given names. After she died, I wouldn't let Daddy call me anything except Mary Margaret." She trembled, and Joshua began to stroke her back.

"Josh? Is she all right?" Sam was standing over them.

"She's remembering." He tried to convey his concern for Maggie with his eyes so that Sam would leave them alone, but his friend knelt beside them.

"Maggie?"

"Sam." Maggie pushed away from Joshua to regard the man who had saved Joshua's life. "You shot Stoney Cox."

"Yes."

"He was an evil man."

"We're going to need a statement from you, honey."

Joshua was surprised at the endearment. Coming from Sam, it was the highest of honors.

"I can tell you everything."

"Maggie's remembered her real name," Joshua explained, "and where she's from."

Sam nodded and stood.

Her voice was stronger. "Mary Margaret O'Hanlon. From Palm Beach, Florida."

Joshua was bending to pull Maggie back into his arms when he caught the dumbfounded look on Sam's face. His friend looked as though he had just seen a man come back from the dead. Or a woman. "Damn!"

"What's wrong, Sam?" Joshua was honestly puzzled.

"Don't you read the papers, for God's sake?" Sam was once again kneeling beside Maggie. "Are you sure, honey? You're not still confused?"

She smiled a little. "As sure as I've ever been about anything. Don't you think I know my own name?"

Sam's laugh was bittersweet. "How did you end up here, Mary Margaret O'Hanlon?"

"I can't fill in all the details because I was out of touch for part of the time." Maggie sank back into Joshua's arms. "I'll tell you what I know, but can it wait a little while? I need some time to pull myself together first."

"That can be arranged." Sam stood. "Josh, get her out of here before the press arrives. They're going to have a field day when they find out who she is."

Joshua was as confused as Maggie had been all these months. He also knew that this was not the time to demand enlightenment. "I'm going to take her back to Skeeter's house for the time being."

"I'll see you both at the station about five o'clock, if she's ready by then. I've got to make some calls to substantiate her story."

Joshua helped Maggie to her feet. She was smiling at Sam's last remark. "After everything, you still don't trust me, do you?"

Sam reached out to stroke her cheek with one knuckle. "What do you expect? Resurrections are more Joshua's line than mine." He turned to Joshua. "Get her home and make her rest."

Maggie looked so drained that Joshua knew Sam's command would be easy to follow. He also understood that his own curiosity would have to wait to be satiated. Maggie was too tired to explain anything. She was still stunned over the events of the morning, still trying to put all the pieces together.

Skeeter had been giving his side of the story to one of the police officers. He came over to join them. "What happens now?" he asked.

"We're going to impose on you a little longer, then I think we'll be out of your house for good." Joshua helped Maggie into the van and settled her on one of the captain's chairs in the back. "Rest now, sweetheart. We can talk all you want later."

Her answer was a tired smile.

"Maggie?"

Joshua came into the bedroom they had so recently shared to awaken Maggie for her appointment at the police station. She was lying on the bed, arms beneath her head, staring at the ceiling. "I'm awake." She smiled. "For the first time in a long while, I'm fully awake."

Joshua sat carefully on the bed, not touching her. "Do you feel up to going down to the station?"

"Yes." Maggie turned her head to examine him. "I feel like talking about it."

"Do you want to tell me now?"

"No." She pulled herself to a sitting position and reached out to put her hand on his arm. "Joshua, love me before we go."

Joshua had carefully avoided any intimacy with her since her memory had returned. Even now he pulled away from her touch. He had managed to comfort her platonically before she fell asleep, but now just the feel of her slender fingers on his arm was making him ache with new need for her. "I don't think that's a good idea, Maggie."

"Look at me." When he didn't, she put her fingers on his chin and turned him to face her. "Nothing's changed between us. I still love you. Only you."

"Maggie." He covered her fingers with his hands and held them against his face for long moments. "You must be terribly confused. You've just gone through a trauma most of us couldn't begin to handle."

"Stop!" She dropped her hands to his shoulders and shook him. "I don't need protecting anymore. I need love. Your love. Can't you trust me?"

Joshua was silent.

"You can't, can you?" She tried to move.

"I trust you. But you need time and space to readjust your life."

"I don't want time. I don't want space. I want you." She dropped her hands and tried to pull away.

Joshua sighed and put his hands on her waist, effectively blocking her humiliated retreat. "Maggie. There was another man before me. What about him? Where does he fit now?"

Maggie saw Joshua's struggle to remain objective. She wanted to soothe him and tell him that there was nothing to worry about. But even more, she wanted to be perfectly honest with him. There had been too many clouds between them. He had to know the truth. Soon he would know everything else; now he must know about James. "I'm engaged to a man named James Darwin."

"I see."

She felt Joshua's hands tighten spasmodically on her waist before he released her. His face showed no emotion.

"James worked with my father. My father owned and managed real estate, and James was his assistant." She drew her knees up to her chin and wrapped her arms around them. "You'd have to understand my background for this to make any sense, Joshua. I was raised in a very cloistered environment. I went to a private school through high school. Then I went to a small women's college. I was shy, and though I dated a little, I really didn't know much about men. I got my degree in child development...."

"That makes sense."

Maggie smiled a little. "And then I taught in an expensive preschool for gifted children. I was living at home. The only social contacts I had were with men my father knew. My father was a wonderful man, but he was also very old-fashioned. I was the light of his life. In another age he would have selected a man for me and told me to marry him. In this enlightened time, he only selected the man and then manipulated us until James and I were engaged."

"It's the twentieth century. You couldn't have been too unwilling."

"I wasn't. James was...is," she amended, "a handsome, clever man. I convinced myself that he would be an ideal husband."

Joshua's face was still carefully blank. "How long were you engaged?"

"Longer than either James or my father thought we should be. I just couldn't make myself set the date."

"Why not?"

Maggie lifted a tentative hand to stroke Joshua's face. He didn't move. "I thought there should be more. James was good to me, very protective and solicitous, but there was no passion between us. I finally told him, and he seemed immensely relieved that I was only worried about such a minor thing. He set out to prove how wrong I was."

"You don't have to go on." Joshua's voice was not as controlled as his features. Maggie heard the lapse.

"I think I do. Evidently it matters to you." She continued to stroke his face. "We only made love one time, Joshua. James convinced me that I would realize what passion there could be if I'd only let him take me to bed. It backfired. Afterward I couldn't abide having him touch me."

"Did you break the engagement?"

She shook her head. "No. I thought I was the problem, not James. He didn't seem to care if I was cold to him. He still wanted to marry me. I thought I'd never find another man that patient and understanding."

"And so you're still engaged."

Maggie shrugged. "I've been away now for seven months. James could be married, for all I know. I hope he is."

"You can say that now, in the heat of the moment. But later, Maggie, how will you feel when you see him again?" Joshua tried to stand. "You're in no shape to be making decisions right now."

"I'm not making decisions. I've made my decision." Her fingers dug into his arm, pulling him back to her. "Love me, Joshua. Doesn't last night mean anything to you? Can you throw away what we have together so easily?"

He couldn't. The rational psychologist disappeared, to be replaced by the man who loved this woman more than he loved anything in the world. He opened his arms and she was in them. Each part of their bodies joined in agonized pursuit of fulfillment. His mouth captured hers as his hands undressed her, making short work of the shirt and jeans that she wore. She undressed him, glorying in the sleek, strong lines of his body. Maggie took the lead, showing Joshua with her lips and her hands what he meant to her. She possessed him in a way that no one else ever had, seeking all the places of his body that would give him pleasure.

Maggie loved Joshua with abandon. Joshua loved Maggie with desperation. When they both hovered on the brink of insanity, Maggie moved on top of him and with a slow, sure thrust of her hips, brought him inside to fill her completely. He watched in fascinated agony as, kneeling above him, she moved against his thighs. The hot sweetness pouring through his body blended with the vision of her, head thrown back and eyes closed in ecstasy as she gave him everything she had inside her.

Her breasts filled his hands, his body filled her emptiness. Each thrust, each twist was a new commitment. "Maggie," he moaned.

Triumphantly, she moved one more time, sending them both to the place where only lovers can go. She collapsed against his chest and he held her, burying his face in her hair.

"No matter what, Joshua. Tell me nothing else matters."

"I'll always love you."

"Nothing else matters."

As much as he wanted to agree, he could only kiss her and hope that she was right.

They were ten minutes late for their appointment at the police station. Skeeter had been asked to come, too, since he had taken such an active part in the search for Maggie's attacker. With Sam's permission Antoinette Deveraux was also to be there. In the car as they traveled to the station Maggie was silent, lost in her memories.

Sam ushered them into a quiet office, probably the only one in the low-slung, sprawling building. The police chief was there and two men in plain clothes who were introduced only by their last names. No reason was given for their presence. Antoinette arrived last, going to both Maggie and Joshua for a quick hug before she settled in a chair against the wall.

Sam made Maggie comfortable, asking her if she would like something to drink. She declined, obviously ill at ease.

"Maggie, are you nervous?"

Joshua had taken a chair next to Maggie's, and he put his hand over hers at Sam's words.

Maggie nodded. "Yes. This isn't going to be easy to tell." For a moment she turned to Joshua. "I couldn't bear to tell this story more than once. Do you understand?"

"Of course." He squeezed her hand, and then withdrew his own. Her story was something that he couldn't help her with. He knew instinctively that his touch was going to distract her. She had to withdraw in order to immerse herself in the memories that had been so long denied.

"Whenever you're ready, Maggie. I'm going to turn on the tape recorder now." Sam's voice was calm. They waited.

Maggie closed her eyes. "My name is Mary Margaret O'Hanlon. I'm twenty-five." She stopped and a tiny smile pulled at her mouth. "Just barely. My birthday was May fifteenth. I'm the only daughter of Chester Gilbert O'Hanlon who was killed by a man named Bob Claiborne."

Joshua saw the two men in plain clothes look at each other and pass a silent, mysterious message.

Maggie opened her eyes. "I'm not sure how much of my history you want. Shall I get right to the kidnapping?"

Sam and the two men conferred as Joshua tensed at her words. "Kidnapping?" His voice was hoarse.

"Be quiet, Josh. Let her tell it her own way. Maggie, can you give us some details about your life? Just a few." Sam smiled encouragingly at her.

Maggie shut her eyes. "I grew up in Palm Beach. We lived in an estate on the water in a Spanish-style stucco house. My mother died when I was six. I went to school at Our Lady of the Americas Academy for Girls and later to Rollins College." She smiled a little. "I had a German shepherd named Trixie who would cheerfully eat anyone she didn't know, and I had countless parakeets. They drove my father crazy. Once I taught one of them to say, 'Chester is a spoilsport,' and I let it loose at a cocktail party my father was having. I was eleven, I think."

"That's good, Maggie. I know this part isn't going to be fun, but we're ready to hear about the kidnapping."

She was silent for a moment, gathering her strength. Joshua wanted to help her, but he could only wait.

"From the time I was a little girl, the possibility of a kidnapping was just something I learned to live with. We had strict security at home, and the nice man who drove me to and from school always carried a gun. If you grow up in Palm Beach, you're always aware of the danger connected with your status. The police department there even has a special 'code red' signal so that if there's a kidnapping attempt, all three bridges to the mainland go up and squad cars cut the coastal road.

"As an adult, I hated the restrictions on my activities. I rebelled, refusing to let my father hire a bodyguard for me. As a concession to his fears, I agreed to learn how to shoot a pistol and I promised to carry one with me if I was out at night by myself.

"My father heard of a man, Bob Claiborne..." She stopped for a moment and swallowed hard. "He lived in West Palm Beach and he specialized in teaching women to shoot to defend themselves. My father had him checked out. Bob Claiborne was an ex-policeman, and as far as my father knew, an upstanding member of the community. Daddy didn't check far enough."

Maggie opened her eyes. "Can I have a glass of water, please?" Joshua knew she was fighting tears.

Sam got her water from the cooler by the door and handed it to her silently.

"Thank you." She sipped as she talked. "I only went to the firing range to please my father. On the last evening of the training, I asked my father to come and watch me shoot. I thought it would relieve his fears. I had become very good with a pistol. Bob said I was his star pupil. My father said he'd come if he could.

"When I got there, no one else was practicing, which seemed strange, but I didn't give it too much thought. I waited for my father, but he didn't come, so Bob said we should get on with the lesson. I shot for a while, and Bob complimented me on everything I had learned. He seemed jumpy, but I really didn't pay much attention because I was so busy trying to do my best."

She had been staring into space, but now she turned her gaze to Sam. "I never thought I'd need to shoot a person. I liked shooting at targets, though. I felt like I was in a penny arcade."

"I understand." Sam nodded at her to continue.

"Bob told me that he had a certificate for me in the back room. I was proud of my accomplishment, and I wanted to show it to my father since he hadn't been able to come. I followed Bob into the back room to get the certificate. He told me to sign my name at the bottom, and when I bent over the desk, he hit me in the back of the head."

She drew a deep breath. "The blow only stunned me. My hair was very long and I was wearing it in a heavy knot on my neck. It cushioned the blow, I guess. I fell, and Bob grabbed my hands and tied them. I tried to fight and he hit me again, but it still didn't knock me out. I began to scream.

"Before he could gag and finish tying me, my father came charging into the room. He fought with Bob." Maggie put her head in her hands. Joshua ached to touch her.

"Bob hit my father with his gun. Then he hit him again. Daddy fell to the floor. He was so pale, and there was blood flowing hard from a gash on his face. I tried to reach him, but Bob hit me again and then I passed out."

Joshua watched as Maggie's shoulders shook with big gulping sobs. He reached to comfort her, but Sam shook his head in warning. Joshua restrained himself, willing her to finish so that he could take her in his arms and soothe her.

Finally she calmed enough to go on. "When I came to, I was in terrible pain. My body was one excruciating cramp and I couldn't move. Later I found out that I was in the trunk of a car, but at the time I didn't know where I was. For a long time I thought I had been buried alive. I could hardly breathe. I kept passing out, coming to, passing out."

"Damn!"

"Joshua, please try to control yourself." Sam's voice was stern. "Go on, Maggie."

"Once I woke up and I was in a motel room. Bob was there and a woman, too. The woman was rubbing my hands and legs to restore my circulation. I was still gagged, but they told me if I didn't try to move off the bed, they'd leave me untied for a while. I was still in terrible pain. I couldn't have moved, anyway. Later the woman took me to the bathroom, but they didn't feed me or give me anything to drink. I guess they were afraid if they took off the gag, I'd scream.''

"Do you have any idea where you were? Can you remember anything about the room?'' One of the men in plain clothes was addressing Maggie.

She shook her head. "They tied me up again, looser this time, and I fell asleep. I thought the worst was over, but later Bob carried me out to the car and put me in the trunk again.'' Tears rolled down her cheeks. "He apologized to me. Isn't that funny? He even put a pillow under my head.'' Her voice broke.

"I don't remember much else about the trip except that I thought I had descended into hell. Every once in a while I'd feel a rush of fresh air and I knew that they had parked somewhere and opened the trunk. Once I heard voices. The woman said, 'She's not going to make it like this,' and Bob said, 'She has to. There's no other way.'

"When I came to again, I was in a room. It was tiny and dark. There was only one window and hardly any light could filter through it. Bob and another man were standing over my bed.'' She stopped and sipped more water. "The other man was Stoney Cox. The woman came in and made me drink something. I vomited and Stoney hit me. Bob tried to stop him, but Stoney enjoyed inflicting pain. He got plenty of chances.'' The hand holding the cup trembled, and she set it down.

"Stoney told me that if I didn't cooperate, he'd kill me with his bare hands. Then they told me that they wanted me to make a tape to send to my father. I couldn't understand that. Bob had killed my father, but when I said that, Stoney hit me again. Stoney said, 'If your old man's dead, we'll send the tape to that pretty boyfriend of yours, but you're going to make the tape.' ''

"And did you?"

Maggie nodded.

Sam leaned forward in his chair. "What did it say?"

"This is Mary Margaret O'Hanlon. I'm safe and well. Please do as you're told and I will remain that way."

The two men in plain clothes nodded at each other.

"Then what happened?"

"A lot of the rest is hazy. They gave me sleeping pills, lots of them, and I slept. At first when I woke up, Bob and the woman were still there, but later they were gone and I was alone with Stoney."

"For how long?"

Maggie shrugged. "A century. I hardly saw him at the beginning. He'd come into the room in the evening, put a plate of food on the bed and take off my gag. Then he'd feed me big mouthfuls as fast as he could stuff it in, and he'd laugh if I choked. Afterward he'd pick me up and carry me to the bathroom. I wasn't allowed any privacy even then. He'd taunt me, and I'd cry."

Joshua was filled with a murderous rage that he hadn't even known he was capable of. For the first time in his life he understood the word "hate."

Maggie went on. "I was always thirsty. I hardly got anything to drink, and I was so weak from the pills and being tied that I could hardly move. One night Stoney came into the room in a rage. He started to call me names, awful names. He said that Bob and the woman who had been with him had been killed trying to get my ransom money. He was furious. He began to hit me. He called me a lying whore and a no-good slut.

"I couldn't resist, but I tried. The more I fought, the more violent he became. Finally I realized what he was going to do." Maggie stopped and turned to Joshua for support.

The expression in his eyes gave her the courage to go on. "He tried to rape me. I knew if I continued to fight him, he'd kill me. I went limp and that seemed to enrage him even more. He hit me over and over again, but he couldn't . . . he couldn't . . ."

"It's all right, Maggie." Joshua reached for her hand. Even if his interference stopped the flood of memories, he didn't care.

She grasped his hand as if it were a lifeline. "After that, he got more and more violent. He was drinking a lot. He'd come into my room and threaten me, call me names. He hated women. He'd ramble on and on. He told me there was a man who was murdering prostitutes and somebody ought to give him a medal. One night he came in with some horrible gaudy clothes and told me to put them on. He smeared makeup on my face and tied a long scarf around my neck. He told me the man who was killing the prostitutes strangled them with a scarf just like that one. He kept tightening the knot until I could hardly breathe. Then he told me he was going to get me some customers."

Maggie watched the emotions on Joshua's face. "It was just a horrible game he was playing with me, but I was frantic. When he retied me, he was so drunk that he didn't get the ropes as tight as usual.

"When he left the room I started to work the ropes loose. It seemed to take forever, but I managed. The scarf wouldn't come off, though. I could barely move once I was free. My legs felt like they were on fire, but I stumbled out of the room. I made it to the front door and down the sidewalk when I heard a car. I hid behind a tree. The car stopped in front of the house, and Stoney Cox got out. When he went inside, I started to run, but I was too weak. I kept falling down.

"The street was dark and it was drizzling rain. It was cold, too, and I kept slipping on the wet sidewalk. No one was around. Once I tried to hide in a yard but the people inside started yelling and a dog came after me. By then Stoney was looking for me. He saw me and I started to run. I'll never know where the strength came from, but I saw streetlights in front of me, and somehow I was running. I was getting close, but Stoney was gaining on me. I could hear him breathing hard behind me and I screamed. Then everything went black."

The room was silent. Maggie continued to grip Joshua's hand and look into his eyes. "And then there was Joshua."

"My God, Maggie. What you've endured." He opened his arms, and in one fierce movement she was on his lap held against his chest.

The police chief was speaking. "What do you think, gentlemen?"

"Parts of her story match what we know to be true. She resembles our photographs, but she's not a dead ringer. She's thinner, her hair's different and so's the nose. We're going to need a positive identification."

Sam stood. "Can we finish the discussion outside and give the lady a chance to catch her breath?"

The men in plain clothes ignored him. "It's time to bring in O'Hanlon himself."

Maggie had wrapped her arms around Joshua's neck, and he was murmuring soothing words to her. Only slowly did the men's conversation reach her. "O'Hanlon?"

Sam shot the men a look that commanded them both to be silent. He came over to Maggie and Joshua and squatted beside them. "Maggie. Are you ready for some good news?"

She nodded, afraid to answer out loud.

"When Mary Margaret O'Hanlon was kidnapped, her father was attacked and beaten by the kidnapper. But he wasn't killed, just knocked unconscious. Chester O'Hanlon is alive."

Maggie just stared at Sam. "Stoney Cox told me that my father was dead. He used to scream it at me. Over and over..."

"It was just another way to torment you. Chester O'Hanlon is alive."

Maggie brought her fist to her mouth, trying to swallow the tears that threatened again. "I can't believe it," she whispered.

"O'Hanlon's daughter was the one who was thought to be dead. You see, the police were notified of the kidnapping, against the kidnappers' orders. When Claiborne went to pick up the ransom, he had a woman with him. The police thought it was Mary Margaret. He had promised to drop her off somewhere after he got the ransom. The police were trailing him, but he got suspicious and started driving at a high speed. He crashed into the side rail of a bridge and went over the side. Both Claiborne and his passenger were killed.''

"They must have gone after the bodies. Couldn't they tell it wasn't Mary Margaret?" Joshua couldn't believe the police would be that incompetent.

"The ransom was dropped off on one of the Keys. The bridge they were on was a huge monster. The car burst into flames when it hit the side and fell hundreds of feet before it even hit the water. It took days to recover the car. What the flames didn't get, the sharks finished." Sam saw Maggie pale. "I'm sorry."

"But my father . . ."

"Chester O'Hanlon is a lost and bitter man." One of the men in plain clothes came up to stand beside her. "We haven't told him about you yet. If you're not who you say you are, we want to spare him."

Maggie pushed away from Joshua and stood to face the man. "Just who are you?"

"We're with the FBI."

Maggie examined him. "You could fingerprint me."

"Mary Margaret O'Hanlon had no fingerprints on record."

"Oh, yes, she did. You'll find a complete set in my elementary school scrapbook. They were made when I was in sixth grade. I was a safety patrol and all of us were fingerprinted. I saved them. Tell Rosie to look on the top shelf of my closet, under the box with my swim team trophies in it."

"Who is Rosie?"

"Our housekeeper."

Something passed over the man's face. He reached out to grasp Maggie's hand. "Miss O'Hanlon, I think you can expect a visit from your father tonight."

The police chief intervened. "Are you sure she's . . ."

"I've seen the trophies myself. Never did get as far as looking through the scrapbook. Rosie was furious that I was poking around in this young woman's closet."

"Please, can I call him now?" Maggie was trembling with excitement, and Joshua put his arms around her to steady her.

"I think, for his sake, that the news should be broken to him gently, Miss O'Hanlon. I'd like to send one of our agents to prepare him."

Maggie nodded reluctantly. "Perhaps that would be best."

"Where are you going to be, Maggie?" Sam asked.

She turned. "Joshua?"

"We'll go to my place and wait."

"Yes. That's a good idea."

"Miss O'Hanlon, if you're feeling up to it, we have some pictures we'd like you to look at. We still don't know the identity of the woman who was with Bob Claiborne."

"I'll be glad to. Anything to get this over with." She followed the FBI man to the door. Skeeter, who had been sitting quietly throughout her entire explanation, stood and put his hand on her shoulder.

"You're a very special lady," he said, bending to kiss her on the cheek.

"And you're my very special friend." She hugged him quickly and then turned to Antoinette. "If it hadn't been for all your help, I might never have remembered."

"You did it, Maggie. I just supported your effort." The two women embraced. "Would you like me to come with you now?" Maggie nodded and together they followed the man out the door.

The police chief and the other FBI man went into another office and Skeeter, Sam and Joshua were left alone.

"Are you all right, Joshua?" Skeeter's voice showed his concern.

Joshua nodded. "The amazing thing is that Maggie is all right. After everything."

"She's one gutsy woman." Sam looked sheepish for a moment. "I'm waiting."

"For what? My 'I told you so'? Forget it. You saved my life today. That's enough to keep you from eating crow."

"Why did you get out of that van when you saw Cox?" Sam asked, genuinely curious that his friend would do something so irrational.

"All I could think about was walking into that Laundromat to see him pointing a gun at Maggie. I didn't even know I was out of the van. I guess I was going to strangle him."

"I'm glad you chose the line of work you did. You'd make a lousy policeman."

"With impulses like that, I make a lousy psychologist."

"So you're human. Now maybe you'll understand some of your patients a little better." Sam clapped him on the back.

"And you, Sam," Skeeter said. "What made you change your mind and trust Maggie enough to follow her to Cox's place?"

"I don't know. I guess I just sensed how genuine her emotions were. She got angry at me a couple of times in the car, and then when she started remembering bits and pieces of her past, I could see how frightened she was. I knew it wasn't an act."

"I'm still having trouble absorbing all this," Joshua admitted. "There's a lot I don't understand."

"Like what?" Sam asked.

"Why did Maggie's father think she needed a bodyguard? Why was she so protected?"

"If you lived in Florida, you'd understand. O'Hanlon owns half the state."

"Maggie said he was in real estate."

"O'Hanlon *is* real estate. He has an empire. Maggie is the heiress to a fortune."

Joshua was silent, his face a brooding mask.

Skeeter understood. "Look, Josh. Just because she's rich, doesn't mean she's anything like Daphne."

"No." Joshua's voice was expressionless. "Daphne was never that rich."

"You know that's not what I meant." Skeeter turned to Sam, trying to change the subject. "I've got a question of my own. Why do you suppose Cox kept her so long after the first ransom attempt went astray?"

"I guess we'll never know, but I have a pretty good guess. Cox was a sadist. He wanted Chester O'Hanlon to think his daughter was dead. I imagine he realized that when O'Hanlon finally found out she was still alive, he'd be willing to pay any price, agree to any conditions Cox made. In the meantime, he had Maggie there to torment."

Joshua made a small sound of pain.

"Then why did he leave her for dead in a vacant lot?" Skeeter asked, his hand on Joshua's shoulder to comfort him.

Sam shrugged. "Maggie said he was drunk. We know he almost killed her that night. By the time he probably realized what he had done, he didn't have any choices. He couldn't carry her back to the house and risk getting caught. Maybe he went back to get her later and she'd already been found. Or maybe he thought she was dead and he wouldn't be able to ransom her anymore."

"And when she didn't die? The papers were full of it."

"He couldn't get to her. She was in the hospital in intensive care and then on a locked psychiatric unit. He was a persistent devil, though. We found out this afternoon that he's been working as an orderly on the late-night shift. I imagine he was trying to get to her even then."

Joshua's voice was bitter. "He did get to her. Nobody would believe it, though. We all thought she couldn't tell her nightmares from reality. Do you know how many times she told me a man had come into her room and tried to smother her? Do you know how many times I ignored her?"

"Don't be too hard on yourself. Even though you didn't believe her, you probably saved her life by getting her out of the hospital. Since then it's just been a game of cat and mouse with Cox trying to find her again to kill her."

"The bastard!" Joshua's voice broke.
"He's dead now, Josh. May he burn in hell."
Joshua could not reply.

Chapter 12

Maggie and Joshua fully expected to find his apartment in the confused state it had been left in. Instead they discovered that Mrs. LeGrand had been in to clean and straighten it.

"It's good to be home," Maggie said tentatively. Joshua had been comforting, but they had spoken little since leaving the police station.

"Yes." Joshua was strangely affected by her words. "Home." Where was home for Mary Margaret O'Hanlon? "Can I get you something to eat? I think I have some cheese. I can make you a . . ."

"Joshua?" Maggie touched his arm. "I have to know something."

He waited quietly for her question.

"Does anything that happened to me make a difference to you? I know that some of it was sordid." She was examining her shoe.

"Make a difference to me?"

She lifted her eyes. "I was never raped, but I know some of the other things that happened were pretty horrible. Does that make a difference to you?"

"Make a difference to me?" He swept her into his arms. "Of course it makes a difference. I realize, more than ever, how precious you are and how tenuous life can be." His lips sought her hair. "It's God's own miracle that you're alive."

They kissed, but Joshua was the first to pull away. "I'll go make those sandwiches."

Maggie put her hand back on his arm. "Then what's wrong? Tell me why you're backing away. If it's not what happened to me, what is it?"

"Not now. Let's eat, then we can talk."

Her eyes began to sparkle with anger. "No! Tell me now. I won't be coddled and led around like one of my four-year-olds. What's wrong?" She followed Joshua into the kitchen, standing firmly in front of the refrigerator.

"I don't want to discuss it now, Maggie. You have your father's arrival to look forward to. Let's not mar it with an argument."

"Now!"

"Are you used to getting what you want?"

She had been ready to give him a list of reasons why they needed to clear the air, but his question stopped her. "Pardon me?"

"Are you used to getting what you want? Has everyone always kowtowed to you? I'm not going to."

"Of course you won't. You're a stubborn, bullheaded renegade who does exactly what he pleases. I'll have to work hard to even make myself heard once we're married." She wondered at the look of pain that crossed his features. An icy chill stabbed through the region of her heart. "Or don't you want to marry me?"

"This isn't the right time to talk about marriage."

She didn't understand. "Don't you want me anymore?" she asked in a soft voice.

Joshua closed his eyes to block out the sight of Maggie's sorrow. "Only a fool wouldn't want you, sweetheart. But

I'm not a big enough fool to believe that there's an automatic happily-ever-after waiting around the corner for us.'' He felt her hands on his shoulders.

"I love you."

It took more strength than he knew he possessed to open his eyes and answer her. "You love what I've been to you. But you may not need what I can give anymore. You may need someone who can fit effortlessly into your life, and I never will. My life has always been lived in a different place from yours, Maggie."

"I see." Maggie dropped her hands. "So it comes down to trust again, doesn't it?" She laughed a little, the sound falling flat in the still room. "Funny, isn't it. When you thought I was a prostitute, you grew to accept it. But you can't forgive me for being rich. In your eyes I've been eaten away by the disease of my father's fortune, and you don't want anything to do with me now that you know." She stepped away.

"It's not that simple."

"Oh, I think it is."

Joshua shook his head. "No one can survive what you've survived in the past months without feeling tremendous emotional stress. You've got to have a chance to consider what you want. You've got to be sure."

"You really don't understand, do you?" Maggie stepped back another pace. "You're the one who has to be sure. You've always been the one, Joshua. Right from the beginning."

"Maggie..."

She lifted her chin but her eyes were filled with tears. "You can't forgive me for being rich. Well, there are some things I can't forgive, either. I can't forgive being blamed for what I'm not. I won't put up with it again. Not ever. I'm not a selfish little rich girl like your ex-wife. I'm the Maggie you've always known. Nothing more and nothing less." She stepped around him to leave the kitchen.

"Where are you going?"

"To my apartment to pack. Don't worry, I won't leave without saying goodbye. You'll know when you're finally rid of me."

The hurt he knew she was feeling blocked the sting of her words. "Don't leave with this bitterness between us. You have to have time," he said gently.

She stopped and turned at the door. "No, you need time. I need you. And that's one thing you've never been willing to give me."

Chester O'Hanlon was a heavyset man of average height. He had Maggie's muted brown hair, and he had blue eyes that Joshua imagined had once been as bright as hers. He arrived shortly before midnight accompanied by a tall, dark man dressed impeccably in an expensive silk suit and one of the FBI men who had questioned Maggie earlier.

"Where's my daughter?"

Joshua knew immediately why Chester O'Hanlon had gotten as far in the world as he had. Power sat comfortably like a visible mantle on his shoulders. "She's across the hall. Come in. I'll tell her you're here." Joshua stepped aside and allowed the men to enter his apartment.

Joshua had checked on Maggie an hour before. She had fallen asleep, tears still wet on her cheeks. Never in his entire life had he felt so torn to pieces. No matter what he had told her, he could not bear to have her leave. He had wanted to scoop her up in his arms and forget his fears. He wanted to tell her that he believed they could make marriage work, that he believed in the depth of her feelings for him. He wanted to tell her that her father's money didn't matter, the differences in their backgrounds didn't matter, her fiancé didn't matter.

Instead he had stood by her bedside and the words had sickened and died within him.

Now he stood by her bed again. "Maggie?"

"Joshua?" She stretched, and for a second she smiled. Then she remembered what was between them and her smile faded. "What is it?"

"Your father is here."

She stood on shaky legs, combing her fingers through her curls and straightening her dress. "Do I look all right?"

"Beautiful."

She crossed the room, and Joshua followed at a discreet distance. He watched her drift across the hallway to stand in the doorway that he had left open. "Daddy?"

Then she was being held in Chester O'Hanlon's arms and both of them were crying. Joshua felt tears run down his own cheeks.

It was later, after she had shared bits and pieces of her story with her father and listened to his version, that she thought to introduce Joshua. She stood, taking his arm as casually as she could. "Daddy, this is Joshua Martane, the man who's helped me so much. Joshua, this is my father, Chester O'Hanlon." She turned to face the man in the silk suit. "And this is James Darwin."

"I wondered if you'd noticed me at all," James said smoothly. He stood to shake Joshua's hand and then held out his arms to Maggie. "Now don't I get a hug and a kiss? I've suffered, too, you know."

Joshua sensed Maggie's confusion. With steely determination he loosened her grip on his arm. She went to James and gave him a kiss on the cheek. Joshua turned away, unable to watch. "Can I offer you something to drink, Mr. O'Hanlon?"

"Nothing. I just want to take my daughter home."

James was pulling Maggie toward the doorway. "If you don't mind," he explained boyishly, "Maggie and I would like a moment of privacy."

The FBI man got up to leave, too. "Well, it's all settled, then," he said. "I'll wait outside." He shook Joshua's hand and then disappeared through the door.

"Martane?"

"Yes, Mr. O'Hanlon." Joshua faced Maggie's father, waiting for him to speak. The signs were all there. Joshua understood that he was about to hear a lecture.

"The FBI briefed me on everything pertinent to Maggie's case. I understand that you and she have been very close."

"That's right."

"Are you in love with my daughter?"

It was the one question that was easy to answer. "Yes."

"Do you also know that she's engaged to be married?"

"I do."

"What are your intentions?"

His intentions? Could the confused knot of objectivity and hot emotions inside him be called intentions? Joshua had never been less sure of his intentions in his life.

Chester O'Hanlon narrowed his eyes. He seemed to sense Joshua's struggle. He was a man who would use almost anything to get what he wanted. "What do you have to offer her, Martane?" He didn't wait for an answer. "Mary Margaret has always had everything she's ever desired. She's not ready for a different life. She could never be happy married to you," Mr. O'Hanlon said decisively.

Joshua had heard the same words before. Years before, Daphne's father had spoken them with far more kindness and consideration. Daphne's father had been correct.

"I don't want you to think I'm ungrateful," Mr. O'Hanlon continued. "But I'll fight for what's right for my daughter and I won't let gratitude stand in the way. I want her to be happy. She's the most important thing in my life."

Joshua smiled bitterly. "Then we have something in common, don't we?"

Surprised, Chester O'Hanlon hesitated.

"Daddy." Maggie stood in the doorway alone, her eyes focused solely on Joshua.

"Are you ready to leave? I can't get you home soon enough to suit me," Chester O'Hanlon said.

Maggie watched the expression on Joshua's face. It gave nothing away. Regret tore through her. Regret that she hadn't been been able to make him love her enough, regret that he was going to watch her walk out of his life without a protest, regret that she would always love him. She regretted the last most of all.

She wanted to stay, to force him to see the truth, but she knew that staying would be the weakest path. This was Joshua's battle. She could not fight it for him. And she would not spend the rest of her life trying to make him trust her love. Caught in her pain, she didn't see Joshua shake his head. She didn't see the expression on his face that proclaimed the end of the most important struggle of his life.

"She's not going anywhere, O'Hanlon." The words were an explosion in the quiet room. Maggie watched Joshua walk slowly to the doorway and hold out his hand. "She's going to stay here and marry me as soon as we can make the arrangements."

They were the words Maggie had least expected to hear. She had gathered all the inner resources she had developed over the past months to help her get through the next terrible moments. But nothing she had learned about courage and survival and patience could help her now. Maggie shut her eyes but the tears spilled out to make sparkling diamonds on her lashes.

"Like hell she is!" Mr. O'Hanlon exploded. "Look at her. You're taking advantage of her confusion. How dare you make demands on her after what she's been through. Mary Margaret, you've got to have time at home to think about this."

"This is between your daughter and me," Joshua said quietly.

No matter how much she loved Joshua, Maggie knew that there were questions that had to be answered. Only then could she be sure. "You know I'm emotionally overwrought right now, don't you?" she asked him, her eyes still tightly shut.

"I do."

"And you know that you're trying to take advantage of my feelings just like my father says?"

"No question about it."

"And you know that my father is as rich as King Midas and I've always done exactly what I wanted?"

Joshua laughed softly.

"And you know that I can be strong willed and difficult to live with sometimes? Almost as difficult as you."

"Open your eyes, Maggie."

She did, and found his. "And you know that there are never any guarantees?" she whispered.

"Yes, there are," he said. "I can guarantee that I'll always love you. I can guarantee that from now on I'll trust your love for me. I can guarantee that I'll spend the rest of my life trying to make you happy. The rest will be up to fate." Joshua continued to hold his hand out to her.

Maggie extended hers and their fingertips touched. "And will you give me all of you, Joshua? The good and the bad? I want it all."

"All of me. Even the parts I hadn't known existed." He pulled her tightly against him, and for a moment they forgot about Mr. O'Hanlon's presence, lost in a kiss that went on and on.

"Well, I'll be damned." Mr. O'Hanlon's voice had lost some of its fury. "You do love him, don't you?"

"Yes."

"What about James?"

Maggie turned to face her father, still held securely in Joshua's arms. "I told James out in the hallway that our engagement has ended. He's in the car sulking. I think he's lamenting a lost empire."

Chester O'Hanlon frowned. "He would have been good to you."

"That's a poor substitute for love."

He tried one more time. "At least think about it overnight. I've got a suite over on St. Charles. Come back with me and we'll talk."

"I'll be there later. Right now I need to be alone with Joshua. You can start making a list of guests for my wedding." Maggie broke from Joshua's grasp and went to her father. "I love you, Daddy. I couldn't even remember who

I was because I thought you'd been killed and the memory was too terrible, but I'm not your little girl anymore. I'm a woman, and I know what I want."

"And you want him." Mr. O'Hanlon nodded to Joshua.

"That's right."

He sighed and his fingers flexed. His struggle was visible. "It seems that I've lost you again." His voice cracked on the last word.

"Perhaps you've lost something, but you've gained something, too," Maggie said softly. "I think you'll come to understand that eventually."

Mr. O'Hanlon turned toward the door and then seemed to think better of it. He turned back to Joshua and nodded his goodbye.

Then Joshua and Maggie were alone.

He turned her to face him, drinking in the sight of her without barriers between them. He lifted his hand and brushed her curls, then he inched her face closer to his, taking his time to find her mouth. He heard her draw in a breath and he saw her eyelids close. Then there was only the taste and sensation of her lips as he brushed them repeatedly with his, finally entering them with his tongue, which seemed, suddenly, to have a life of its own. He had only wanted to seal his words, not begin an avalanche. They had to talk. He had to explain.

Still, he couldn't pull away. His intentions were the best, but Maggie's body was welded, now, to his. Her arms had crept around his back, and he could feel the sensuous movement of her hips against his thighs. He was a man who had walked the line between rationality and emotion for too long, a man who had tried to follow his head when his heart cried out for a different road. What caution still existed inside him was evaporating in the heat their bodies made together.

"Love me, Joshua."

"I do, Maggie."

"Show me." Her dress rustled against his legs, which were bare below the shorts he wore. He could feel her breasts under the sheer cotton, her nipples rigid beneath their covering. They repeatedly brushed his chest. He ached to feel her skin against his. Sensing his desire, she moved away just far enough to watch his face as she unbuttoned tiny pearl buttons and let the dress drop to the floor. In a minute she was naked.

Her body was a marvel of symmetry and softness. He wanted to lose himself in it forever. "Maggie, my love. I have to explain. Everything has to be right between us." His words were a hoarse plea. He could not take his eyes off her.

"Let no words come between us, Joshua."

He pulled her close and he felt her fingers unsnap the catch of his shorts. He tugged off his shirt, and they melted together. He lifted her and she wrapped her legs around him. His hands traveled her body. Even in his white-hot anguish to join, he wanted it to be perfect for her. It was Maggie who finally made them one. She was impatient for all of him, more than ready to share herself. At the feel of his body in hers, she shook with a release so profound that it defied all logic.

Joshua carried her to his bed, and whispering endearments, he came to her again. He watched her face as he led her to another, different place, a place gained by slow inches and subtle, loving torture. When she reached the glorious peak, he did, too. Maggie cried his name and he felt tears wet his cheeks. He gathered her against him and felt her heart beat. They rested, wrapped tightly in each other's arms.

Later he felt her stir and reluctantly he let her go. She moved only inches. "Are you awake?" she whispered.

"Just," he admitted, lifting his head to kiss her.

"Do you still want to talk?"

"No, but we should." He propped his head on his elbow and traced designs over her shoulders and around her breasts. In fascination he watched the immediate transformation that occurred. "You're so incredibly responsive," he murmured, his mouth seeking the evidence of her awakening desire.

"If you keep that up, we aren't going to have that talk." She didn't sound concerned.

With a sigh, he lifted his head. "You've forgiven me, I know. Still, I'd like you to understand what was driving me."

"You were afraid."

He sighed again, tilting his head to meet her gaze.

"I don't think that it's easy to be you, Joshua. You have such high ideals. You want to be everything to everybody. It's the minister that's still in you. It's been hard for you to admit you have needs. I think I frightened you because I understood that."

He smiled, brushing her hair back from her forehead. "Yes. But it's even simpler than that, really. I wanted you so much that when I finally had you, I was afraid I'd find out you weren't real."

She puckered her forehead. "I am terribly real. I have a real Irish temper and a crooked nose and I'm addicted to old Orson Welles movies."

"And you love me."

"With everything inside me."

"That's all that matters."

"I'm also rich."

"I can live with your money. It's not your fault you were born with a handicap." He avoided the playful poke of her fist.

"And I can live with your pride and your arrogance. But, Joshua, I don't intend to lean on you. This marriage is going to be a partnership."

"No more minister. No more psychologist. No more bodyguard. Just a man who needs his woman." He bent to find her mouth for a long, slow kiss. "And I do need you, Maggie. More than I'll ever be able to show you."

"I think you should try, anyway," she said, her hands threading through his hair.

With a humid caress, the New Orleans summer night closed softly around them, enveloping them in the dark protection that is a gift to all lovers.

Epilogue

In the beginning there was nothing. An absence of form and sound. An absence of pain and fear.

Then there was the voice.

"Joshua. Joshua, wake up." Maggie opened her eyes and rolled over, contacting his hard, unyielding body with her own. "Joshua, it's your turn to get up with her."

"I was hoping you wouldn't remember."

"I keep a mental list. This is the two hundred and tenth time she's awakened me from a sound sleep. I got up for number two hundred and nine."

"If I'd known the baby was going to inherit your Irish temper, Mary Margaret Martane, I'd have thought twice about conceiving her." Joshua pulled Maggie against him so that she fitted perfectly in the curve of his body. He shut his eyes again. "Do you suppose if we ignore her, she'll forget she wants company?"

A loud wail from the other room answered his question. Joshua buried his face in Maggie's abundant curls and then pushed himself into a sitting position.

Maggie lay with her hands propped under her head as she waited for Joshua to bring three-month-old Bridget Marie in to be nursed. Tiny fingers of light announced the arrival of dawn. As she watched, the big old room turned rosy and the lace curtains at the tall windows blew gently with a cool breeze.

"I love waking up in this house," Maggie told Joshua as he came into the room carrying his daughter, football-style, in front of him. "I love waking up with you."

"Well, you're getting plenty of chances these days." Joshua nuzzled Bridget's neck before he passed her, with noticeable reluctance, to her mother.

Maggie settled back against the walnut headboard and propped Bridget's head on one arm. In a moment, the little girl was hungrily devouring her early-morning breakfast.

"For all the years I lived in this house," Joshua said, watching them, "it never seemed so much like home."

When Joshua and Maggie had discovered that they were expecting a baby, they had decided to renovate Joshua's boyhood home in the Irish Channel, which he had held as rental property since his mother's death. The house, chopped into apartments years before, had taken extensive work but had yielded to loving care and skilled workmanship. Now it was a gracious example of what patience and attention to detail could do.

The neighborhood was filled with houses just like it, some under renovation, some waiting for the right owner to see their potential. Maggie and Joshua felt that they were at the forefront of a private urban renewal project that would help beautify the city they loved.

"I can't believe I start back to work today," Maggie said, switching Bridget to her other breast.

"I can't wait to have you there." Joshua traced a line up the side of Maggie's arm with his index finger. Then he slid closer and put his arm around her shoulder. Somehow, he never tired of watching her nurse their child.

"How many fathers get to have their wife and their child so close by? You can zip down and see us any time you get a break."

"Thanks to your father."

"Yes." Maggie handed Bridget to Joshua, and he laid the baby gently against his shoulder.

Mr. O'Hanlon, in gratitude to the hospital that had saved his daughter's life, had made a substantial donation to renovate the wing for the day care center. Maggie, with Millie Taffin's recommendation, had been hired as its new director, and she had been privileged to oversee the changes. Now the center cared for sixty children in facilities that were second to none.

"Kiss your daughter good-night." Joshua held Bridget's tiny face under Maggie's nose.

"Do you think we ought to put her back to bed? We'll only have to wake her up in a little less than an hour to take her to the hospital with us."

"I can think of some wonderful things we can do in that time if the baby goes back to sleep." Joshua's voice held promises.

Maggie kissed Bridget and then snuggled back under the covers to wait. Joshua was back in bed in a moment. "As much as I love that little creature," he said, "I still need lots of time alone with her mother."

Maggie smiled and opened her arms to him. "Dr. Martane," she said softly, "I have this recurring dream I wanted to tell you about."

Joshua began to trail kisses down the side of her face to her neck.

"I keep dreaming I have everything that anybody could ever want. Then I wake up and I can't tell my dream from reality." She moaned as his mouth found the place that their baby had just abandoned. "What do you think?"

"I think" he said, his lips against the silken skin of her breast, "that I should spend the rest of my life making sure that you never know the difference."

"I think," she said with a deep, contented sigh, "that I'll just have to go along with that treatment plan."

Silhouette Intimate Moments

COMING NEXT MONTH

MAN FOR HIRE—Parris Afton Bonds

Alyx needed to hire a man to help her rescue her kidnapped daughter. Khalid Rajhi was a desert sheikh who gave not only his help, but his heart.

THE OLD FLAME—Alexandra Sellers

Sondra had always recognized the power Ben held over her, and never more clearly than now, when there seemed no way to escape him, on the job or off.

SWEET REASON—Sandy Steen

Laine had no intention of falling in love while on vacation in Mexico, much less getting involved with a case of espionage. But Drew Kenyon had a way of blowing intentions and expectations to the wind.

WHEN WE TOUCH—Mary Lynn Baxter

The FBI wanted Blair Browning back, and they knew just how to get her. Caleb Hunt wanted Blair, too, for a very personal reason—and he, too, seemed destined for success.

FOUR UNIQUE SERIES
FOR EVERY WOMAN YOU ARE...

Silhouette Romance

Heartwarming romances that will make you laugh and cry as they bring you all the wonder and magic of falling in love.

6 titles per month

Silhouette Special Edition

Expanded romances written with emotion and heightened romantic tension to ensure powerful stories. A rare blend of passion and dramatic realism.

6 titles per month

Silhouette Desire

Believable, sensuous, compelling—and above all, romantic—these stories deliver the promise of love, the guarantee of satisfaction.

6 titles per month

Silhouette Intimate Moments

Love stories that entice; longer, more sensuous romances filled with adventure, suspense, glamour and melodrama.

4 titles per month

SIL-GEN-1RR